MAN IN QUEUE

SHANDI BOYES

Illustrated by
SSB COVERS AND DESIGN
Edited by
MOUNTAINS WANTED PUBLISHING

Sugar and Spice

Lady in Waiting

Man in Queue

Couple on Hold

Enigma: The Wedding

Silent Vigilante

Bound Series:

Chains

Links

Bound

Restrained

Psycho

Russian Mob Chronicles:

Nikolai: A Mafia Prince Romance

Nikolai: Taking Back What's Mine

Nikolai: What's Left of Me

Nikolai: Mine to Protect

Asher: My Russian Revenge

Nikolai: Through the Devil's Eyes

RomCom Standalones:

Just Playin'

The Drop Zone

Ain't Happenin'

Christmas Trio

Falling for a Stranger

Coming Soon:

Skitzo

Trey

Alex

a collective gasp rolls through the church when the deranged woman's weapon of choice is exposed. Thankfully, it isn't the dangerous arsenal I expected—but it is the reason her Sunday shoes are covered with vibrant red splotches.

Regan stops talking when a dissected pig's heart rolls across the pristinely clean church foyer. Her eyes lock with mine for several long seconds before they lower to the woman squealing like a banshee. I can tell she is grateful her stalker has been detained, but she is confused as to what it all means.

She's not the only one lost. Her stalker's threat was highly graphic, one of the most disturbing I've ever seen, so I expected her to be more creative than harassing Regan with a pig's heart. Her arrest is simple and done without harm to either Regan or herself. It almost seems too easy.

When the lady I have pinned to the ground spews vitriol in Regan's direction, I scan the muted church for the gentleman I spotted earlier, hoping for some assistance. I can't keep the assailant contained and comfort Regan at the same time. I also have no jurisdiction in Texas. A local cop needs to arrest her to ensure all the loose ends are adequately tied. The last thing I want is for her to slip prosecution because I failed to follow protocol.

Although I don't know the man I am seeking any better than the churchgoers staring at me, I've lived amongst law enforcement officers my entire life, so I know a cop when I see one. He is one of us; I'm certain of it.

Upon discovering the man I'm hunting tucked in the far corner of the church, I jerk up my chin, wordlessly requesting his assistance. He briskly shakes his head before slumping low in his chair. His endeavor to hide comes too late. Numerous attendees' eyes followed the direction of my gaze when I nudged my head. His hope to fade into the background was lost the instant he was spotted by a local, because he is one of them as much as he is an officer of the law.

Recognizing his cover has been blown, the blond-haired, brown-eyed man stands to his feet and heads my way. The gasps of the crowd keep coming when he unlatches a set of cuffs from his belt at the end of the aisle.

The reason for their surprise comes to light when Regan mutters, "Ayden? What the hell are you doing?"

Regan's eyes dart to her father when Ayden kneels down to secure cuffs on the subdued woman. Hayden shrugs at Regan, as confused as every other attendee gawking our way.

Confident he has the woman contained, Ayden helps her stand to her feet. He dips his chin my way, his greeting more to hide his snarl than a formal introduction.

After an apologetic glance directed at Regan, Hayden, and Sally, Ayden guides the assailant down the church aisle. "Danielle Thomas, you are under arrest for breaking and entering a property with the intent to cause grievous bodily harm. You have the right to remain silent. Anything you say can and will be used against you in a court of law . . ."

His words soften the farther he guides Danielle through the crowd of people glaring at her with the same disdain they issued Regan only an hour ago. I stop awarding him the same confused stare when Regan's scent infiltrates my nostril cavities.

"What the hell is happening?" She stops to stand next to me.

"You tell me," I reply, a little lost. "Do you know that man?" I nudge my head at the man who was reluctant to break his cover for the greater good.

Regan nods. "He's my baby brother." The dryness impinging my throat intensifies when her massively dilated eyes stray to mine. "Seems like we aren't the only ones keeping secrets. As far as my family was aware, Ayden was set to graduate Lennington College next month."

Alex

"You okay?" I ask Regan as my backside joins her on the two-seater couch in her family living room.

She halfheartedly nods. "It's just weird, you know." She stops cuddling her knees so her head can crank in the direction her family is seated. "I don't know why he needed to keep his career a secret. We're his family. If he can't be honest with us, who can he be honest with?"

Her response surprises me. She's been quiet since we left the church three hours ago, but I thought her wish for privacy centered around the detailed report local authorities drafted in front of her parents, not her brother's secret. Regan is confident and forthright, but just like me, she keeps parts of her life hidden from those she cares about. She's not doing it to be mean; she's protecting them as I always will her.

Going off a hunch, I say, "Ayden may not have had a choice but to lie." My last word muffles from Regan smashing a pillow into my face.

After a growl exposes her anger, she leaps from the couch and bolts up the stairs. I understand her annoyance—Danielle arrived at Luca's memorial with the intent to publicly shame her. I just can't fathom why all her fury is directed at Ayden. Although his break in cover meant confessing to a yearlong secret, he did that to protect Regan and her family, so she has no right to be angry at him.

Unless...

I take the stairs two at a time, barely crossing the threshold of Regan's bedroom before her door slams shut.

"You're supposed to be on the other side," Regan snarls, exposing my intuition is spot on. She's not mad at Ayden. She's upset with me.

She stops wearing a hole in the carpet when I grip the top of her arms. She could pull away, but even someone as strong and unbreakable as Regan can't deny the attraction teeming between us. The rise in her temperature when I grabbed her wasn't from anger. It is the same reason her pulse is fluttering against my fingertips. She's mad, but she's still responsive to my touch.

I wait for my silence to coerce her eyes to mine before asking, "Why are you angry at me? I haven't done anything wrong."

Frustrated at my inability to read her every thought, she breaks away from me. Her angry steps move her across the room to her suitcase left open on her bed.

Although grateful she's packing for our flight that leaves in under two hours, I have no intention of going anywhere until we sort this shit out. Our return to Ravenshoe means facing the biggest battle in our relationship to date. Hayden's aversion to me getting cozy with his daughter will seem like child's play when I come clean about mixing business with pleasure to Theresa.

I'm not willing to face that shitstorm without ensuring Regan and I are solid. If we don't put our best foot forward, our relationship will be squashed before it's official. That isn't a probability. It is a certainty.

Regan stops shoving clothes into her bag like a madwoman when I say, "If you want to yell at me, Rae, yell at me. If you want to slam a door in my face, slam it in my face. But if you want me to help you with whatever is eating you alive, you need to talk to me. I am many things, but I am not a mind reader."

"That's half the problem, Alex. I don't know who the fuck you are." She points to her bedroom door as if it is a paradox to the universe. "Only two nights ago, you told me the only thing I'd ever do in your bed was sleep. Then we. . ."

"Fucked?" I fill in, hating the word, but not as much as I loathe her inability to describe what we have as something more than just a physical connection.

"Yes!" She throws her hands into the air, firmly holding her ground. "Then you were all alpha possessive with my dad like no one would ever come between us, before you went and. . ."

"And. . .?" I prompt, lost on the direction of her conversation this time around.

The anger on her face morphs to dislike. "You took Ayden's side by excusing his lies the same way you do yours."

"I didn't excuse his lies. I accepted them. That's different."

She lets out of frustrated squeal before she starts packing

again. "A lie is a lie; you're not supposed to use them on the people you love."

One word, and I'm feeling more emotional than angry. Her "L" reference could be directed at Ayden, but after the day we've had, it seems more aimed at me.

Testing a theory, I ask, "So you've never hidden a truth to save a loved one heartache? Or kept someone's secret just because they asked you to?"

I know I've hit the nail on the head when the resentment in her eyes fades with each question fired from my mouth.

"Ayden was deceitful, Rae, but he didn't intentionally set out to hurt you. I've only just met him, but I know protecting you and your family comes before anything else."

"You don't know that," Regan barely whispers, her words forced through a sob sitting in the back of her throat. "You don't know him. You barely know me."

That hurts to hear, but it doesn't stop me from saying, "I know you, and although I've only just met your family, nothing will stop me from keeping them safe, because I know how important they are to you. Furthermore, Ayden has your blood in his veins, Regan. That automatically makes you his number one priority."

She remains quiet for several moments while my thoughts run wild. I'm skating on thin ice here. One wrong move and I'm either history or heading for greatness. I rake my fingers through my hair while contemplating what to do next. I could dismiss Regan's frustration as a family issue, but deep down inside, I know Ayden's confession isn't the sole reason the little vein in her neck is working overtime. Some of the blame rests on my shoulders.

I exhale a deep breath. *Fuck it. I'm already sitting in a very deep hole, so what's a few more inches between friends?*

After removing the designer garment from Regan's hand, I dump it on the ground before pulling her into my chest. The annoyed grunt she releases when her beloved dress lands at our feet gives me an excuse for the extra thump of my heart when I say, "Don't ever doubt someone's love because they're required to keep minor details from you. Let actions speak on behalf of the words they can't express."

I was originally referring to Ayden and his disclosure, but the heavy sentiment bouncing between Regan and me shifted my focus. I'm not surprised. I can't have her this close to me and think rationally. It is impossible.

I silently will for Regan to open up to me. When she doesn't, I plead, "Talk to me, Rae. Let me help you."

The hope in my tone compels her head to pop off my chest. If I had any doubt about how profoundly this woman has crawled under my skin, I am certain now. I thought love was supposed to be blind, not smack you upside the head?

After a quick swallow, Regan faintly whispers, "My parents are good people; they don't deserve to have all their children lying to them."

As the truth smacks into me, I nod. This isn't about Ayden, Danielle, or me. This is about Regan, and the secret she's been carrying the past eight years.

"Did you lie to hurt them?"

Regan angrily swipes at a tear careening down her cheek before shaking her head.

"Then it's okay. They'll forgive you—"

"They can't forgive me if I have no intention of telling them I lied."

I smirk, hearing the deceit in her tone a mile out. She is so close to cracking, she just needs a little more confidence. This weekend has been as good for her as it's been for me. Peering down at her now, I barely see the hurt, tormented woman I witnessed staring at the sky every night at precisely 10:03 the past six months. That woman is nearly gone, almost vanished.

This may make me sound conceited, but I feel partly responsible for the drastic upshift in her personality. Not because I'm a giver and she's a taker, but because for every boost she gives me, I return it. Despite social status or amounts in our bank accounts, we are even.

"If you don't ever tell your parents what happened the night of Luca's accident, that's your choice, Rae." She attempts to interrupt me, but I keep talking, "But if one day you want to get it off your shoulders, I'll be right at your side, supporting you."

She tugs her blouse sleeve over her hand before using it to clear a few tears stranded on her cheeks. Once she is confident her face is moisture-free, she cautions, "You shouldn't say stuff like that to me."

"Why? Does it make your insides all gooey?" The jest in my tone lightens the tension in the room.

"No." Regan arches a brow. "It makes me want to run for the hills. I don't do. . . *this*."

The gag she releases when forcing "this" out of her mouth makes me smile. "*This*? You don't do *this*?"

I tug her in close before dragging my bristle-covered jaw down her neck. Although she squeals, the extra thump of her heart is the only thing I hear. She wants this. She's just too scared to admit it.

"What about *this*, do you do *this*?"

Her girly squeal switches to a moan when my teeth graze her budded nipple through her shirt.

Throwing her head back, she moans, "Oh yeah, I definitely do *that*."

I give her a look, a glaring stare that warns of my bubbling jealousy.

"With you. I'll do *that* with you," she whimpers, reading me better than any woman ever has.

I bang my chest with words instead of my fists. "That's right. Me and *only* me."

Ensuring she can't protest my underhanded demand we go exclusive, I seal my mouth over hers. Our kiss starts out innocent, a flurry of playful nips and furled lips, keeping it somewhat harmless, but the instant Regan's tongue slides along mine, things become out of control.

She coaxes me to the dark side with gentle strokes and prolonged tastes of her mouth. Then, when I think our exchange can't get any hotter, she drags her cheek down my beard, combining our scents in a way that can't be seen as any less than unified. I knew she wanted *this*. She wants it as badly as me.

When her hands move to the buttons of my shirt, we stumble toward her bed. Our movements match ones we made when rolling in the grass earlier today. They are fast and with purpose.

As our tongues tangle, I grind my erection against her pussy. Her desperate breaths allow me to explore her mouth, tasting and sampling every inch of her, loving the moans rolling up her chest.

Just when she thinks she'll never breathe unaided again, I lower the devotion of my lips to her erratically thrusting torso. I bite her nipple through her thin blouse before lavishing it with my tongue to lessen the sting.

When she moans my name, sparks fly as desire makes our exchange snowball. I toy with her breasts, biting, sucking, and squeezing them until the intoxicating scent of her pussy becomes too great to ignore.

I drop my lips to her under-boob, then her stomach, until they come to a stop at the top of her milky white thighs. I'm about to tell her I want her sweet pussy on my mouth, but she beats me to the task. With a smile that has precum seeping into my trousers, she drags up her skirt until it bands around her waist like a belt before hooking her panties to the side. The sight of her naked pussy nearly makes me lose my mind.

Fuck me. She's saturated.

My hand darts up to cover her cries of ecstasy when my tongue spears her glistening pussy lips. I understand her wild response. I'm overcome with pleasure, by the seductive flavor stimulating my taste buds.

"Oh god, yes," she purrs, her thighs parting wider.

Getting carried away in the phenomenal sensation, I knead her breasts through her shirt while completing a rapid set of licks to her swollen-with-need pussy. We've been so impatient, we haven't removed an article of clothing. I'm still in my despised JC Penney suit, and Regan is wearing the black skirt and white fitted blouse she wore to Luca's memorial.

My cock hardens more, aroused by the brave, strong woman she represented today. She didn't shed a single tear—not one!

Wanting to ensure the only cries she releases today are ones made in pleasure, I grip her ass with my left hand before guiding her legs over my shoulders with my right. She moans my name in a throaty groan when I blast her pussy with greedy licks and pulse-quickening plunges of my tongue. I eat her as if she is the most decadent piece of dessert I've ever tasted, because she is.

When I slide two fingers inside her, her back arches off the mattress. "You're so wet for me. So tight and snug. I fucking love it."

My assurance relaxes the strain of her thighs, allowing my fingers to glide in and out of her without hindrance. I increase the speed of my pumps, finger-fucking her until she is on the verge of orgasm.

When I suck her clit into my mouth, I nearly see a blistering of stars form in front of her eyes. "About fucking time," I growl against her soaked sex, pleased by the way she roughly yanks my hair while succumbing to a climaxing trance.

Waves of pleasure cascade down her body as violent shudders reduce her to a quivering, sticky mess. Her orgasm seems to command the use of every muscle in her body, but instead of fighting against it, she submits to the madness.

My chest swells, confident this is the first time she's ever submitted. The cries tearing from her throat expose her inability to deny me, but just in case she isn't hearing things as lucidly as me, I up the ante.

Her thighs continue trembling in the aftermath of orgasm when I place her onto her feet before spinning her around to face me. After tugging my trousers to my knees, I sit on the edge of her bed. With our eyes locked, I perform a long, determined stroke of my cock.

I'm not trying to get hard—my cock is thick and covered with angry veins. I'm not even teasing her as she always does me. I'm forcing her to respond—to show me what I mean to her. If I am going to give up everything I have for her, I need to make sure she's willing to do the same for me. That includes her need for control.

"See something you like, Rae?" My voice hitches when my thumb glides over my knob to gather a sticky bead of precum pooled at the end.

Regan hesitates for barely a second before she nods.

"Then come get what you need."

The raw huskiness of my voice intensifies the dampness between her legs. She is dripping wet, her sheer panties unable to contain all the moisture. Her eagerness adds to the girth of my cock.

"Nuh-uh," I groan when she slips her panties to the side before attempting to straddle my lap. "If we're doing this, we're doing it evenly. Right?"

The confused cinch of her brows smooths when I nudge my head to the carpet beneath my feet. I brace myself in preparation for her to dart to the door, so you can imagine my surprise when the only response I get is a ball-clenching smirk.

Pleasure shoots through me when she falls to her knees to replace my hand with her own. She didn't protest my demand for a minute—not even one damn second.

A groan of satisfaction vibrates her tongue when she laps up my precum before sliding her pillowy lips down my shaft.

When her mouth stops halfway down, I grunt, "Close, baby, but I think you can do better."

Regan rolls her eyes at my term of endearment, but her lips stay circled around my cock—*where they belong.*

After scrunching her hair into a tight fist, I slowly roll my hips forward. I watch her closely, ensuring the pain fettering her features is more from taking a man of my size to the back of her throat than actual pain. The delicious moans ripping from her mouth assure me she is finding this as pleasurable as I am, but the moisture in her eyes keeps my peacock feathers tucked away.

I must tread lightly. Today has been tough on her.

Regan is the most confident woman I've ever met, but it flourishes even more when I praise her stellar cock-sucking skills. She strokes and sucks me harder, which only increases my grip on her hair.

I use her hair as leverage to guide her speed, my pumps as frantic as my lungs are sucking in air. "That feels so good, baby. Your mouth sucking my cock as greedily as your pussy does is pure fucking heaven."

Another surge of blood rushes to my cock from her throaty garble of approval. She takes me deeper, her cheeks hollowing as she sucks me so fiercely my knees wobble.

Just as the sensation drawing from my balls to the crest of my cock becomes too great to ignore, Regan's lips move to my sack. Her nips and sucks cause them to grow heavy with need, aching for release. She works me as if she's been dying for this day as long as I have, as if her attraction is just as intense.

My plan to hold back until surrounded by her warmth comes undone when she rakes her fingernails across the sensitive skin between my balls and ass. She smiles when my cock begins to jerk in the seconds leading to it coating my knob and her curved lips with a milky substance.

While her tongue laps up my spawn, one of her hands cups my balls while the other works my shaft. She doesn't give in until every drop of my cum has been spilled. It is pure fucking heaven. The best head I've ever been given.

Until we're interrupted by a grizzly bear.

"Daddy, don't. . ."

Regan's plea comes too late.

3

I stop scanning the isolated surroundings for familiar focal points when the heat of a gaze captures my attention. Alex is watching me from afar, studying me as closely as my father is eyeballing him in the rearview mirror of his truck. He's worried about my silence, petrified it's based on the unbelievable connection we shared a mere hour ago.

He shouldn't be. My silence has nothing to do with the whirlwind of emotions he's been hitting me with all weekend, and everything to do with haunted memories. They're crashing into me hard, surrounding my heart with the four walls Alex has been trying to bust down since he waltzed into my life with a cocky grin and a skull-cracking head.

For every step I take forward in my grief, I feel like I'm thrown back another three. Today's trip to the airport is by far the biggest leap I've taken thus far. I'm just waiting for the repercussions to surface, knowing they will inevitably happen.

The first ten miles of our trip was made in silence; even the

16

tick of my dad's jaw couldn't be heard. The next ten miles was occupied assuring my dad he could take the most direct route to the airport so Alex and I wouldn't miss our flight. And the final ten miles have occurred with Alex's hand curled over mine.

He didn't speak when we drove past the tree that bears Luca's name, but words weren't needed to relay his empathy. Him squeezing my hand spoke volumes, much less how he pressed his lips to my temple.

It was a bold move on his behalf. He barely survived my father's wrath when he was dragged out of my room by the collar of his shirt. He may not have if Ayden hadn't stepped in.

I don't know why Ayden felt compelled to assist Alex. More times than not, he's dishing out the punishments with my father. There is only one reason he chose a different route this time: law enforcement officers can sniff out their own.

Alex's dominance, self-assuredness, and cunning ability to be two steps ahead of the game significantly narrowed down his possible job titles the past forty-eight hours. My list that was once a mile long now only has three occupations remaining. He is either an undercover cop, a CIA agent, or a fellow member of my brother's new found career: an agent at the Federal Bureau of Investigation.

Although I'm confident I could force the truth from him, I won't. A person harboring a lifetime of secrets can't ask others to disclose their own secrets. Until I'm willing to come clean about all the secrets I'm keeping, I can't expect those around me to. For that alone, I rest my head on Alex's shoulder, accepting the silent comfort he is offering me without hope of a reward.

Ignoring my father's warning growl, Alex's lips brush my

temple for the second time this evening. "Are you okay?" he asks a short time later, put off by my silence but longing to ease my pain.

I nod, answering him with the same number of words we've shared since our foray in my childhood bedroom. I'm not quiet because I'm frustrated. Who in their right mind would be? Alex's arrogant, controlling crash into my life frustrates the living hell out of me, but there isn't a word in the dictionary that can describe what I feel when he devotes his attention on me.

This afternoon, he was bossy and domineering—the hottest I've ever seen him. That notion should scare me. I've been on my own way too long to find dominant, superiority-seeking men appealing, but there is something about Alex that has me seeing things differently.

He's not assertive because he's placing me below him. He's striving to show me he can handle a woman as fierce and independent as me. He doesn't want to change me; he wants to protect me. If that protection comes without a side dish of babying, I'm open to the possibility. . . *maybe?*

Attraction is a scary thing. It bolts through your body without warning, exhilarating your veins with a lethal combination of thrill, excitement, and need. It makes you heedless. Giddy. Sometimes a little stupid. But once the attraction is requited, it generally moves on. We stop skipping down the street and making sickening ga-ga faces at random strangers who have no idea we've been jabbed in the butt by Cupid's arrow. Life returns to normal.

Usually.

That hasn't happened with Alex yet. The nervous butterflies

in my stomach and the flighty feeling in my head are still present, so much so, I'm wondering if Cupid is peering down at me, laughing his ass off. He must have struck me more than once, otherwise what other excuse could I have for what I'm feeling? I don't do. . . *this.*

Ignoring my heart's painful squeeze of denial, I clamber onto the sidewalk outside of the domestic terminal on Alex's heel. After scooting past his wide shoulders, I throw my arms around my daddy's neck. I hug him as fiercely as I did my mom and Ayden an hour ago. Mercifully, he returns my embrace. I wasn't sure he would after what he walked in on.

"Come back soon, baby girl, *please?*"

Tears prick my eyes from the plea in his tone. "I will. I promise."

He clutches me for a few minutes longer, ensuring he gets a year's worth of hugs in one visit. I understand his plight. Remorse has made my trips home very sporadic the past eight years, but I don't see them being so few and far between anymore. It will always hurt coming back here, but with good memories replacing some of the bad, it will be easier to return.

"Weston's birthday is next month. His momma is organizing a spit. Why don't you come back for that? He'd love to see you."

I pull back from my daddy's broad chest. "I'll try, but I have to check Isaac's schedule first."

The squint of Alex's gaze eases when my dad grumbles something under his breath. They've never met, but my dad's disdain for Isaac is as profound as it is for Alex. Not knowing the entire story, he blames Isaac for my dwindling contact the past eight years.

He couldn't be further from the truth if he tried.

I've lost count of the number of times Isaac has offered to charter me home in his private jet. He even said he'd drive me if my reason for not visiting centered around a fear of flying. He wants me to heal just as much as both Alex and my father.

"Do you think Kate would mind me adding a plus one to the invitation?"

Wild nerves take flight in my stomach when I shift on my feet to face Alex, ensuring my dad is aware who I'm referring to. "What do you say, Mister Fancy Pants? Are you up for some more farmyard antics?"

"Rae. . ."

My dad's warning snarl quickens my pulse, but it is barely a blip on the radar when Alex nods without pause for consideration. I never thought I'd see the day. An olive branch offered and accepted between us without bloodshed. *Who could have predicted this?*

After a final promise to return more frequently—and a wordless request for leniency—I give my dad one last hug before Alex and I make our way to the check-in counter. With my father's lecture on being respectful under his roof exceeding its usual thirty-minute timeframe, we arrive at our gate with barely a second to spare.

Fortunately, the airline representatives are more accommodating of tardiness when you're a priority customer.

"Welcome back to business class, Ms. Myers. Can we start your service with a beverage? Perhaps a glass of sparkling wine?"

James greets after takeoff, his smile widening when he spots Alex sitting next to me, caressing my hand in his.

"A drink would be lovely, but I'm more a martini girl. Shaken, not stirred. Skip the olives."

With a wink revealing he heard the underlying message in my request, James skedaddles to the back of the plane. With Alex and me the only business class flyers on this redeye to Ravenshoe, he has no other guests to accommodate.

The fine hairs on my nape prickle when Alex presses his lips to my ear. "If you're aiming to make me jealous, you missed the boat with James. His Tinder details are still in my wallet."

My eyes snap to his so fast, our lips briefly brush. "I wasn't flirting with James. I was setting the mood."

Alex remains quiet, somewhat confused.

It clears when I ask, "Care to become a member of the mile high club, Mr. Rogers?"

His groan is as sexy as his sinfully handsome face. "Are you propositioning me, Ms. Myers?"

"Depends?" I reply with a shrug.

"On?"

His quick reply reveals his eagerness. I just don't know if it is eagerness to accept my invitation or discover my terms. *I guess there is only one way to find out?*

"On whether or not you're going to accept my proposal. I've never thrown out an invite like this before. I don't want it tossed back in my face."

My teeth grit, hating the need in my voice. I'm not a clinger. I'm independent and strong. . . and horny as fuck, so I really hope he hasn't misread my eagerness as vulnerability.

My worst nightmare comes true when Alex mutters, "I don't

21

know if this is a good idea, Rae. Today has been tough on you. I already stepped over the line twice. I don't want you to think I'm taking advantage of you—"

"If you so much as mention the word vulnerable, or anything along those lines, I'll stab you with my fork the instant James serves dinner. I'm a grown ass woman who has no troubles differentiating horniness from grief. I'm horny, goddammit, but since you're clearly not up to the task, I guess I'll have to take care of business the old-fashioned way!"

I slam my purse onto the table separating our seats before making a dramatic dash for the bathroom James is steering clear of. After shutting the door with force, I lean my back against it.

Okay, maybe I'm a little stressed.

At least this time, it isn't just Luca's memorial hammering me. It's everything. Danielle and her crazy plan to replace my heart with a pig's because supposedly mine is malfunctioning. The statement I was forced to give in front of my parents about how I discovered Danielle had been in my apartment, and uncovering I'm not the only Myers keeping secrets. Ayden has bucket loads of them, and Raquel's are only just surfacing.

I also feel guilty. Today is supposed to be about Luca, but all I'm worried about is gobbling up the scraps Alex is tossing my way before he returns to the "no touch" rule he instituted before we left for Texas. That's why I invited him to Weston's party. Taking him back to Texas may be my only chance of securing a second round with him.

Ugh! Now I'm more mad than horny. I've never been more pathetic in my life. My momma raised me to take no shit from anyone. She knocked my dad's pegs down an inch or two when he sauntered into her life anticipating a wallflower but discovering a tigress—and instead of emulating her, I wilted under the heat.

Screw Alex and his above-par bedroom skills, way with words, and panty-wetting face. I was perfectly fine before he waltzed into my life, so I'll be perfectly fine when he saunters back out.

After scowling at the two-faced liar glaring at me in the mirror, I pivot on my heels and throw open the washroom door. I don't make it one step out of the zesty-scented space. Alex's imposing frame is blocking my exit. It is more rigid than usual since it is hardened with anger.

I realize I still have a lot to learn about the man standing in front of me when he charges for me. The crash of our lips is so violent, James's head pops through the curtains separating business class from economy. Upon spotting Alex's fingers weaving through my hair as his tongue strokes my stunned mouth, James once again disappears into the abyss.

In a flurry of bites and kisses, I somehow end up pinned against the wall of the bathroom with my skirt wrapped around my waist and Alex's cock nudging between the folds of my pussy. I don't know where my panties went. One minute they were there; the next minute they were gone.

I call out in an erotic purr when Alex sheaths me in one quick motion. Stars blister in front of my eyes as his name topples from my lips. This is what I need. This and only this. I need to be claimed. Taken. *Loved.*

As if he heard my private thoughts, Alex grunts, "The next time you need me, Rae, tell me. Don't badger me to force a response. Don't run from me so I have to chase you. Run to me." He jackknifes his hips, creating a wave low in my womb. "Because no matter what you say or do, no matter how bad things get between us, I'm not going anywhere."

He stares straight into my eyes, the possessiveness in them piercing my heart as well as my senses. "And neither the fuck are you. Do you understand me? I'm here, Rae. I'm right fucking here."

He fucks me greedily, knowing my desires will subdue me enough that my heart can hear the truth in his words. The emotions powering our exchange are too much. The sensation, the energy, and the enlargement of my heart, it's all too much. I can't handle this. I shouldn't be having feelings like this for any man, let alone one I hardly know. The last time I felt like this, the man I loved said he could never love me back. He killed himself the night I confessed my undying devotion, preferring to die than disappoint me.

Alex's thrusts slow when an unexpected sob tears from my throat. I try to cover it up with a moan, but he's too perceptive to accept another lie. While his pumps switch from a man fucking in a wildly possessive rage to those of a man in love, he coerces my eyes to his.

I fight his pull. I don't want him to see me like this—defenseless and raw—but his pull is too intense. When I give him my eyes, he peers straight into them, not the least bit worried by the moisture teeming in them. He caresses my cheeks, lips, and neck with the same tenderness his cock bestows on my pussy. He accepts the utter rawness beaming from me without any hesitation crossing his features. He cherishes me, devastating lows and all.

"I've got you," he mutters when my body chooses its own

response to his silent assurance by nuzzling into his neck. "And I'll never let you go."

He doesn't. He cherishes me the remainder of the flight, making me the most unhinged and vulnerable I've ever been.

I knew this man was dangerous.

It isn't solely my life in his hands, though.

It is my soul.

4

"*A*re you sure you don't want me to walk you to your door?"

Regan's eyes stray from her apartment building to me. One of the little nicks that hit my heart earlier tonight stops gushing when I fail to register any pain in her eyes. They are clear and bright, as free and open as she has been the past three hours.

I never went into the bathroom with the intention of breaking her. I was merely banging my chest, acting moronic. It was only when our eyes met for the quickest second did I realize she wasn't vulnerable because of Luca's memorial or Danielle's threat of harm. She was vulnerable because for the first time in years, her heart was open and willing to accept the numerous invitations I've been handing it the past forty-eight hours. She wanted to let me in.

Although I hate seeing her so raw, it guarantees that every step I take from here on out will be a step in the right direction. She's caught up in an investigation she doesn't belong in. She is as innocent as Dane was that night on the hill five years ago, so I'll do everything in my power to ensure her life isn't impacted as badly as Dane's was.

I'll even walk away from the role I was born to fill if it assures her safety.

"It's fine. It's late; Danielle is in custody, and we both have important tasks to undertake tomorrow," Regan replies, drawing me from my somber thoughts. "Besides, we have to go back to reality at some point, right?"

"Not if you aren't in a fantasy," I deny, shaking my head. "This is the most real I've ever been. . ."

My words trail off from Regan pressing her lips to mine. "Save the morality statement for when you're not waking up in a made-up life with a fake license and job description."

Her lips curving against mine stuff my retaliation down my throat, but it doesn't stop me from saying, "I could always become an accountant? Then I can work with you and your boss crunching numbers all day."

The creepy feeling on my skin from mentioning Isaac isn't as noticeable this morning. Probably more to do with the fact that Regan's lips are hovering over mine than my dislike going away.

She draws back so she can see my eyes. "You could, but. . ."

She leaves me hanging as badly as she did yesterday morning.

"But. . .?" I encourage.

Her face screws up. "My boss has a very strict non-fraternization policy."

I huff to hide my desire to throw my fists into the air. "So you've never. . .?"

I'd like to pretend I left my question open for her to answer how she sees fit, but in all honesty, I can't stomach the idea of her with Isaac, much less articulate it, meaning the gag that ended my question was very much real.

The bile scorching my throat eases when she answers, "God no. That'd be like having sex with my. . ." Her reply stalls as quickly as my question, her gag as authentic as mine.

She takes a few seconds to clear the horrified expression from her face before asking, "What about you? Have you ever played office shuffle with your boss?"

The crinkle her nose gets when she is jealous is fucking adorable—adorable enough for me to smash our mouths together. I kiss her long enough to quench my desire to have her beneath me for another thirty seconds, but not long enough for her to forget our mutual interrogation.

She arches a brow, demanding I answer her the very instant we stop playing tonsil hockey. "There is only one way I'll ever lie on the same bed with my boss—when we're buried beneath the same pile of dirt."

"So your job is dangerous?" Regan stammers out, hearing something in my confession I didn't mean to reveal.

I shouldn't love the worry clouding her eyes, but I do. "Yes," I reply honestly. "But not in a way I can't handle."

My cocky affirmation alleviates the fret brewing in her eyes, but it doesn't wholly erase it. "Is your position to blame for the scar on your knee?"

The air sucks from my lungs. I try to speak, but I'm lost for words. We've fooled around three times in a little under twenty-four hours, but with the exception of the time she scared the living daylights out of me, she's never seen me fully naked.

Not even two seconds later, reality smacks into me. "Ah, you saw my scar when you were on your knees."

Regan rakes her teeth over her lower lip, her pose as seductive as her scent. "I wanted to ask you about it then, but I was a little occupied."

I clutch my chest, feigning battle wounds. "A *little* occupied. Dear god, please save my ego."

She rolls her eyes, taking my comment as I intended: playfully.

"I'm sure your ego is perfectly fine." Her lustful eyes glide down my body in a slow and purposeful probe, only stopping when they reach the wound responsible for my six-month stint in rehabilitation. "Did it hurt?"

I wait for her eyes to return to mine before shaking my head. "Not in the way you're thinking." Wounds doctors couldn't heal are my biggest battle—some I'm still battling to this very day. "Does my scar bother you?"

Regan's brows furrow. "Why would it bother me?" Her eyes dance between mine before she mutters, "Visible scars have nothing on the ones people can't see." She leans in close, bringing her nose to within an inch of mine. "Besides, scars are as sexy as fuck because only big, strong, sexy men have them." Her growled words have my cock thickening as rapidly as my tongue.

After giving me a flirty wink acknowledging she's seen the growth in my pants, she twists her torso, throws open the back passenger door of the cab we're sitting in, then graciously slips

out. I spot her tease from a mile out. She's leaving me hanging
—*again.*

Her saunter to her apartment building slows when I roll
down the cab window and shout, "Will I ever live it down?!"

"Not any time this century," she replies, proving beyond a
shadow of a doubt that she knows me better than anyone. "You
don't kiss a girl like me then run off like I gave you cooties
without suffering the consequences."

"But we share the same cooties now. Doesn't that mean my
penance has been paid?"

That forces her to turn around and face me. With a grin as
devilishly wicked as her beautiful face, she replies, "I don't know?
Maybe we should discuss it over a bottle of wine this evening?"

Even though the dip in her tone reveals her hesitation to ask
me on a date, her confidence doesn't falter in the slightest.

"What time? I'm not sure how late I'll be tonight."

I wish I were lying. Standard work hours aren't a thing for
FBI agents, much less when one is about to confess to half a
decade of sins.

Not turned off by the unease in my tone, Regan suggests,
"Come around when you've finished."

"It could be late," I warn her honestly.

I'm ready to hand in my badge immediately when Regan
replies, "That's okay. I'm not going anywhere. Right?"

The relief that crosses her face when I nod makes my chest
swell.

After a final wave, she enters the door the doorman is
holding open for her. I wait until she is whisked away in the
elevator of her apartment building before signaling for the taxi

driver to go. Before he gets two feet from the curb, the door Regan exited only minutes ago pops back open. A small part of me—mainly my egotistical side—is hoping it is Regan. Unfortunately, my luck appears to have run dry today.

"Theresa, what the hell are you doing here?"

After requesting for the cab driver to circle the block, Theresa swings her narrowed eyes my way. "Shouldn't I be asking you that? It is. . ." Her eyes drop to the expensive time-piece circling her wrist. ". . . 3 AM. I'm all about the early bird catching the worm, but you're not scheduled until tomorrow morning. And as much as we wish it weren't the case, Ms. Myers isn't known for her early morning theatrics. Her after-hours antics, though. . ." The mocking laugh she uses to finalize her sentence raises my hackles.

"That's not true. The surveillance team hasn't spotted Regan with any *companions* the previous two months." My teeth grit from my tone dipping at the "companions" part of my statement.

"Hmm. True." Theresa taps her index finger on her painted lips. She is either starting her day early or hasn't laid yesterday to rest just yet. "It's quite comical when you think about it. Just as you started working her case, Ms. Myers' long list of men tapered off. Anyone would swear she was aware she is under surveillance."

Even knowing she is goading me doesn't stop me from retaliating, "There has never been a list. I scoured the reports you gave me with a fine-toothed comb. Other than being photographed having brunch with Isaac, no other male associates have been noted in Regan's file."

"Until now," Theresa adds on, her voice arching as high as her penciled brow.

Tension runs through my veins when she thrusts a manila folder into my hand. I don't need to open it to know what is inside. The sardonic expression on her face answers all my questions. *Smug bitch.*

Recognizing I have no intention to hammer the final nail in my coffin, Theresa throws open the confidentially marked document. A knot tightens in my stomach as I scan the photos inside. The dozen or more snapshots don't just reveal the kiss Regan and I shared in the back of a taxi mere minutes ago; they're a timeline of our trip to Texas—romp in a grassy field and all.

Our pull and thrust routine of the past forty-eight hours is displayed in vivid detail: the tears she shed in the plane when memories of Luca became too much, our argument near the tree that claimed Luca's life. Even the leverage her mother's Jeep gained when we were launched into the air are displayed in graphic detail.

"I must say, I didn't think you had it in you. When I told you to go in hard, this wasn't what I was anticipating," Theresa mocks as her eyes absorb a picture of Regan and me wrestling in the cow dung-stained meadow.

"So. . ." She snaps the folder shut and pries it out of my hand, which is virtually impossible with how hard I am clutching it. "The next question is, where do we go from here?"

I expect her to demand my resignation be on her desk by 9 AM, but she shocks me for the second time in under ten minutes when she says, "You've knocked down her wall of trust; now you need to weasel your way into her inner circle."

My eyes snap to Theresa's. "What? I wasn't with Regan to—"

"What are you saying, Alex? Spit it out. We're all friends here." Although she is demanding I speak, she continues talking, "Are you saying your actions this weekend weren't for the good of the agency? That you soiled not only the reputation of the Bureau but the legacy of your family for *that*? A romp in a grassy field with a woman way below your league?"

I don't usually react in anger. Theresa is making me reconsider more than just my position in her team. I've also never had the desire to smack a woman before, but once again, Theresa has me considering a new approach.

"Is that what you're saying, Alex? Surely I'm mistaken. You're a dedicated agent—a highly sought-after member of my team." The sneer in her praise ensures I can't mistake it as sincere. "You don't break the rules for anyone because you understand what's at stake. Am I right?"

My lips move, but not a word escapes them. In this very moment, I recognize Theresa's game plan. She's not an *ask questions, hope for a good response* agent. She crash tackles her mark, stunning them with half-assed assumptions in such quick succession, they believe they're factual. That shit doesn't work with me. Why? Because it's the process I usually run with.

Although my silence should reveal to Theresa her game plan is up, she refuses to acknowledge it. She continues chipping at my armor until she produces a hit so hard, it winds me.

"This isn't just about you and a five-year long obsession, Alex. This goes way deeper than that." She smiles in a way that displays the evil running through her veins before handing me a second folder. "If you've truly placed Ms. Myers above your legacy and your team, this may force you to reconsider your objective."

My nostrils flare when I scan the article inside the folder. It is the contract I negotiated with the Bureau for Dane to be placed on Theresa's team as a consultant. It is up for renewal at the end of the month.

"Dane has nothing to do with this." My words mince through grinding teeth. "He's an agent—"

"*Was* an agent."

I continue talking as if Theresa never spoke, "Who has given countless years of service to the Bureau. His family relies on this money, Theresa. They can't survive on his disability insurance. He lives in the most expensive state in the country."

Blood floods my cheeks when Theresa says sardonically, "I guess he'll have to move."

"Move?! He can't move. It cost hundreds of thousands of dollars to have his house fitted with the equipment he needs to live a standard life. He's over six feet tall; his wife can't be expected to carry him up a set of stairs."

She looks down at me, her hideous, evil eyes scanning my face. "All facts you should have considered before traveling miles across the country with a target—"

"Regan isn't a target!" My voice is so loud, a lady entering a bakery next to us balks. After calming the anger scorching my veins with a few quick breaths, I say more respectfully, yet sternly, "She is a victim caught up in a world she doesn't belong in."

"If that is true, what harm will be done proving that?" Theresa asks, her tone lowering to a more understanding one.

I remain quiet, not trusting her, but having nothing to fall back on. I know Regan is innocent, so proving that isn't an issue. It is the lying I'm struggling with. My plan today was to come clean to Theresa about the conflict of interest I have in this case. Then, once the dust settled on that, confessing my line of work to Regan was my next step. Now. . . I'm fucking lost.

I am to blame for Dane's injuries, so shouldn't I sacrifice my happiness to ensure he lives the best life possible? If you had asked me that same question only days ago, I would have answered yes without a smidge of doubt. Now I'm torn. I want Regan more than anything, but I owe Dane *everything*.

"What do you need?" My voice is laced with so much anger, I have a hard time recognizing it.

"Names, dates, anything we can use to take down Isaac," Theresa answers quickly, her briskness exposing her eagerness. She wants to take Isaac down almost as badly as I do. I just haven't figured out why.

I rub my hand across my tired eyes before asking, "And that's all you'll do with the information? Take down Isaac?"

Theresa's pause should riddle me with hesitation, but with my head not responsible for my thoughts, I pretend her dipping chin is in good faith.

It is stupid of me to do, but not as stupid as it is for her to underestimate me.

5

"What can I say? She's a freak, and not in the way I like them."

A halfhearted laugh escapes my lips as I slouch into my chair. "I wouldn't let Kristin hear you say that. She'll have you hung by your nuts."

"Wouldn't be the first time." Dane's laugh is more genuine than mine. "Won't be the last."

When a deep *oomph* barrels down the line, my first smile of the day cracks onto my lips. I should have known Kristin was by his side, supporting him. Excluding the day she gave birth to their second daughter, Addison, she hasn't left his side since that fateful night five years ago. She's the adrenaline pumping through his veins. The reason he wakes every day. *She's his Regan.*

I wait for Dane to finish laughing before asking, "Did you forward the footage from Regan's apartment to the DA handling Danielle's case?"

Dane hums the start of his reply. "She said it wasn't required, but I still shared what I found."

His reply is short, but it doesn't stop me missing the words he didn't say. "You also believe Danielle will get off lightly?"

Dane's second hum isn't as strong as his first. "Most likely. It's a sticky case. Your grubby mitts didn't help."

"What was I supposed to do? Let her attack Regan in a church full of witnesses?"

My reply is equally shocked and peeved. Shocked he doesn't understand my objective—Dane protects his wife as fiercely as I guard Regan—and peeved he's reading Regan's stalker case in the same manner as me.

"Yeah, pretty much," Dane replies, snubbing the fury in my tone. "Then the case would have more evidence than just a partial fingerprint discovered in a glove several floors down from the crime scene and the word of two scorned women."

"Regan isn't scorned—"

"She is listed as the spouse of the deceased. Even if Danielle's claims of an affair with Luca are false, the jury will still see Regan as a scorned woman, meaning Danielle's claim of being harassed by Regan after Luca's death is plausible."

My deep exhalation nearly drowns out what Dane says next: "You know the odds in these cases, Alex. For every juror we dismiss for their disdain of cheating, we have another who's a glorified adulterer. I hate to tell you, man, but the odds are against you on this one. Danielle is claiming self-defense."

Anger hits me like a hard blow to my chest. "How can she claim self-defense when *she* was the one who arrived at church clutching a pig's heart?"

"The same way you should have refuted Theresa's claims of being insubordinate—severe emotional distress."

A *pfftt* noise vibrates my lips. "Severe emotional distress, my ass. Nothing I did this weekend was done under protest."

"I know." Dane's tone isn't as high as mine, his voice not as stern. "But Theresa doesn't. She placed you in a predicament you weren't trained for, therefore you didn't know how to act. A simple mistake—any good union rep will argue the same on your behalf."

That's easy for him to say. He doesn't know what Theresa is holding over my head. It isn't just my job on the chopping block if I go against her. Dane's livelihood is also at stake.

Believing my silence is due to contemplating his suggestion, Dane says, "You called for my advice, so here it is: go the deflective ruse. It's an easy excuse. I glanced at the surveillance images logged this weekend. If I were there, I would have *soothed* Regan in the same manner you did."

The last half of his sentence comes out in a flurry from Kristin's fist stealing the air from his lungs. It is lucky she's quick to retaliate, as my response wouldn't have been anywhere near as subdued.

A door being slammed shut rumbles down the line before Dane quickly pushes out, "Stop being so hard on yourself. Do you truly believe you're the first agent to dive beneath the sheets with a target? It is a part of our industry."

His reply stumps me—wholly and without constraint. I know him well enough to know his comment wasn't metaphorical. He's talking from experience.

"What the fuck, man? Does Kristin know?"

I try to hold in my anger, but, in all honesty, I can't. Kristin is so much like a sister to me, anger minces my words, making me sound the most volatile and unhinged I've ever been.

"Don't be an idiot." Dane laughs as if we're at a comedy club. I don't know what the fuck he thinks is funny. This shit isn't funny.

When I say that to him, he replies, "You need to remember who you're preaching your godliness to. I heard the rumors. I know how you climbed the rankings so fast."

Fury builds in my gut. "What the fuck are you talking about? I got where I am on my own merit. No one gave me shit."

His mocking laugh adds to the wobble of my top lip. "Uh-huh, you keep telling yourself that, bro."

When he disconnects our call, I clutch my cell as if it is his neck. This isn't the first argument we've had, but it's the first time I've regretted carting him down the meadow on my back. That man I was arguing with is not my brother. The Dane I know idolizes his wife. His girls are the apples of his eye. He'd rather die than hurt them. He doesn't cheat and lie. He loves. I can't put it any simpler than that.

I sit in silence for several minutes, torn on where I go from here. I called Dane because I needed advice on what to do with Regan. Our conversation started in the right direction until Dane gave me an update on Danielle's charges. There is solid evidence that Danielle has been in Ravenshoe the past two months. She admitted to the arresting officer that she has a "strong dislike" of Regan, but the DA is still going in soft.

At this rate, she'll barely get a slap on the wrist, let alone the sentence she deserves. It is like five years ago all over again. They're handed the perp wrapped up in a shiny red bow, but instead of believing the evidence presented to them by a dedicated and well-respected member of law enforcement, they side with the criminal.

I guess that excuses my heated conversation with Dane. We're both on edge. Dane has a bout of extensive physical therapy coming up—it's costly and excruciatingly painful—and I'm still twisted up in knots over my somewhat arrangement with Theresa.

I don't trust her. She'd throw a baby under the bus if it guaranteed she'd get her man. That's not someone I want to side with. What I said to Dane was straight up honesty. Everything I've accomplished in my career I achieved myself. No one gave me a lending hand or a sneaky payment under the table.

My dedication to my job is why I'm at the office at god knows o'clock on my day off, seeking evidence in Isaac's case. I know what I'm searching for is here; I just have to find it.

And I'll do it without prying into Regan's private life.

A few hours later, I throw an evidence folder onto my desk in frustration before raking my fingers through my hair. I'm fucking exhausted. With my run-in with Theresa playing on my mind all morning, I didn't get a wink of sleep before starting an impromptu sixteen-hour shift at the office.

I'm also dying to call Regan, but since I'm striving to keep the lies to a bare minimum, I don't know what I could say. Even asking her something as simple as how her day was could substantiate corruption when I eventually come clean. Her day-to-day life intertwines with Isaac's, so until that is unraveled, a humble conversation is out of the question.

I've never felt so fucking torn in my life, and Dane's confession isn't helping matters. He cheated on his wife. Like. . . fuck. If he can do that, what else is he capable of?

Now I understand what Regan meant about not lying to the people you love. I'm hurt by Dane's betrayal, and I'm not the one he deceived. And although my deception isn't as deep as Dane's, at the end of the day, I'm still lying to Regan.

Under different circumstances, I'd come clean. Not just to Regan but Kristin as well. Obviously, my knee wasn't the only thing that got shattered in that field all those years ago. Apparently, my integrity was destroyed right along with it.

When did I become this man? Was it when I lied under oath to save a woman I didn't know? Or when I pledged to Dane I'd never stop hunting the man responsible for his injuries knowing he was sitting directly across from him, vowing revenge?

This weekend, I thought I regained a part of me I had missed the most. Now I'm realizing all I did was half unmask him. I'm no better than I was five years ago or six weeks ago. I'm broken. Fractured. Fucking lost.

I'm drawn from dangerous thoughts when the creak of a door sounds through my ears. Cranking my neck, I spot a man approximately mid to late twenties standing at the entrance of my office. Well, I shouldn't say *my* office. The damp, sooty basement the Bureau seconded for Theresa's team doesn't have any internal walls, and the dusty windows lining one side only peer out to a derelict warehouse that houses just as many rats. It is a bunker that represents Theresa's operation to a T—bland and boring as fuck.

Noticing the unnamed intruder is standing next to an

industrial-sized vacuum, I gesture for him to enter. He does—albeit hesitantly. I understand his unease. Usually, the instant the clock strikes six, a mass evacuation occurs from this floor. The techs don't put in the same hours we agents do. They've got women to go home to. Kids to bathe. *Sheets to mess.*

If I weren't seeking evidence to take Isaac down without Regan's help, I would have left hours ago—although sleep would be the last thing on my mind. Who needs rest when you have a woman like Regan waiting for you?

Not anyone sane.

When my eyes return to the stack of evidence in front of me, a few hours of shuteye doesn't seem as impossible as it did seconds ago. My sleep deprivation must be making my vision blur, because if I were to believe the reports in front of me, Isaac is a brilliant business man who is filthy fucking rich, but not corrupt.

If that isn't a clear sign for me to call it a night, I don't know what is.

When I stand to gather my jacket from the back of my chair, I notice the janitor is still loitering by the door. He has dropped to his knees, the large vacuum cleaner he's wrangling as uncooperative as my heart has been the past seventy-eight hours.

"Did you check the fuse? Relics like her still have the original equipment they were designed with," I ask, stopping at his side.

He mumbles something about it not being the fuse. His sharp grumble reveals his disinterest in my help, but if that didn't, his quick change in position is a sure-fire indication.

Must be asshole appreciation day today—everyone is super moody.

After taking in his sandy blond hair, the part of his face not hidden by a cap, and dainty hands, I head for the door. I'd wish him luck, but he's not the only one struggling with anger issues today. I have plenty of them—in abundance.

Halfway to the door, my pace slows. His hands were dainty, *dainty*—almost feminine. I don't know why it bothers me—his girly hands are more a problem for him than me—but recalling that fact has my heart rate kicking up.

Just before I exit, I scan the notch in the wood the janitor's frame reached when he entered. It is inches below my line of sight—making him a good head shorter than me.

Once again, his small stature is no concern of mine, but yet again, it has my heart rate soaring. His age, height, and lithe frame must make his position difficult. He'd barely hit 130 on the scales. The vacuum he's trying to fix weighs nearly that much.

I don't know whether to laugh or groan when my polished dress shoe snags a cable on the ground. The cord from the vacuum cleaner is sitting halfway out the door—nowhere near the closest electrical outlet.

"Might start if you plug it in." My deep timbre is hindered by annoyed laughter.

I don't have time to tell others how to do their job. I'm having enough trouble maintaining my own work ethic.

Bobbing down, I pick up the cable before spinning around to face the janitor. Halfway there, a glimpse of silver flashes before my eyes.

Then all I see is blackness.

6

*M*y eyes stray from the screen of my phone to Isaac when his throaty cough rumbles through my ears. He doesn't have a cold; he's merely announcing he's noticed my disturbance without words. I've been a little preoccupied the last half of our meeting. By a little, I mean a lot. Alex never said he'd make contact before arriving at my apartment tonight; I'm just hoping he will. Isaac works odd hours. Considering he is my sole employer, I bend my schedule to fit him. I forgot to factor our meeting in when I invited Alex over to share a bottle of wine, so I'm worried I'll miss his visit.

I freeze as fear hardens my spine. I've become one of them: those needy, clingy women who stare at their phones for hours on end, willing for them to ring.

Ugh! I'm going to be sick.

Is this why Alex hasn't made contact in over eighteen hours? He said he'd be late, but I didn't realize he meant this late. If he is loitering because of my forwardness, he doesn't need to fret.

Asking a man to share a bottle of wine is the equivalent of slipping him my hotel room key. It doesn't equal a lifetime commitment. It means I'm horny.

Mostly.

Somewhat.

Not even.

Argh! This is the exact reason I didn't want to go to Texas. I barely knew the man who bumped heads with me in the elevator, but that didn't stop me from thinking about him twenty-four-seven for the two months that followed. If that didn't already have my radar hollering, the fact I agreed to go home with him on the weekend of Luca's memorial should have been all the indication I needed to know I should stay far away from him.

Perhaps I'm having a midlife crisis? I'm not thirty for another three years, but after everything I've been through, some days I feel like I'm fifty. Don't get me wrong, when my thoughts stray to Alex, sex is on the forefront of my mind. But occasionally, everything he said and did this weekend also makes an appearance.

You couldn't see his eyes when he held me after our foray in the business class bathroom. We were in the most unromantic venue you could possibly imagine, the zesty scent filtering the air constantly reminding us of our location, but nothing could take away from the emotions exchanged between us during that moment. It was beautiful—*horrifyingly disgusting*—but beautiful nonetheless.

My dinner stops creeping up my esophagus when a stern gaze secures my devotion. Isaac is glaring at me. It isn't his *make your knees wobble with nothing but a sideways glance* stare. It is

45

more frightening than that. He wants to talk, and it has nothing to do with business.

Pretending I can't read him as well as he can read me, I prop my hip onto the makeshift desk before glancing down at the business proposal displayed across it.

"I like it. Not sure I'd pay to enter the dance club, but desperation makes people stupid. So. . ." A shrug finalizes my reply.

Not believing my sudden interest in the nightclub designs he's showing me is genuine, Isaac arches his brow. I act oblivious, my skills clearly unimpressive considering how narrow his eyes become.

"It's nothing," I eventually succumb, throwing my arms into the air. "It's just a guy I met. He's as confusing as you."

Isaac takes my swipe at his ego with a smile. "Did you meet him while home for the weekend?"

My eyes rocket to his. *How does he know I went home?*

"Your credit card," he fills in, smirking at my wide eyes and gaped mouth. "My accountant fills me in on any expenses charged—Every. Single. Morning."

Misreading the anger in his tone as exploitation, I pledge, "I transferred my fare on the way here. I'm not expecting you to foot the bill—"

Isaac swipes his hand through the air, cutting me off. "I don't care about the money. Your expenses are covered as part of your employment—travel included." He waits for me to nod in agreement before continuing, "I'm more interested in your decision to return home *this* weekend. How long has it been?"

He already knows my reply, but I pretend he doesn't.

"Nearly a year since I've been home. Eight since I've stepped foot in that church."

Hearing the quiver in my words, Isaac moves around the desk to join me on the other side. He's removed his suit jacket but kept on his beloved vest, giving him the enticing ruthless businessman look every woman craves—*well, ones not suddenly obsessed with Viking men with devastating blue eyes and hairy chins.*

Isaac's eyes dance between mine, his lips unmoving. He doesn't need to speak to express his questions, though. I can see the concern in his eyes, hear the elongated beat of his heart. He is so clued in on every aspect of his employees' lives, he knows precisely what occurred this weekend. I just hope his sixth sense is honing in on Luca's memorial and not the other equally heart-clutching events of the weekend.

"How was it?" Isaac asks a short time later when he sees the remorse in my eyes switch to something else—something I'm striving to ignore every time I catch sight of my reflection.

I'll never regret a single moment of my time at home, but I do regret not doing it sooner. Even with Danielle's batshit crazy idea that I'm a heartless wench in need of saving, the past weekend was good for me. I combatted hurt, resentment, and the fear of being unworthy of love all while surrounded by people who actually love me. It makes a lot of sense when you think about it.

"It was . . . *good*. Not really an ideal setting for a naughty getaway, but it went okay." A frisky wink chops up the concern in my tone to more manageable pieces.

Isaac laughs, thankfully accepting my jest in good faith. I want to update him on all the juicy and not-so-juicy tidbits of my weekend, but since I'm not eager to add more worry to his plate, I keep quiet.

The more successful Isaac becomes, the more he has needed to stay on his toes. Unless they're featured on *Sixty Minutes*, people don't like to hear others' success stories. Jealousy, suspicion, and even sometimes distrust come into play when people believe someone has succeeded them.

That's why I was so gung-ho about Alex's comment on two alphas not able to co-exist unless they're planning to take each other out. Why can't there be more than one successful person in a relationship?

Take my friendship with Isaac as an example. I don't loathe him because he's rich, handsome, and successful. I want to emulate his achievements. And since Isaac's views are similar to mine, I'll achieve them even sooner than anticipated.

Isaac isn't a greedy man. He shares his wealth and knowledge with those closest to him. It's the reason we're standing in a derelict warehouse near midnight. This rundown factory is our first joint business merger. I have a thirty percent stake in Isaac's latest venture. I am a silent shareholder, but I'm not worried. A man as astute and business-conscious as Isaac would never make a stupid business decision. Furthermore, I drew up our agreement. If anyone is in danger of coming out of our deal a loser, you can be assured it isn't me.

"When will the refit be finalized?" I ask Isaac, hoping to get our conversation back on track before I crash.

I'm not like Isaac. I usually wake before the sun, pound the pavement for two hours straight, then start my day, which means I'm usually in bed no later than 11 PM. The redeye Alex and I took last night already stole hours of my sleep, much less how many times Alex has occupied my thoughts.

Isaac flashes a brutal grin. "He tried for six weeks, but I scaled him back to three."

I smile at the ruthlessness in his tone. His builder isn't lucking out—he just wrongly assumed working for Isaac would be a walk in the park. It won't take him long to adjust. Isaac will ride you like an inmate serving life, but he pays well if you produce what he needs.

"Alright. I'll get these documents finalized this week before scheduling acquisitions for the parcels of land on each side of ours." I roll up the blueprints and hand them to Isaac. "Are you still chasing that bakery a few blocks over? I had a chat with the planning commissioner last week. We may be able to switch the zoning from commercial to industrial, meaning the owner will have no choice but to close up shop, but I wanted to check with you first."

Isaac's pause for consideration is shocking. Usually he's on the ball when it comes to all things business. "Let me speak with Cormack. My plans are for Ravenshoe to prosper, not run businesses out of town."

I wryly grin, loving the honor in his tone when he talks about Ravenshoe. No matter what the crazies tell you, this town belongs to Isaac.

"Okay. I'll advise Mitch to hold on any mergers until I get word from you."

I shadow Isaac out of the makeshift door his builders blasted through a double bricked wall earlier today. A smile crosses my face when I spot Hugo, Isaac's righthand man/body guard, leaning on the front panel of Isaac's Mercedes. Hugo is a handsome man in his early thirties. His dark hair contrasts with his white face, making his gleaming white teeth even more noticeable. He is a similar build and height to Alex, so I'm certain he's equally appealing out of his clothes as he is in them, although I could never testify to the fact.

What I said to Alex in the wee hours of this morning is true: Isaac has a stern nonfraternization policy he demands his staff follow. But even if he didn't, I don't ever see Hugo and me dancing beneath the sheets. He's a little annoying—kind of like the big brother I've never had. He's handsome and fun to hang around, but I'm more interested in strangling him than seeing him naked.

A prime example of why we'll never do the naughty rumba presents when Hugo curls his thick arm around my shoulders to noogie my head. "Didn't think I'd ever see the day. Little Ms. Prim and Proper getting down and dirty in the club scene."

His comment makes me smile—*on the inside.* I can't let him think he got under my skin by smiling for real. He falsely believes my sky-high shoes, pretty dresses, and perfectly made-up face make me a goodie two shoes.

He's so far off the mark, he's one of the "girlfriends" I referenced when I said I should have recorded my romp with Alex in the meadow. City slickers often underestimate us country girls. When we get down and dirty, we don't just get our heels a little smudgy. We get downright filthy.

Hugo's laughter is cut in half when my elbow becomes friendly with his ribs. Using his distraction to my advantage, I dip under his arm, spin on my heels, then dash for the bustling street in front of me.

I barely make it six paces when the heat of a gaze slows my

steps. Isaac's overprotectiveness is so obvious, I don't need to hear him speak to feel his concern.

"I'm fine. I've got mace in my purse," I assure him, not bothering to spin around and face him and his stern glare.

"And. . .?"

Hugo's high tone forces me to spin. He's giving me the same rueful glare as Isaac, and suddenly it's like going from one younger brother to two overbearing older ones.

When Hugo's dark brow becomes lost in his hairline, I murmur, "I've also got your gift." I pat my clutch shoved under my arm.

Hugo doesn't give fancy bottles of perfume or generous checks like Isaac every Christmas. He hands out mace, knuckle-busters, and pretty little guns that slip right into a regular-sized purse.

"No one will mess with me tonight. . . *not unless they want a knuckle sandwich.*" I say my quote with the same drawl Hugo's voice regularly dons. It is a weird cross between a New Yorker accent and a Bostonian. "Now go on, get, before I make you shadow me on that 4 AM run you've been promising me since last year."

Hugo grimaces. I barely see it with how quickly he dives into the driver's seat of Isaac's town car.

Unfortunately, Isaac isn't as eager to leave. "Are you sure you don't need a ride? I'm going straight past your penthouse."

"Certain. I'm not going home." I waggle my brows.

He spots my lie a mile out but pretends he doesn't. Hating that I've placed him on a list he doesn't belong on, I hit him with straight-up honesty. "I missed my run this morning. It's playing havoc with my emotions. I need to burn off some

51

energy, so I figured a late night walk might do me some good."

Hearing the truth in my reply, Isaac dips his chin. "Okay, but stay on the main roads. I'll have Hunter trace your steps."

Stealing my chance to announce I don't want his head of security following my every move, Isaac slips into the back of his car. I glare at him through the heavily tinted window for several moments, only breaking contact when it dawns on me he has no intentions of leaving this alley until I'm out in the open, wild and free for his hacker/security guard to trace my every step.

With a huff, I continue for the street. Only once I merge onto the sidewalk do I lose Isaac and Hugo's scrutiny. *Thank god.* I handled enough machoism this past weekend to last me a lifetime. I don't need any more. And I'm not solely referring to Alex.

Needing a quick breather, I duck into the little alcove of the nightclub Isaac and I are building. I'm not tired; I've barely walked five steps. My body is just kicking up a stink about the number of times Alex has entered my mind today.

I wish my heart was my only body part being uncooperative. My brain is being just as perverse. I swear I can smell Alex's schmexy scent right now. It's virile and hot, making me so desperate, I'm five seconds from calling him a pathetic loser.

Ugh! Step it up, Regan. Desperation is your ugliest attribute.

Agreeing with the voice in my head, I move out of the alcove. I complete two whole steps before a deep groan scares the living daylights out of me. There is a homeless man sleeping under a soiled blanket near a dumpster on my right. He's moaning and groaning as if his body can't decide whether to vacate the contents of his stomach or bowels first.

Although I feel sorry for anyone required to sleep in an alleyway, Alex's stance on not giving money to the homeless alters my steps. Instead of walking toward the man in need, I pace away from him. I'm not going far, just to the convenience store on the corner. A bottle of water and some Advil may help ease his pain.

Before I leave the alley, the homeless man grunts something under his breath. I freeze, certain I heard him wrong. If he uttered the name I believe he did, he isn't just a random homeless guy. He's someone extremely important to me. Someone who hasn't left my mind all day.

With my heart in my throat, I jackknife back. My worst fears come true when I spot a snippet of blue snaking out of the blanket tossed over the man's head. He isn't a beggar living on the streets because he has no money. He's Alex.

"Oh my god, what happened?"

I rush to his side, my steps as frantic as my heart rate. My stomach heaves when I toss the blanket off him. His ruse of acting homeless is more authentic since he's sleeping in pee-scented bedding.

The desire to sanitize my hands for the next year flies out the window when I raise his slumped head. He has a large gash on his right temple sending a stream of blood down his cheeks, his thick and bushy beard a perfect sponge to absorb the mess.

I gag again as my head grows woozy. *I don't do blood. Blood and I are not friends.*

"Wait here; I'll get help."

I twist then stand, my charge across the asphalt only slowing

53

when Alex faintly murmurs, "No." For how fast my heart is raging, I'm shocked I heard him. "No police. Help me up." His words are separated by long, painful groans.

Over a dozen curse words roll through my head when I bob down to aid him from the ground. He either drank two gallons of whiskey for dinner, or the bump on his head did a real number on him. He can barely stand upright.

"Whoa. Slow down," I plead when he stumbles toward the dumpster he was resting on. *If he falls, I may never get him up.*

I watch him toss aside pee-stained blankets and soiled cardboard as if they're feathers as he hunts for something in the trash next to the dumpster.

"What are you looking for?" I ask when his furious growl vibrates both my chest and the area between my legs.

After scanning the alley, he shifts his eyes to me. "They took my gun."

"They?"

I want to act shocked at his admission he owns a gun, but we both know it would be a woeful waste of time. I've known since the day we bumped heads that he carries a weapon—now it's just a fact instead of a hunch.

"From what I heard while drifting in and out of consciousness, there were at least two perps."

"Perps?"

I swallow harshly. I'm more worried about him being unconscious than knowing how many men jumped him, but just like I'd never let Hugo believe he got one up on me, I can't let Alex know how profoundly he's crawled under my skin either. Not yet. *Maybe never.*

My hand slides into my clutch when Alex nods. The cool

metal under my fingertips soothes me enough I can scan the alley without fear. The men who assaulted Alex better be long gone, or they're about to find out the lengths Myers go to protect those they care about.

Mistaking the heavy groove between my brow as fear, not shock he's already on a short list of men I'd draw blood for, Alex advises, "They're not here. They left ages ago." His lips quirk in confusion. "What time is it?"

He curses when I twist my wrist to show him it is nearly 1 AM.

"What the fuck did he hit me with? I was out cold for nearly two hours."

Unsure if he wants me to answer, I shrug. "Are you sure you don't want to call the police or go to the hospital? You're bleeding—*profusely*."

I'm surprised at how confident my voice is. My stomach doesn't match. It's five seconds from tossing.

"No police. I don't want a turf war," Alex answers.

I keep my expression just as passive as his, hoping it will hide my confusion about his reply. What turf war is he talking about. . .? *Oh no. He's not a gangbanger, is he?* The Italian mob has been trying to get a foothold in Ravenshoe for years. Only Isaac's friendship with another notorious syndicate leader has stopped it from happening. The same can't be said for the towns bordering us. Hopeton has been riddled with gang violence the past twelve months.

My focus shifts to Alex when he asks to borrow my cell. Nodding, I rummage through my purse. Since I'm all thumbs, it soon falls to the ground, exposing Alex isn't the only one packing heat.

"What the fuck?" Alex's voice is as firm as his fists clench when he spots my gun. "Where did you get that? Is it legal?"

I shrug. I didn't ask Hugo for the deets when he gifted it to me. I just shoved it in my purse, where it has remained until now.

"Give it to me." He summons me with two fingers like I'm a dog being commanded to heel next to its owner.

He may be injured, and I may be on the verge of a panic attack, but you can be assured I'll never be a spineless wench who jumps on queue. With a sneer, I shove my dainty weapon back into my purse before clutching it into my chest. "No, it's mine."

Alex steps closer to me, suffocating the putrid scent lingering in the alley with his seductive *I can't wait to drink it all up* smell. "Open carry is illegal in Florida. You need a fucking permit."

His expression twists with anger, but it has nothing on the worry crossing mine. Just the pain smoldering in his eyes when they met mine reveals it took him an immense amount of effort to retaliate to my childish reply—nearly as much as it's taking him to remain standing.

Realizing this is a fight for another day, I thrust my purse into Alex's chest. My swing is barely a fairy tap, but it is enough to send him stumbling backward. I barely catch him before he crashes into the dumpster, which is a mammoth effort considering he is nearly double my weight.

Some of the anger on Alex's face fades as he regains his footing. He's not grateful I stopped him and the ground from making kissy faces; he's pleased I submitted to his demand without complaint.

"Did you drive here?"

I wait for him to straighten his polo shirt before shaking my head. It takes everything I have to leash my anger when a furious growl bubbles in his chest. He gives me a look, one that advises a prolonged talk on personal safety has been placed on my upcoming agenda. *Goodie—not!*

Through gritted teeth, I say, "There is a taxi stand half a block up. We'll get a cab back to my apartment, then we can attend to your wound."

My tone is sharp with worry. I'm not concerned about taking him back to my apartment. It is the blood oozing from his wound causing my fretful response. The more anger thickens his blood, the wider the vibrant red streak down his cheek becomes.

After scanning the alley for the third time, Alex replies, "We can't stay at your apartment. We'll go to a hotel."

I want to argue, but the slur of his words squashes the need. He's on the verge of collapse, minutes from succumbing to his injuries. The only reason he hasn't surrendered is because he's too panicked about protecting me. How do I know this? He has the same horrified expression on his face my dad did when he arrived at Luca's accident scene eight years ago.

The howl he released when he thought I was in the car was horrific. It shredded my heart just as violently as it did when the medics pulled Luca from the wreckage. He was right. I was sitting in the passenger seat of Luca's car that night. I just hid from him as I wish I could Alex right now.

Don't misconstrue my lack of empathy. I don't want to hide from Alex because I'm an uncaring, selfish bitch. It is the very opposite that has me running scared. Bit by bit the past weekend, the wall around my heart crumbled. I tried in vain to build it back up today, but all the bricks I stacked toppled the instant Alex reappeared.

I'm feeling things I shouldn't be feeling—things I haven't felt in years. That's why I tried to protect my heart, to rebuild the wall he pulverized, because if I don't do something to salvage the wreckage, this man could destroy me.

I don't know how.

I don't know why.

I just know he will.

7

*M*y mouth burns as if I have swallowed acid, and my head is thumping, but the ache that's been stabbing my chest the past twenty-plus hours has vanished because Regan is sitting beside me—safe and uninjured. In the seconds leading to me passing out, she was the first person to enter my mind, and she never left.

At a time where I should have been concerned about my safety, all I could think about was her. That's not surprising. I'd rather take a bullet to the skull than see her hurt—especially if I am the man causing her pain. The absolute terror clouding her eyes when she tossed off the blanket covering me matched the fear they held when she stood up on the podium at Luca's memorial to give her eulogy. I knew she wanted this; I just didn't realize her desires were as profound as mine.

A hiss parts my lips when the taxi driver takes a corner so sharply my brain collides with my throbbing skull. I honestly don't know what the perp hit me with. It had to be something significant as I've been fading in and out of consciousness the past two hours.

From the quickest flash of silver I saw before I was knocked out cold, I was suspicious of the vacuum cleaner, but the man who assaulted me was waif-thin, his frame feminine. He could barely lift the vacuum, much less strike me over the head with it.

That's how I know there was a second assailant—that and the fact I heard two voices when I was moved from my office to the alley outside. I don't know why they needed to move me. There is nothing in my office but paperwork, files, and a whole heap of surveillance images. . .

My inner monologue trails off as a disturbing thought enters my mind.

Fuck.

My wooziness doubles when I drop down low to snag Regan's purse off the cab floor. I slide open the zipper with force, not the least bit worried about its squeals of protest. Unappreciative of me manhandling her belongings, Regan snatches it out of my grasp. I barely get out half a protest when she thrusts her cellphone into my hand, proving she knows me better than anyone.

After giving her a quick smirk in thanks, I slide my finger across the screen. When it requests a lock code, my eyes drift to Regan.

"Zero, zero, zero. . ." She swallows numerous times in a row at my stern glare before forcing out a final, "Zero."

The deep gash in my brow stings when I arch it high. She hammered me for not having a passcode, yet she has the most generic one there is.

"It's better than none," she grumbles under her breath while I dial a number known by heart.

Uneasy about having this conversation in front of Isaac's lawyer, I twist my torso to the traffic streaming by the taxi we're sitting in. Although I trust Regan, I don't know how deep her loyalty to Isaac runs. I also don't want to put her in a compromising situation.

Theresa answers my call a mere second before it goes to voicemail.

"Send a crew to HQ. I believe our operation has been compromised."

Theresa fumbles something out, but Regan's deep gasp drowns out what she said. It is for the best. My head is pounding too severely to deal with a verbal slinging match with the devil's spawn who wears Prada.

"I was jumped at HQ before they moved me into the alleyway. The perps wouldn't have done that unless they were seeking something significant at my location."

Theresa's deep sigh exposes she understood my coded response. "It's our target. I guarantee it. He knows we're on to him."

I murmur in halfhearted agreement. This feels like something Isaac would do, but it's not sitting right with me. I trust my gut, and it's warning me to remain vigilant. Until I work out what its caution pertains to, Isaac will merely remain the top man on my list. He just isn't the sole listee.

"I'll have men directed there now." Theresa coughs as if pained to ask her next question: "Are you injured?"

"Not enough for you to worry."

She laughs, more amused I wrongly think she cares than

charmed by my dry humor.

My eyes stray to Regan when Theresa's second question comes out more sincere than her first, "Will you be in tomorrow?"

I take in Regan's wide eyes, quivering chin she's trying to control with a scowl, and clasped hands. "No. I'll take a few days off. My head is thumping like a bitch." *Not as much as my heart*, but I won't tell Theresa that.

Theresa's disdainful groan is the last thing on my mind when I stretch my empty hand across the cracked leather dividing Regan and me. I hold it out palm side up, leaving Regan with the decision of whether she wants my comfort or not.

I exhale the big breath I'm holding when her sweaty hand slips into mine two seconds later. My heart does a weird thump when her head comes to rest on my shoulder a few seconds after.

See? What more proof do you need? She wants this. Even scared—and perhaps a little peeved—she can't deny me or my support.

I can give her both; I've just got to work out a way I can do it without compromising Theresa's investigation. Theresa wants Isaac—*as we all do*. When I hand her her man, her vendetta against Regan and Dane will stop. It's that simple. . . I just wish it wasn't taking so long.

Isaac is clever at hiding his steps. Unfortunately, I'm not one hundred percent convinced he's the only person covering his tracks. The woman beside me is beautiful, smart, and highly intelligent. If anyone is qualified to keep their client out of trouble, it is her.

Recognizing I'll never ease my confusion *or jealousy* by siding with the bane of my existence, I say down the line, "Call me if you need anything. . ."

Theresa's laugh is the last thing I hear before she disconnects our call. After pulling Regan's cell from my ear, I stare down at Theresa's number on the screen. My finger hovers over the delete button, but for some reason, I can't erase it. What if tonight ended with me blacking out from more than just a concussion? Regan knows nothing about my life or the people in it. If she didn't find me tonight, she would have believed I stood her up after our naughty weekend. I don't want that.

She means more to me than just a random hook up, so the last thing I want is for her to believe that's all she is. I'd rather be busted in a lie than have her think she means nothing to me. For that reason, and solely that reason, I hand Regan her phone with Theresa's number still stored inside. If I disappear off the face of earth, she'll have a way of discovering what happened to me.

Regan remains quiet the rest of our trip to the hotel. She doesn't speak a word when I hand the taxi driver an extra-large tip to cover the cleaning bill for the droplets of blood in the back of his cab, or when I request a midfloor room at our hotel. She doesn't utter a single syllable until we enter our room nearly twenty minutes later. Then, it's like a word explosion.

"What's going on? After the incident in my apartment, you wouldn't let me check into a hotel room. But here we are—in a fucking hotel room after you were attacked! You're bleeding—a lot! You said they took your gun, then you called some mysterious female who seemed more concerned about herself than you. Who calls a whiny two-faced bitch for help when they're in trouble?! Not anyone smart!"

I can see she has so much more to say, but thankfully, my cupping of her jaw steals her words.

"We're at a hotel because it is the only place I feel comfortable having this conversation. You're here with me because you're one of a few people I trust. They did take my gun, but I don't need a weapon to keep us safe. . ." I wait for her to see the honesty in my eyes before adding on, ". . . I also had no choice but to call my boss. The men who attacked me wanted something. If I didn't give her a heads up, and they found what they were looking for, my position would be in jeopardy."

My first sentences ease the heavy groove between her eyes, but my last one put it straight back in place. "Why would your position be in jeopardy? You were attacked. Even if the assailants stole a truck load of gold bricks under your watch, you aren't to blame."

"That is true. . . under normal circumstances. My boss is anything but normal," I reply, giving the only excuse I can find.

Things are more complicated than that. If Theresa's hunch is right, and tonight's escapades were performed by someone in Isaac's crew, I have a shit load more than just my position at stake. If the internal affairs department, or someone more highly ranked than Theresa, finds out about my interactions with Regan in the leadup to our operation being infiltrated, they'll assume corruption. If they assume corruption, guess which way their fingers will point first? I'm a sitting fucking duck, waiting to be shot.

"If your boss isn't doing things above board, you need to report her. Or even better, sue her," Regan suggests, following me into the tight yet spotlessly clean bathroom. "You won't believe some of the payouts I witnessed during law school from employees suffering severe emotional distress after workplace incidents. You have rights, Alex. Use them."

My eyes roll before I can stop them. What is it with people citing "severe emotional stress" to me today? I'm not fucking stressed. I'm angry. Furious. On the verge of hunting down the men responsible for Regan seeing me like this and snapping their fucking necks. Then I'll go after the real culprit—the master behind the minions. If this is Isaac's doing, I'll make him pay.

I stop scrubbing blood and dirt from my hands and face when Regan places a three-finger serving of whiskey on the vanity. I was so caught up unjumbling my confusion, I didn't notice she had exited and reentered the bathroom. That is unacceptable. It shouldn't matter what is happening, she should always be on the forefront of my mind.

Although I appreciate her trying to ease the fury blazing through my veins, I can't drink; I'm on the job. When I tell Regan that, she replies, "You *can* drink because you're on leave —remember?"

Her eyes drop to the blood-stained vanity when I stand my ground. I'm not being stubborn. I'm keeping on my toes. Regan's threat and my attack occurred too close for this to be a coincidence. There is something I'm missing, but for the life of me, I can't work out what it is. It is clear our relationship is being watched—the evidence Theresa presented yesterday morning proves this without a doubt, but I'm hesitant to believe the only eyes on us belong to a woman.

I'm drawn from my dark thoughts by Regan's deep swallow.

Her massive gulp was compliments of watching a droplet of blood drip off my chin and roll down the vanity. The contrast between the white sink and my blood is a vivid reminder on how quickly someone's life can end. One bullet can change everything. I'm just fortunate tonight was not my night.

Feeling the heavy sentiment in the air the same as me, Regan seizes the glass of whiskey to throw down the burning liquid with one quick swallow. After slamming the empty glass back on the vanity, she locks her eyes with mine. She doesn't say anything; her eyes just drift over my face before stopping at my beard that looks more reddish than usual compliments of the blood mottled throughout it.

"I can do this," she mutters, more to herself than me.

With a yank on my shoulder, she spins me around to face her. She steps forward until I am crowded against the sink. When she scoots to the left to snag a washcloth off a glass shelf, her breasts scrape my arm. It is only the briefest touch, yet the violent storm swarming us evacuates.

"You don't have to do this."

She wets the washcloth before carefully dabbing it on my right temple, ignoring me, her focus determined.

The more blood she clears, the closer we become.

Within minutes, there's barely an inch of air between us, and I'm hovering on the brink of insanity. I can't have her this close to me and not touch her. I'd rather face corruption charges than give up the crazy, unimaginable sensation that forever bristles between us.

She'll be worth losing everything for, because she is worth *everything*.

I sweep my fingers down Regan's hips slowly, a teasing

66

touch that is so soft, it's hardly registered. When she fails to protest, I drop one of my hands to the slit in her skirt and glide it up her thigh. As my fingertips graze her swollen cleft, her head falls forward, bringing the tip of her nose resting against mine.

I brush the back of my hand down her panties, loving that they moisten under my touch. She calms down as much as she ramps up, my touch dispelling her worry as quickly as it entices her excitement. We breathe as one for several minutes, the angry tension in my veins exchanged for a more enjoyable one.

Once Regan's panties are damp enough to cling to the folds of her pussy, she murmurs, "We shouldn't be doing this. You're hurt."

Her breathless words spoken with worry shouldn't turn me on, but they do. It means she cares for me, which also means she needs this as much as I do. I want her to know she's not responsible for what happened tonight just as much as I need confirmation of it. She wasn't in the alleyway because she knew of Isaac's plans. It was a coincidence. *Wasn't it?*

"Why were you in the alley tonight, Rae?" I ask as my fingers strum her dampened slit.

With her eyes on me and her throat purring, Regan answers, "I was working."

I rub her clit with my thumb, circling it in a way that drives her crazy before slipping her panties to the side to inch two fingers inside of her. Her pussy clamps around my stationary digits, wordlessly begging for them to move while also notching them in a few millimeters deeper.

Although this isn't an interrogation tactic I've used before, I'm excited to test it out. People are most honest when they're

67

blinded by lust. You can't get any rawer than this. My fingers are in her tight canal, my thumb is on her clit, and her beautiful green irises are boring into mine. She's exposed and vulnerable —the most beautiful I've ever seen her.

"You were working? What case can you work on in an alley at 1 AM?"

Regan's breaths rattle when she replies, "It's a business venture. A new nightclub. Construction started last month. I was on my way home when I found you."

My stomach fills with heat from her reply. She's being honest. Numerous blueprints and cash transactions have been added to Isaac's file the past four months. It was earmarked as expenditures for a new operation in the Ravenshoe area.

Although my woozy head had me taking the long route to discover what two plus two equals, Regan's confirmation helps me see things more clearly. The dungeon-like room I've been working out of the past six months is across the street from a bunch of buildings Isaac owns. If he's planning to turn one of them into a nightclub, Regan's admission makes sense. She works for Isaac. She goes where he goes... unless she's with me.

"So you were with your boss tonight?" My interest can't be contained—neither can my jealousy.

"Uh-huh." She swivels her hips, unappreciative of the still-ness of my fingers. "We crunched numbers for hours." With a seductive smirk, she squeezes the walls of her pussy, hugging my stationary digits. "A true accountant would have creamed his pants by now."

"We both know I'm not an accountant—"

"Just like we both know my thoughts on numbers men." Regan's brow is as high as the confirmation in her tone.

I stare at her in shock. *She's aware of the afternoon I pretended to be a doctor?*

When her brow rises even higher, as if to say, *you bet I do,* my heart rate triples.

It is lucky my fingers are in her greedy pussy and my thumb is circling her clit, or she'd have me by the balls. It is also fortunate she doesn't scare easily. This is the exact reason I'm willing to fall onto a knife for her. She's not just the woman I've been seeking the past five years. She's the one I've been searching for my entire life. She gets me—bad points and all, yet she's still not running.

Bottle me up as this brew is done!

"Stand back, baby; I want to see your face."

My breaths come out even harsher when Regan does as requested without any hesitation. She licks her lips when I adjust the angle of my wrist, so I can hook her pussy to my hand as it's never been. I can take her even deeper now, but I still want more.

"Lean your back against the wall and rest your foot on the toilet."

With the bathroom being small in size, Regan can do as requested without my hand breaking contact with her glistening slit. Thank fuck – as my fingers haven't stopped pumping in and out of her the past five minutes, meaning her moans have ramped up a few decibels.

"Now open up your shirt. I want to see those gorgeous tits."

Her wide eyes glide over my sweaty forehead, down my inflamed cheeks and across my bristle-covered jaw before she does as requested. Her delay didn't stem from her concern I'm too injured to participate in a vigorous activity. She needed time to work out whether she wants to gift me the reins or not.

Her quick removal of her blouse proves she does, but her demand two seconds later reveals it is only a partial share. "Your turn."

With a smirk, I grip the back of my shirt and drag it over my head. Because I'm reluctant to remove my fingers from her snug canal, my shirt puddles around my wrist, hiding the enticing visual of her bald pussy being claimed by my fingers. Caught up in the wickedness of our exchange, I remove my fingers from one warm hole, dump my shirt on the ground, then stuff them into an equally inviting location.

Regan balks for the quickest second when her seductive taste coats her tongue, but the husky purr vibrating my fingertips two microseconds later makes up for her shortage of eagerness.

"You taste too fucking good not to share."

Stealing her chance to misread my comment—or hear the slur of my concussed head—I lunge for her mouth. As our tongues share her delicious taste, I toe off my shoes before tackling the belt holding up my trousers with the assistance of my erect cock.

With Regan's help, they're soon dumped on the sparkling clean floor beside our intermingled shirts.

"On or off?" I ask Regan after dragging my mouth from her kiss-swollen lips to lower my eyes to her fitted skirt.

When she peers at me, confused, I elaborate, "We're taking this show into the shower. On or off."

Her teeth graze her bottom lip, torn. She loves the idea of being taken so hard and fast, she doesn't have time to remove her clothes, but she doesn't want her prized possessions getting ruined in the process.

"Tick tock, Rae. My dick is aching for you."

My comment makes her decision on her behalf. Her leap into my arms starts the process of her skirt being removed, so I add a few tugs to help it along.

By the time I switch on the shower faucet, it sits in shreds on top of my trousers.

"This better be worth it," Regan snickers over my lips.

"You know it will be."

To amplify the cockiness of my reply, I brace her back against the wall the water is spraying on, part her thighs with my hips, then drive home. Her eyes close as she struggles to contain the emotions fueling our exchange. Tonight, I'm not the agent who rushed in and saved her from a deranged stalker any more than she's the lawyer who prepared to defend me from thugs when I felt like my brain was about to explode. We are a man and a woman unifying as one. We are even. Equal. Together. *Complete.*

After a few long pumps, I nip Regan's nipple, returning her eyes to mine. She whimpers from the sternness of my bite. It's more a cry of ecstasy than pain. Good. I don't want to hurt her. I just want her to see what her honesty does to me. She could have lied earlier. She could have told me anything I wanted to hear just to ensure our exchange continued on the path it is, but she didn't. She went for honesty. Now I need to do the same. . . after I've taken care of business.

I circle my tongue around Regan's hardened bud before sucking it into my mouth. The hot water siphoning from the showerhead masks her floral scent, but her skin tastes the same.

It is seductive and sweet and has my hips grinding upwards in quick, crafted strokes.

The louder Regan moans, the further her head descends into the water. Gushes of hot water trickle down her platinum hair, straightening her usually wavy locks before gliding across her collarbone and through the dangerous valley between her thrusting breasts.

I tighten my grip on her sharp hips before increasing my speed. I want to see her tits clap in reverence of our performance. The little jiggle and bounce routine they're doing now is nice, but nothing will compare to seeing her body used as it was built for. She was designed to be fucked, and considering this is the first time I've taken her without clothing, I want to cherish every minute of it.

Within seconds, Regan's breasts do the twirl/clap routine I was aiming for. Let me tell you, it is a fucking riveting visual. Her pert pink nipples sit high on the generous swell of her breasts, and the bloom across her chest isn't solely compliments of the heat bouncing between us. I drive into her even harder, taking her to the very brink of ecstasy.

"Oh, god, I can't fucking breathe," Regan murmurs a short time later, her usually smooth voice hardened with lust. "I've heard sex can take your breath away, but this is utterly ridiculous."

With her effort to suck in precious air hindered by the steamy conditions, I switch off the faucet and head to the main area of our hotel room. Not a step is taken without my cock impaling her in some way. We move from the bathroom to the bed without losing contact. . . until I place Regan on the bed.

"My turn."

With her legs curled around my waist, she flips us over so she's straddling my hips—a maneuver I've only seen in A-grade defense classes. I almost voice a protest, but the beautiful curve of her back steals my words. She thrusts her tits my way as she strives to find her rhythm. The rise and fall of her exquisite body as she rides my cock is a captivating visual. The way her stomach clenches with every descent and the sweat rolling from her neck to her breasts keep me enthralled for several long minutes.

I love that she's confident enough to take charge, but with my night not starting as I would have liked, I need to bang my chest a little—assert my authority. So with that in mind, I execute the same maneuver Regan did on me ten minutes ago, except I keep the aggression on the downlow—although she doesn't seem to notice that.

With a grunt, she flips me over once more, commanding the reins without a word spoken. Since we're out of mattress, we land on the floor with a thud. Our brutal crash doesn't deter Regan in the slightest. Before all the air in my lungs has vacated, she straddles my hips, guides the crest of my cock between the folds of her slick canal, then slams down.

I bite out a string of curse words. Her pussy isn't just wetter than it was in the shower; it's also tighter. "You feel so fucking good."

"Then stop fighting for control and enjoy the ride."

Her words aren't snarky—far from it. They're too nurturing to display anything but sincerity. She's not being dominant because I'm failing to give her what she needs. She's taking charge so I can relinquish it. She's identified that I'm struggling and showing she's strong enough to take the reins when needed. If that doesn't prove her ability to destroy me, nothing will.

My fingers dig into Regan's hips with violence when I adjust her position. I'm not fighting to be top dog. I want to show her what her support means to me. She wants us even—I'm assuring we are.

Regan's scream of frustration shifts to a moan of pleasure when my cartwheel-like maneuver has her swollen-with-need pussy landing on my mouth. I crank my neck forward, smashing my lips against the succulence responsible for the delicious scent lingering in the air.

"Oh. . . you shouldn't. . . I can't. . . Fuck. . ." The rest of Regan's reply is a garble.

Her nails dig into my thighs as her head flops forward. She's at my mercy, her body incapable of denying the sensation roaring through it. She quivers and shakes as the most seductive fucking taste I've ever sampled smears my tongue. Her orgasm is quick to arrive but less eager to leave. It takes several long, perfectly addictive minutes before her shaking subsides. And even then, she's only at half-strength.

While Regan works through the exhaustion screaming through her body, I suckle her clit into my mouth, easing its frantic throbs. My speed is slow and patient, a teasing pace full of admiration and mutual respect.

After regaining control of her limbs, Regan returns my devotion with the same agile moves. Her sweaty palm glides down my erect cock before her pouty lips nestle my weeping crown. We suck, lick, and fondle each other for the next several minutes, our exchange only ramping up when the tension in my sack grows too great to ignore.

In a nimble roll, I enter Regan from behind. As we work together to find a rhythm fast enough to be satisfying but slow to starve off my desire to come, I slide my fingertip over the soaked opening of her pussy. With our sideways position letting my chin rest on her nape, she feels the curve of my lips when the strum of her clit causes her hips to jerk forward.

"You better not be laughing at me, Mister Fancy Pants." Her use of my favorite nickname weakens the sneer of her words, but it doesn't completely erase it.

"I'm not laughing. I'm smiling. Those are two entirely different things." After circling my thumb over her clit three times, I add on, " I love the way your body responds to my touch. It's more vocal of your needs than you are."

"That's because the only needs I have are for you to fuck me well enough that I come. . . *again*."

I burrow my head into her neck. I'm not hiding my face in shame but concealing my smile from the dip of her tone when she said "again." Anyone would swear she's never had back-to-back orgasms before. I know that isn't true. Our romp in the field had her firing back-to-back shots. It was beautiful, too perfect to have only happened once.

Unless. . .

"Oh, baby, if I had known, I would have aimed for more than two."

Regan cranks her neck back to peer at me. My chest swells when I see the confirmation I am after in her eyes. I may not have been the first man she slept with, but I was the first to award her multiple orgasms. And you can be assured I'll be the last.

"Step off the soapbox, Alex. You can't bang your chest until you've delivered the goods."

Her sassy words muffle into the thick carpet pile when I adjust her position once more. I heard the challenge in her voice, saw it flare through her eyes. Finding the right balance has always been my biggest issue with Regan, but that never enters the equation when we're fucking. Right here, in this environment, logic defies. We're not dueling; we're forging peace. I've struggled to find my place in the world for years, but that will never be the case when I'm balls deep inside her. I'm the hunter claiming his prize. The first place winner stepping up to the podium to collect his medal. I'm her motherfucking other half.

I stop banging my chest without fists so I can raise Regan's glorious ass high into the air. She purrs a throaty garble when I slam my cock back inside her. It vibrates all the way up my shaft when my hand bounces across the pasty white globes bobbing up and down in front of my face.

As a fiery jolt scampers across the taut skin of her ass, Regan calls out in a grunt, her eyes rocketing to mine. "Again." Her voice is unlike anything I've ever heard. "Spank me again."

A lifetime of injustice is corrected when I answer her request without a single qualm. She shouts my name as her pussy bleeds my cock of precum, its frantic squeezes begging for me to join her on the dangerous ride that borders the brink of insanity. If I weren't still seeking a way to relocate my ego, I'd happily jump on board, but right now nothing but discovering how many ways Regan can scream my name is on my mind.

That. . . and striving to unearth why the angry red handprint on Regan's glowingly white ass has my attacker's identity smacking into me at this very instant.

8

I wait for the shower to switch on in the hotel bathroom before snagging Regan's cell phone from the side table and dialing a frequently called number. An operator at FBI headquarters requests my name and badge number two rings later.

"Alex Rogers, ID 3415673, seeking information on a Brandon James, technician at—"

"Patching you through to his cell now."

"Or that'll work too," I mumble to myself, annoyed.

I'm not bothered by the operator's quick thinking. I'm frustrated as hell that I have to deal with this now. Tonight has been the best night of my life. The past ten hours with Regan have been phenomenal. We fucked. We laughed. We ate room service while sitting on the floor with our legs intertwined before she fell asleep in my arms for the most peaceful four hours of my life.

And I did it all without letting on to her that she is responsible for my assault last night. She didn't clock me over the head before stealing my wallet, badge and gun. She was just her—a woman so perfect men can't understand why they can't have her.

I stop watching steam float under the bathroom door when Brandon's groggy voice sounds down the line. I'm shocked by the huskiness in his tone. He sounds as if I woke him. With Theresa's team dwindled to half a dozen men, I thought she'd have all available agents working on my case. It's what I'd do for a fellow agent. You don't rest until the case is solved. That's why my sleep has been so lacking the past five years.

Deciding to end one pandemic before starting another, I say, "We fucked up."

Although I could place all the blame on Brandon's shoulders, some of it belongs to me. I was so caught up unlocking years of frustration, I didn't adequately assess what was happening. We didn't go to Regan's ranch for a naughty weekend. We went there because Regan's life was threatened. Her safety should have been my only concern. Instead, years of restlessness and unrealistic promises were on the forefront of my mind.

I'll never regret a single moment I've spent with Regan, but I'll forever regret that my stupidity almost cost me everything. I'm not talking about my life, either. I'm referring to Regan's.

"We agreed the assailant was five foot eight with sandy blond hair and a waif-like build."

Brandon murmurs, either in agreement or because he's still in the process of waking up.

"Danielle was recorded as five foot seven on her arrest documentation. . ." Brandon attempts to talk, no doubt to assure me an inch difference in a mental calculation of a perp's height is not uncommon, but I continue speaking, foiling his endeavor to lessen my anger. ". . .and she has mousy brown hair."

"She could have dyed it."

I work my jaw side to side. "It was also noted in her file that her hands smelled of bleach—"

"Because she cleared Regan's apartment of evidence Friday night," Brandon interrupts, speaking to me as if I am an idiot. "That shows our case was thorough, not done in haste."

"No, it doesn't." I furiously shake my head even though he can't see me. "Danielle smells like bleach because she works at a poultry farm. Her main task is to clean the feeders each day—with bleach."

Brandon takes in a sharp breath, but I can tell he isn't one hundred percent persuaded by my evidence. That's okay, I'm confident the next fact I hit him with will have him climbing over the fence.

"The constant wet conditions her hands are immersed in is the reason they're covered with dermatitis. They're scaly and red—nothing like the electrician's hands we captured on surveillance."

"Fuck," Brandon murmurs, the truth smacking into him as perversely as it did me when I stared at the angry red welt on Regan's pasty white skin last night. "But we arrested Danielle. Her fingerprint was in the glove canal. That evidence can't be undone."

"The evidence is right: Danielle was in Regan's apartment Friday night. She just wasn't alone."

I give Brandon a few minutes to absorb the facts. I'm not

doing it because I understand sometimes you need a breather. It is because I also need a moment. The facts were right in front of me, staring me in the face, but I ignored them. Even with my job on the line, and Dane's livelihood at stake, it was the most idiotic thing I've done this week.

After a few silent seconds, Brandon asks, "What do you want me to do? I could run video evidence back through an analytic recognition software via an expanded search. Even without his face, shoulder width, height, and the way he walks, we could discover a match."

My lips twist, impressed. I didn't know we had software capable of tracking someone by their swagger. If I did, Isaac would have been arrested years ago. You can't have attitude like his without the pompous walk to back it up.

Realizing I'm reflecting my anger in the wrong direction, I return my focus to Brandon. "Run the data, but use the footage obtained last night. We may have his face on camera."

"Footage?" Brandon asks, clearly confused. "I don't know what footage you are referring to."

"From the incident at HQ. . ."

Silence—lots and lots of silence teems between us.

"Where I was assaulted. . ."

More silence.

"I was jumped on my way out of the office last night. How do you not know this?"

"You were assaulted while on duty?" The shock in Brandon's tone exposes his confusion is authentic.

Even though he can't see me, I nod. "They took my gun and badge. I don't even have my cell."

I'm not sure why I added the last comment. Probably more

to ensure he's aware my phone is compromised than wanting it cited in my report.

"When did this occur?" Brandon's words are barely heard over the stomping of feet.

"Approximately 11 PM. I was out cold for a few hours, so I could be a little off on the timeframe. I was found in the alley by Regan just before 1 AM."

Brandon's heavy stomps stop. "You were discovered by Regan?"

My jaw tightens from the worry in his tone. He doesn't need to worry about Regan. That's my job.

Pushing my idiotic neurosis to the side, I reveal, "Regan just happened to be visiting the building directly across from HQ. The same building our office windows face."

I swear I can hear Brandon's brain ticking as he works through the facts. "You weren't scheduled yesterday."

A hum vibrates my lips as I nod. "I wasn't due on deck until this morning."

"So the assailant had no idea you'd be where you were at the time of the assault?"

"Uh-huh," I groan as the tick in my jaw ramps up.

"So he wasn't there for you. He was there for. . ."

"Regan," we say at the same time, my voice filled with more anguish than Brandon's.

"He had dainty hands, was a few inches shorter than me, and has sandy blond hair. The fucker we let slip the net Friday night is still free and capable of stalking Regan Monday afternoon. We fucked up."

"We did," Brandon agrees, "but I'm more interested in discovering why Theresa didn't report the incident last night. I was on call. Your contact is the first I've had from a member of our team the past twelve hours."

I take a few moments to contemplate before spitting out, "IA?"

"Huh?" Brandon's voice is so loud I wouldn't be surprised to discover Regan heard it in the shower.

After moving onto the balcony attached to our room, I murmur, "Theresa may be keeping things in house as she's worried about IA. It's the only plausible excuse I can find. With my shit and Regan's shit intermingling, we've got a lot of shit going on. Shit Theresa doesn't want internal affairs becoming aware of."

Brandon pauses again. It isn't long, but it is extremely revealing. He wasn't aware of my relationship with Regan. Although stunned, I'm not wholly shocked. This is the exact reason he's been left in the dark. Theresa has trust issues, and Brandon is new to our team. He's not privy to half the shit she does every day, much less all of it.

"You and Regan?" Brandon doesn't say any more, although I can tell he wants to.

I lick my dry lips. "It's complicated and not something I have time to discuss right now." There's even less time after I hear the shower faucet switch off.

"Alright." I purse my lips, shocked at how quickly Brandon gives in. "How shall I contact you if I get any results?"

He sounds skeptical, but I pretend he doesn't. "Use this number. I'll be out of the office for a few days."

Pen scratching paper sounds down the line at the same time Brandon's breathing weakens. He must be jotting down Regan's phone number.

His deep exhalations return when I say, "And Brandon?"

"Yeah."

I don't know him very well, but I must trust him when I request, "Keep this conversation between us."

Usually, I follow procedures to the letter, but there is a niggle in my gut warning me to remain vigilant. Regan's attacker could have assaulted me and left, but he removed me from the premises. That has my suspicion piqued. He wants Regan, but she isn't the only target on his wish list.

After Brandon agrees to keep things on the downlow, I disconnect our call and head back inside. My timing is better than a perfectly laid out skit when Regan walks into the main area of our room two seconds later.

I do a double take when my scan of her body reaches the luscious curves of her thighs. She's not wearing any pants. She's wearing nothing but my short-sleeve shirt and a smirk sultry enough to buckle the knees of the world's strongest man.

With her eyes on me and her lip caught between her teeth, she murmurs, "It's lucky a majority of my work is done from home. Imagine the coronary my boss would have if I turned up to work like this?"

I grumble under my breath that a coronary will be too easy a death for him if he *ever* sees her like that.

I thought I said my sneer softly enough it was only audible to my ears, but the streak of lust blazing through Regan's eyes weakens my hypothesis. "A marathon romp with a record-breaking number of orgasms and you're still playing the jealousy card. God—I'd kick up a stink if it didn't make my insides quiver."

If my cock wasn't already standing to attention from her

comment, it has no chance of staying down when she shoves me onto the mattress before straddling my lap. I growl. Pants aren't the only piece of clothing she is missing. She's also not wearing any panties.

"Nuh-uh." She slaps my hand away when it sneaks up to grip her ass. "We've been there. Done that. *Multiple times.*"

I grin and waggle my brows at her last comment. Sex is the one thing I can give her without holding back. It is something we share that is solely for us. No one can control it, demand we adjust it, or alter the inane connection that comes with it. When we're together like that, unified as one, I feel as if I can take down the world with my bare hands.

My cocky smile droops an inch when Regan murmurs, "I really wish you'd let me call Raquel. If we don't address your wound properly, it could scar."

I cup her hands in mine, removing them from an old scar hidden behind a scruffy chin and overdue-for-a-trim hair. "Won't be my first scar, unlikely to be my last."

I issue my comment in jest. Regan doesn't take it that way. "I don't like this."

She isn't the only one harboring dislike when she removes herself from my lap, taking the seductive heat warming my cock right along with her.

"This isn't me. I don't watch someone I care about be assaulted and do nothing about it. I fight. I win. I make culprits pay. I wouldn't act like a bimbo who stupidly believes sex is more important than discovering the people responsible for dumping a man in an alleyway with no concern for his life. Normal Regan would stop this. I'm not exactly sure how, but I know she wouldn't be holed up in a hotel room with her boyfriend, acting like nothing happened." She suddenly stops talking as her eyes dart to the partially cracked open curtain.

My heart drums against my ribcage as I encourage her to repeat her statement. "Holed up with her. . .?"

She doesn't play along as nicely as she has the past ten hours. She remains perfectly quiet and painstakingly still.

"What did you call me, Rae?"

Regan's brows cinch. "Nothing. I didn't say anything."

Why she decided to become a lawyer, I have no idea. She's a terrible liar, her poor skills only second to her inability to hide her emotions. She wears them on her sleeve, visible to the entire world.

"I won't let anyone hurt you, Rae. Not even me."

Her chest rises and falls three times before she faintly whispers, "I'm not worried about me."

She flattens her ear on the bedding we're lying on before slanting her head my way. It feels like the world implodes in my stomach when she locks her glistening eyes with mine. She is worried about herself, but not in the way I first perceived. She's worried what will happen to her if something were to happen to me. That's not surprising. It's been eight years since Luca passed, and she's still picking up the pieces of her life. Just the thought of going through that again has her skin clamming up and her eyes watering.

"Come home with me."

That clears the fret from her face by replacing it with pure, unbridled fear. . . *or is it fury?*

"What?!"

"Come home with me," I repeat, acting as if she is hard of hearing.

85

She heard me; I'm just unwilling to accept the denial streaming from her eyes. This is the perfect solution for our predicament. An impromptu trip to my hometown will get Regan off her stalker's radar long enough for Brandon to work his magic, while at the same time surrounding her with more law enforcement officers than Theresa has on her team. It's perfect—a true win/win... if I can convince Regan.

"I can't—"

"Can't or don't want to?" I question, using her words against her.

Her lips quirk as she struggles to hide her smile. "Both." She raises to a half-seated position. "This is absurd. We're grown adults, for crying out loud. We don't rush home every time we get a boo-boo."

"Rae..."

My grumble of her name isn't because I disagree with her. It is a warning that I'm five seconds away from pinning her to the bed to convince her with the tactics I used Saturday morning.

"We need to do this."

"No. *You* need to do this. There's no *we* in this scenario."

She rushes to her feet. I don't know where she's going; there are literally a few feet of carpet between us and the door.

I smirk when she walks three paces before spinning on her heels to retrace the steps she just took.

"You pace when you're frustrated."

Her wide eyes stray to mine. "No, I run when I'm frustrated. But since I don't have clothing, I'm doing the next best thing. Count your blessings, Mister Fancy Pants. If I had the means, you'd never catch me."

There she goes with her poor lying skills again. The clothing part of her statement is accurate, but I know she has no intentions of running from me. If she was planning to bolt, she would have the instant she found me in the alley. Regan has never hidden the fact she finds relationships confusing. I'm nowhere near as worried. It's new—everything new takes some adjusting.

A wry grin crosses my face as I switch tactics. "You said Normal Regan wouldn't sit by and watch a person she cares about be assaulted without doing something about it. I'm doing something."

Regan's face screws up as if she vomited in her mouth. The reason behind her disgust comes to light when she asks, "Your plan to combat being assaulted is to hide as if you're a coward?"

"No!" I lower my voice, which in turn reduces my anger. "I'm drawing out the perp. Forcing him away from his comfort zone."

She throws her hands into the air. "By running home to mommy and daddy with your tail between your legs."

My smirk morphs into a genuine smile. She's extra cute when she's riled up with jealousy, but it has nothing on her spit-fire attitude when she's preparing to fight. She has her fists up and is ready to grapple, except she isn't defending herself. She's protecting her man.

Her step slices to half its natural stride when I stand to my feet. Unlike her, I haven't put on a single stitch of clothing. I am as naked as the day I was born and as stiff as I'll be the day I'm laid in my final resting place.

"Alex. . ." Regan stammers in warning, stepping back. "I'm not some naïve twit you can wave your magic wand at and put me under a spell."

I continue toward her with slow and purposeful strides. Her eyes narrow as she scrutinizes my face. The curl of my lips and the spark in my eyes reveal I took her magic wand comment as a compliment.

She pops out her hip, highlighting the seductive swells of her body. She's mad, but it only makes me more determined. I'd rather her be angry and horny than harmed and unbreathing.

"Two nights—tops. Then we're even."

She looks at me like I'm insane. "Even? How will this make us even?"

A crass grin stretches across my face when her eyes drop to my cock to take in its twitch. "I saw yours, then you saw mine." I wait for her eyes to float back to my face before adding on, "I've been introduced to your parents, so now it's only fair you meet mine."

"I didn't invite you to meet my family. You forced an introduction."

Her strong words weaken when I reach her, twist her, then arch her over the chair tucked into a small writing desk at the front of our room. I grind my cock against her ass without shame, my earlier releases a forgotten memory.

I can tell by her expression that it's taking everything she has not to respond to my grind. Her teeth gritted and exposed, but the warmth between her legs can't be contained.

"I had planned to stay at a hotel; you wanted to stay at your family ranch. How is that a forced invitation?" My words are strained from a heavy tongue, my quest to have her beneath me nearly overtaking my endeavor to do things my way.

Regan waits for my hand to finish skating around her quivering stomach before she replies, "I never wanted to go to Texas. You *forced* me to go."

She balances on the balls of her feet when my index finger pierces the folds of her pussy. "Are you being forced now, Regan?"

I keep my fingertip perched at the entrance of her pussy. Not quite penetrating the area responsible for the seductive scent wafting in the air, but close enough its presence can't be ignored.

When she shakes her head, I lower my chin to skim my lips across her ear. "Because you're too strong to ever have *anything* forced on you."

Her eyes rise to mine. The lust in them grows from my confession. She heard the honesty in my tone; she knows I'm telling the truth.

"That's why I asked you to come with me, Rae, instead of telling you it was what we were doing. I want you to come home with me because you want to, not because I'm forcing you."

"Is that so?" When I nod, she asks, "Then why is your cock grinding my ass while your finger skims my pussy?"

"Because I can't help but touch you. Your body was built for this. You know it." She purrs in agreement. "I know it." We moan in sync when my thumb grazes her swollen clit. "And after our efforts last night, I'm fairly sure every guest at this hotel knows it."

She smiles, not the least bit concerned people heard her in the throes of ecstasy. Good—because if I have it my way, they're about to hear her all over again.

"So you're touching me merely because I'm your drug of choice, and you're due for another hit?"

"Uh-huh, except I'm not a random junkie picking up B-Grade shit from a skittish dealer on a corner. I'm going for the premium stuff, the superior stuff on the top shelf no one else gets to have. I'm talking the cream of the crop, baby."

"Cream you want curdled by uncomfortable dinners, awkward glances, and god knows what other shenanigans occur at family meet and greets. I haven't avoided them since my teen days for no reason, Alex. I don't play well with others."

The openness in her tone surprises me. She truly thinks our time home will be uncomfortable and awkward. She couldn't be further from the truth. After getting over the shock of me bringing home a woman for the first time, my family will love Regan. I'm one hundred percent certain of this.

When I say that to her, her face pales even more. "I'm not a girl you take home to meet your parents, Alex. I'm the one you invite to functions when you want to make an ex jealous, or your coworkers drool in envy. I'm not parent-certified."

She groans when I step back so she can spin around to face me. She does, although hesitantly. I attempt to fire off a remark, a comment that any man would be fucking blessed to have her in his life, but she beats me to the task, her comment more pained than pleasant. "Parents have a knack for knowing good people. They'll smell my rotten insides from a mile away. Luca's parents did."

Finally, the truth smacks into me. She's not opposed to meeting *my* parents. She's recalling bad memories.

"Do you really think I'd take you home to be ridiculed?" Stealing her chance to reply with one of the many grievances firing through her eyes, I quickly add on, "I'll walk away from everyone I know before I'll *ever* let that happen."

Her eyes dance between mine as if shocked by my declaration. This is one notion I can't understand. Why in the world would anyone as perfect and beautiful as Regan think she'd be second best? I wasn't lying when I told her dad I didn't care if our relationship was two hours old or over a decade long, she'll always be my number one priority.

"Two nights, Rae, give me two nights of the real you, and I'll do the same. No holds barred. No secrets. No lies—"

"No omissions of truth."

I smile then nod. "Just two people hanging out like we did at your ranch."

Her smile matches mine, her memories just as fond. We only left her ranch a little over twenty-four hours ago, but it feels more like a lifetime. I'd give anything to go back to that moment in the field where we became us.

After a deep breath that expands her chest, Regan locks her eyes with mine. "Truth?" She only says one word, but the hundreds streaming from her eyes express more than real words ever could.

Even panicked I'm mere hours from losing her, I nod. It's time for me to be honest. I just need to bring her stalker to justice first. If I confess right now, she'll never let me protect her. She may not even let me see her again. I don't want either of those things to occur, so although I'm pledging honesty, it must start from now. I can't confess to old sins just yet.

"Okay." Regan releases another big breath before stepping closer to me. "I didn't take a shower."

My eyes dart to her hair that's bone dry before scanning the little pockets in her collarbone. They don't have a single drop of moisture on them.

When I return my eyes to Regan, she confesses, "After the first time we. . . *fucked*, you went a little quiet. I knew something was off."

Although pleased at her uncomfortable wording, it does little to ease my agitation. "So instead of asking me what was wrong, you spied on me?"

"No." She shakes her head. "Well. . . not technically."

Catching my stink eye, she adds on, "I intended to take a shower. I switched on the faucet. . . I just never got in."

"Did you press your ear against the door?"

Her lips quirk into a smile. I really wish they wouldn't. I can't stay mad at her when she's smiling at me. It is impossible.

"Yes." She chews on the corner of her lip, enhancing her sexpot look. "When that didn't work, I used a glass."

I smirk, half-impressed, half-peeved. "What did you hear?"

Her smile drops as her eyes narrow. "More my raging heart than anything."

I exhale a relieved breath.

It is quickly withdrawn when she adds on, "But I know you're hiding something from me, Alex, so until you come clean on what that is, I refuse to go anywhere with you. Trust is a two-way street. You either give it to me fully or cross the road, leaving me on the other side."

This. . . this is the exact reason I know she is the woman for me. She gets me. Even while masking my confusion in a way I've been trained to do, she sees through it. She sees the real me.

Now things are about to get even more real.

9

I stare at Alex, confused and complexed. I thought he'd be frustrated at my lack of trust, but the crinkle in his brow isn't there because of what I said. It is there *because* of me. I went the honesty route because I thought it was the right thing to do. I've lied so much the past decade, I'm having a hard time distinguishing between truth and dishonesty.

I was also hoping a little bit of honesty would encourage Alex to do the same. If the uneasy crinkle in his top lip is anything to go by, I'm skeptical.

After curling his hand around mine, Alex guides me to the bed we spent a majority of our night wrestling on. The frustration slashed across his face jumps onto mine when he enters the bathroom to put on a pair of boxer shorts and plain black trousers.

He throws open the partially open curtain of our patio before joining me on the bed. The late morning sun sends hues of yellow and white dancing across his packed stomach and smooth pecs. I thought he was opening the curtain to let natural light into the room. Only now am I realizing that isn't the case. He wants me distracted.

Before I can announce I am on to him, he twists his torso to face me. The worry in his eyes secures my devotion even more readily than his sexy six pack.

"I need you to know, nothing I am about to tell you is your fault."

The fact he feels compelled to say that piques my suspicion. It also assures me this is one hundred percent my fault.

"There was something off about the man who assaulted me last night."

I give him a look. It's my *duh* face. "Clearly, only an insane man would go against one as strong and determined as you."

My compliment has the effect I am aiming for. His somewhat deflated chest swells as his lips tug high. I had wondered last night if his silence stemmed from shame, but then I realized someone with confidence like Alex would never feel shame. He was mad about what happened, and frustrated by it, but from the details he shared, he's aware size, shape, and vitality doesn't matter when you're victimized inside your comfort zone. That's why he took me back to Texas after my home invasion. He knew my ranch was where I'd feel the safest.

"It wasn't his stupidity that made him distinguishable. It was his mannerisms and size."

I'm dying to jump in, but I'm truly lost. From the snippets of conversation I heard through the bathroom door, Alex used words like "waif." Don't get me wrong, I know size doesn't matter when it comes to strength, but it seems pretty futile right now.

Recognizing that he is at point B, whereas I'm still struggling to find my way to point A, Alex rips the Band-Aid off in one quick succession. "I believe the man who assaulted me last night was the same man in your apartment Friday night."

"Huh?"

I want to say more, but I'm too shocked to string words together. That doesn't make any sense. Nothing he is saying makes sense. Danielle threatened me. When I failed to adhere to her threat, she turned up at Luca's memorial with a pig's heart. Alex arrested her, and she got carted off to jail, meaning my stalker case is now shut. It's been solved. Done and dusted. Never to be mentioned again.

My brain stops trying to unjumble the evidence when Alex says, "My place of employment is at 4756 Marcotte Avenue." He waits, giving me time to retrieve the Ravenshoe map stored in my head before continuing, "The windows in my office face the alleyway where you found me."

"That proves nothing." The drumming of my heart on my ribs echoes in my reply.

Although frustrated by my lack of trust, Alex continues chipping away at it. "What time did you arrive for your meeting last night?"

"A little before 11," I answer, unsure what that has to do with anything.

"And where did your meeting occur?"

I lick my dry lips before answering, "In an office at the warehouse my employer is remodeling into a nightclub."

"An office that happens to face Marcotte Avenue, with windows that can only be peered through from an elevated position, such as the office building across the street?"

My pulse thrums faster with each word Alex delivers.

"I wasn't scheduled to work yesterday, but even if I were, my office is usually empty by 6 PM. Excluding janitors, it is rare to find anyone on the premises after dark."

My pride rises to the occasion, but a voice in my head tells it to remain calm until we've gathered all the facts. "That's circumstantial evidence. It will never hold up in court."

Alex smirks, apparently amused at my attempt to switch our conversation from personal to business. I was, but it doesn't mean he needs to laugh about it.

"I'm not here to convince members of a jury. I'm just hoping my *girlfriend* will hear me out."

He stares straight at me when he says the dreaded "G" word, but I act coy. "No matter who you're trying to convince, you need more evidence."

Alex grumbles. "The person who assaulted me had dainty hands. . ." Before I can interrupt him with the assurance that a lot of men have dainty hands these days, he quickly adds on, "His size, hair coloring, and build match that of the assailant we caught on surveillance entering your apartment Friday night."

A bolt of shock rattles my core. "Hold on, what? Go back a minute. You have surveillance of the person who entered my apartment Friday night?"

Alex smiles to hide the curse words streaming through his eyes before he dips his chin.

"How?" When he looks at me, confused, I reveal, "The owner of my building had his security personnel scour the tapes Saturday morning when he discovered my warped door. He said they didn't find any evidence of a break in but requested I check my possessions just in case."

My furious eyes dance between Alex's for several minutes before I spit out, "I wasted two hours of my precious time this morning with an insurance agent going over the inventory of my apartment to ensure nothing was missing when I knew without a doubt nothing was stolen."

Although peeved I lost time I'll never get back, I preferred it over telling Isaac what really caused my door to get out of whack. With my stalker case closed, I didn't feel the need to burden him with old issues.

"Segments of the tape from that night were accidentally corrupted. . ." My brow quirks from Alex's desolate tone. "But footage of the suspect was transferred to a secure server before it was wiped."

I remain quiet for several long minutes. I'm torn. Knowing there is footage of Friday night's incident fills me with both panic and gratitude. I'm panicked because I'd rather sell a lung than have Isaac discover what truly happened, but grateful because if Alex's theory is right, and Danielle isn't to blame for what occurred in my apartment, that footage could be my only means to seek justice. Even if I weren't a defense attorney, I know video evidence is damning in cases like this.

Over the next ten minutes, Alex updates me on everything he knows. He gives me a play-by-play rundown of what occurred before he was knocked out, before he switches to the data still a little blurry in his head.

By the time he has finished updating me, I'm still only halfway over the fence. I've looked at the facts objectively, so I can comprehend his anxiety, but I need a few more t's crossed and i's dotted before I can fully regard his idea. It isn't because I'm stubborn. I'm just. . .

Stubborn.

"So can you understand my request to go home, Rae? If this man is the same man who threatened you, he knows your routine. He recognizes your strengths and weaknesses, but he'd never anticipate this move."

"No one would anticipate this move—not even my momma."

Alex grins, hearing my comment as I had intended: playful. I was hoping a bit of wittiness would dispel some of the tension in the air. It seems to have the opposite effect. I'm more panicked now than I've ever been, but my worry isn't caused by the person determined to hurt me. It is the plea in Alex's eyes.

"I don't know if I can do this, Alex. I have my job. Friends." *A testing inability to say no to you.* "I can't just pack up and leave town for a few days. People rely on me."

"And who do you rely on, Rae? Who has your back?"

I nearly say him, until I realize it is an utterly ridiculous thing for me to say. He's a stranger, a man I've fucked more times the past forty-eight hours than I've been sexually active the past two years, but that's not the point. Gaining enough trust to be someone's crutch takes years. It isn't something you achieve over a weekend.

I attempt to tell Alex that, but something stops me. I want to say it is the plea in his eyes, but a flash of red unconcealed by bad lighting harnesses my lie. If he is right, and our attackers are one and the same, his assault is my fault. He was injured because of me.

Although his injuries are nothing compared to what Luca suffered, they still have guilt eating me alive. For that reason, and that reason alone, I lock my eyes with Alex and say, "We're staying at a hotel. If your parents hate me, don't blame me. If they demand you leave Ravenshoe or burn at the stake, don't blame me. If your sisters, cousins, or any other female relative says I am to blame for their husband's wandering eyes, d—"

"Don't blame you," Alex fills in. "Got it."

"I don't think you do. You haven't seen this in operation around other people." It is conceited of me to do, but I swipe my hand down my body. "People get agitated around things they don't understand. I am often misunderstood."

Alex tugs my bottom lip out from under my teeth, saving it from being gnawed to death. "Stop it. You're fucking perfect. My family will love you."

It seems like he wants to say more, but before he can make a foolish mistake, I save him for the second time this week by sealing my mouth over his.

My nerves spike when Alex rounds the hood of the taxi before clambering into the seat next to me. His packing expedition took one tenth the time of mine. I barely sucked in three breaths between his departure and return. I know why he is eager. He wants to get me to the airport before I change my mind for the eleventh time this morning.

Isaac was fine with me taking time off. His quick reply was more to do with his inaccurate assumption that my request centered around the anniversary of Luca's death. But even if it didn't, he still would have granted my request because he knows I wouldn't ask unless it was important.

"You ready?" Alex draws my focus to him.

I shake my head. "But that won't save me, will it?"

"Probably not."

He does up his seatbelt before leaning across my torso to do the same to mine.

"Do you really think a sliver of material will stop me from escaping if I choose to run?"

Alex's chuckle makes me hot and needy.

"Probably not," he repeats, "but I packed my running shoes just in case."

If I hadn't seen the honesty in his eyes, I'd assume he was joking.

With it being a Tuesday morning, our commute to the airport isn't as hair-raising as the one we made Saturday. Commuter traffic is still at a standstill but since we're heading in the opposite direction, it doesn't hinder our progress—*unfortunately.*

I drag my sweaty hands down the flare of my skirt before asking, "Do your parents know we're coming?"

When Alex shakes his head, concealing his smirk, I whack him in the bicep. It is not a smart thing for me to do. His arms feel like they're made out of concrete, and they make my *needs* even more urgent.

"Why didn't you tell them?"

Before he can answer me, my phone buzzes, advising I have a new text message. My eyes only skim the first line before Alex snatches my cell out of my hand.

Unknown Number: *No video evidence of your assault was located.*

"Are you fucking kidding me?"

Since Alex isn't talking to me, I don't reply. Lucky, as I wouldn't have gotten a word in between his index finger smashing the screen of my phone as he dials a known number, and his angry roar bellowing down the line. "What do you mean there's no evidence?!"

He waits, grunts, then waits some more.

"You know she's full of shit, right?"

Another long pause.

"Because this is the crap she pulls."

This pause is the longest of them all.

"I don't know. I guess I'll have to find another way?"

When he swings his eyes my way, I dart mine to the scenery whizzing by our window. My attempt to act ignorant comes too late. Alex spotted my snooping ways, but instead of lashing out in anger, he subdues my curiosity by holding out his hand palm side up.

Not even thinking, I accept his gesture. It was a smooth move for both of us. Just his fingers intertwined with mine calm the erratic beat of my heart and stop his fists' clench and unclench routine.

He doesn't wait for his phone companion to quit squabbling before he suggests, "Send the footage to Dane. Even if it's been cut and removed, he'll find it."

After a few more grunts and a jerk of his chin, he disconnects his call and hands my phone back to me.

"Bad news?" I ask, stating the obvious.

Heat slicks his face as anger pulses through him. "It's just the same shit, different day."

I nod in understanding. "That's been my life the past eight years. I am stuck on a hamster wheel. Same emotions. Same monopolized day. Same acquisitions. There's just one difference this week: I have a new sidekick." I bump him with my knee to ensure he knows whom I am referring to. "Is there anything I can help you with?"

Alex shakes his head for barely a second before his brow arches. "Does the warehouse across from my building have any surveillance installed?"

I twist my lips. "Most likely. Isaac is pedantic about security."

Alex appears more displeased than happy—even while asking, "Do you think he'd give me access to his security servers?"

Lines of worry indent my forehead. Isaac isn't cautious about security for no reason. He has millions and millions of dollars' worth of assets to protect, much less items you can't place a monetary value on.

Spotting my apprehension, Alex assures, "I don't need access to his servers. Just the footage from the alleyway. He could burn it on a CD or... *thingy*."

His deficient computer knowledge compels a smile onto my lips, but it doesn't award him a reply.

"Please, Rae." He purposely uses my nickname as he knows how much I love hearing it. "This could close your case sooner, meaning you'll be back on the hamster wheel before you know it."

His smart ass remark isn't helping to plead his case. If anything, it has me wanting to say no. I'm scared shitless about meeting his family, but a little part of me—a teeny, weeny tiny part—is a tad bit excited.

Before Luca's accident, I was an adventurous, fun-loving

person. If there was a party or social gathering, you could be assured I would be the first person there. Well, not first, as everyone knows it's more fashionable to be late than early, but you get what I mean. I lost part of who I was when Luca's life perished way too early. With Alex's help, I'm rediscovering who I've always wanted to be.

Incapable of ignoring Alex's flopped head and lowered lip for a second longer, I breathe out an exasperated sigh. "I'll call his head of security before we take off." When he gives me a flirty wink, announcing my pledge of assistance will be well-rewarded, I forewarn, "But don't get your hopes up. I'll need to give Hunter way more than a smile to get him to agree to this."

My tease has the effect I am aiming for when Alex grumbles under his breath. He does the same thing anytime he's jealous. His inaudible grumbles remind me of Muttely, the cartoon dog from *Wacky Races*. It's cute and endearing, enough to send any girl's pulse racing, even while she's in the process of facing her worst fears head on.

10

"*P*eanuts," Regan hisses under her breath for the fifth time since we disembarked the plane and entered our rental car. *"Peanuts."*

She stops fastening her seat belt, her narrowed eyes straying to mine when I say, "You could have had pretzels."

She doesn't find my humor amusing. The heavy groove that settled between her brows when I told her we were flying economy remains as strong as ever. I didn't refuse the travel agent's offer of an upgrade for no reason. I did it to settle Regan into normality before she hits the streets of suburbia. She might have grown up on a farm, but Regan is as glamorous as they come. If the price tags on the unworn dresses she packed "just in case" are anything to go by, she left the norm a very long time ago.

Don't get me wrong, I fucking love who she is—sparkling dresses and all—but she won't get that here. Here, she'll get a belly full of food and a heart full of love. Everything else stops at the door. It's real. It's gritty. It's the Rogers way.

Regan wiggles in her seat the next thirty miles, her senses shifting into high gear the more unpopulated the streets become. She won't find the farm she is seeking—just a hidden pocket of perfection on the outskirts of Washington DC. My childhood home has been in my family for decades. It's been handed down generation after generation—just like my job title.

"Wow." Regan's breath expels without the quiver her jaw has had since we exited the tarmac at Ravenshoe Airstrip.

After taking in the swinging sign advising we've arrived at The Manor B&B, she shifts her eyes my way. "Never took you as a bed and breakfast traveler. Sleazy two star motels seem more your style." A frisky wink accompanies her slam.

"Up to your standards?" A wicked smile crosses my lips.

She sucks in a wild breath before nodding. "Very much so."

I've barely come to a stop at the end of a long driveway when Regan pops open her door. Her hand protects her eyes from the late afternoon sun so they can absorb the pre-war features of concrete and stone. The entire lower level of The Manor is constructed with Braddock's rock, dug from a quarry not far from here. Each piece was carefully selected to ensure it fit with the previously set rocks.

The veins of earthy red tones throughout the rock contrast against the white shutters and restored timbers of the top floor, making The Manor one of the most architecturally sought-after homes designed in the pre-war era. It is a house you'd expect to find in the countryside in the United Kingdom. The big, expansive verandas are a testament to the man who built the home—as are the current owners.

"Have you stayed here before?" Regan asks, her voice picking up suspicion from the valet greeting me by name.

My shoulder touches my ear when I shrug. "A few times."

I curl my hand around Regan's before climbing the eight stairs separating the footpath from the full-length patio numerous guests are putting to good use. Grayson leans against the railing, his gaze wide with amusement as he eyeballs our approach. He's my eldest brother. The deal maker. The deadly marksman. The all-round playboy. He has the same rugged grin as me, carved facial features hidden by a few days' growth, and an appreciative eye for fine ladies.

His long gaze at Regan's svelte frame leaves no doubt to my last confession. Grayson's interests are piqued, but not enough for him to leave his mark. *Someone else must have his attention.*

Placing my hand on the curve of Regan's back, I guide her toward the side entrance of The Manor, barely saving her from the quirk of Grayson's curious brow. He was happy appraising her from afar until I blew the calm, collective ruse I was working with by placing my hands on Regan. Now he's shadowing us into the private entrance of our home, his interest as notable as Regan's.

"Don't we need to check in?" Regan asks, stunned I've guided her into the core of The Manor via the back entrance.

Before I can answer her, a loud squeal pierces my ears. "Alex! What the bloody hell are you doing here?! I thought you weren't due home until Christmas!"

Darcy, all one hundred and ten pounds of her, darts off a stool at the kitchen island to head my way. Regan's eyes, which were back to their normal width seconds ago, narrow when Darcy leaps into my arms and plants her lips on my cheek. She is so excited to see me again, she's failed to notice Regan standing beside me. It's probably for the best. If she catches sight of the death stare Regan is giving her, she may not survive its wrath.

The longer I return Darcy's embrace, the tighter I have to grip Regan's hand. She appears two seconds from running, and she isn't even halfway into the series of surprises I have planned for her.

After placing Darcy back onto her feet, I jerk Regan forward until she is once again standing at my side. She stops taking in Darcy's bare feet, short denim shorts, and midriff top when I say, "Darcy, this is my girlfriend, Regan." Regan's screwed up nose from me calling her my girlfriend smooths when I quickly add on, "Regan, this is my baby sister, Darcy."

Regan's eyes rocket to mine, certain she heard me wrong. She didn't. Even with her British accent in full swing, Darcy has the same sandy hair as mine, bright blue eyes, and mischievous grin.

The grin announces she has finally noticed Regan's scowl. She's more amused by it than disgusted.

"Darcy is an actress. She's preparing for a role, hence the accent."

Air evicts from my lungs when Darcy backhands my chest. "I'm an *actor*." She says her last word sharply. "There is no discrimination in *my* field of expertise." She doesn't need to spell out what her remark means. She loathes my family lineage as much as my mother does.

Speaking of mothers, I've just spotted mine darting past the kitchen. "Mom!"

Regan grips my hand so fiercely, her fingernails pierce my skin as effectively as they did my back last night. "You said we were staying at a hotel."

She expresses her comment softly enough neither my mom, aunt or . . . *I do a quick head count* . . . four cousins will hear her.

"We are. The Manor is kind of a hotel."

"Owned by your family."

Her words are issued with a glare hot enough to melt ice, but a stranger wouldn't know that. She has a perfect smile plastered on her face, and her shoulders are high and without tension. If I didn't know her as well as I do, I'd assume she knew of my intentions to bombard her with all my family in one sitting.

It's a pity I know her very well. She's not just planning to dissect my nuts the instant we're alone; she'll boil them up and feed them to the hounds. *Even more reason for me to keep her occupied.*

After introducing Regan to my mom in the same manner I did Darcy, we make our way to the rest of my family standing frozen, gawking at us. They're not stunned by the way Regan carries herself with grace while her eyes scream troublemaker. They want to know what caused the drastic shift in my dating stance between Easter and now.

A few months ago, I declared the odds of me coming home with a date at Christmas would be zero to none. Now, I'm striving to work out if Regan and I will do Christmas at The

Manor or just New Years. I guess it will depend on which cele-
bration is more important to Regan's family. Mine will be
happy with either. As long as there is enough food to sponge up
the copious amounts of alcohol they consume, they'll celebrate
the day as if it is the best day of the year.

We make it through an additional six introductions before
Regan returns her focus to my mom, who is leading the
campaign to assimilate her into our tight family dynamic with
the gusto of a tigress. "Is there a bar here? Or anywhere within
a ten-mile radius?"

My mom slaps Regan's arm as she steps into her private
bubble, popping the only defense Regan had left at her disposal.
"Do you think any of us would be here if we didn't?" My mom's
eccentric words change Regan's fake smile to a real one. "Why
do you think we're loitering in the kitchen? We're waiting for
the clock to strike five."

Regan bumps my mom with her hip, making the admiration
in my mom's eyes grow tenfold. "It's five somewhere in the
world, am I right?"

"Hell yes, sister. Then let's do this," Darcy squeals, happy
someone else has taken over the troublesome reins she usually
controls.

I'm left hanging in the kitchen when my mom and Darcy
curl their arms around Regan's waist to drag her toward the
fully stocked bar. It isn't a hard feat considering Regan has been
seeking a way to flee from me since we arrived.

Within seconds, Grayson and I are the only Myers left
standing in the once bustling space. "You know you've lost her
for eternity now, right?" His black boots clip the wooden floor
as he spans the distance between us. "They've been seeking a

new member to join their unit since Lorraine left for college last semester."

He pops his hip on the kitchen counter, bringing his six foot four height closer to my six foot two stature. "Is she really your girlfriend?" His eyes say the words he can't express: *Or is she your mark?*

"Have you got a few hours? Because it will take at least that many for me to work through my own confusion before I can tackle yours."

Grayson nudges his head in the opposite direction from where Regan and our female relatives just went. "I've got more than a few hours. Let's hustle."

He heads out the door we entered only twenty minutes ago, not bothering to turn around and check if I'm following him. He knows I'll follow, but he wouldn't care if I didn't. Grayson isn't called the game player for no reason. He knows everyone's strong points and weaknesses. That's how he plays the game so well. If you're on his team, you're set. I wouldn't recommend getting on his bad side, though.

Six beers later—*Grayson, not me*—my older brother slumps into a wicker chair in one of the many screened patios of The Manor. "Are you certain the guy from Regan's apartment is the same man who assaulted you?"

I nod. "What other reason would he have to clock me over the head?"

"I can think of a few." Ignoring my squinted gaze, Grayson rests his feet on the glass table holding his empty beer bottles.

"Your girl is right: you ain't got shit in evidence. If I hadn't seen the little vein in your forehead working overtime as you recited the facts, I would've believed this was a ruse to force her here against her wishes." He uncrosses his ankles and leans forward to grab another beer from a cooler at his side. "What about that techie you mentioned? Has he found anything more concrete?"

I drop my eyes to Regan's phone that I haven't let out of my sight for a single minute today. There are no messages, emails, or missed calls—*unfortunately.*

My disappointed sigh must answer Grayson's question on my behalf. "Give me the afternoon to get clearance, then I'll run some searches."

"You'll do that for Regan?" Shock resonates in my tone.

Grayson is the first to tell you his time isn't free. If you want it, you better be willing to pay for it, so I'm shocked he's offering to help without additional stipulations being discussed.

I yank away from Grayson when he tugs on the clump of hair on my chin. "I'm not doing it for your girl. I'm doing it for you."

I wait, knowing there is more. I'm proven right when he says, "On one condition."

I'm not happy, but I jerk my chin up all the same. I'll even go as far as pretending I haven't noticed him eyeballing a beautiful redhead from the corner of his eye the past two hours if it gets me one step closer to unearthing the person striving to hurt Regan.

I stop trying to figure out why the redhead seems familiar when Grayson says, "Call Bennett. He's struggling with his new placement." He taps my shoulder, takes one final glance at the redhead, then enters The Manor via a squeaky screen door.

I wait for it to stop swinging before punching a frequently dialed number into Regan's cell. I've never believed in delayed gratification, so I may as well tackle Grayson's demand now.

Bennett doesn't answer my call, but his voicemail is extremely concerning.

"Hey, you've reached Dok. Leave your name and number, and I'll get back to you."

Dok? Who the fuck is Dok?

11

For every minute I spend drinking and chatting with Alex's family, the chances of him waking up tomorrow morning still breathing increase. I should hate him for the predicament he placed me in. I should castrate him as a warning to any man thinking about strong-arming me, but when he waltzes into the room, his brows furled in confusion, the last thing I want to do is hurt him.

Kiss him. Fuck him. Do wickedly naughty things to him with my tongue. They're the top items on my agenda. Then, after a quick rest, I'll let him return the favor. I could blame the tequila in my veins for speaking on my behalf, but I had most of these ideas hours before alcohol hit my system.

A whoosh of lust shoots through me when Alex notices my heated stare. He dips his chin, his lips furling more than his brows as he makes his way across the room. The bustling chitchat filling the bar only moments ago fades to barely a whisper. All the guests are too enamored by our pull-thrust routine to continue with their conversations.

I'm not surprised by their interest. People I hadn't been formally introduced to bombarded me the instant I was out of Alex's earshot. Their questions all honed in on the one focal point: was I really Alex's girlfriend? I should have told them Alex can't afford me, but something stopped me from doing that. I dropped the "B" word first, so I can't be angry at Alex for running with it.

"Hey." Alex presses his lips to my temple, causing the crowd surrounding us to let out a collective sigh. "Settling in okay?"

I drag my hand along the countertop, revealing my last three hours have been well spent. If I wanted to add to the groove between his brows instead of erasing it, I could pretend alcohol is the only cause for my giddy state, but recalling his pledge for us to be honest this weekend has me saying, "Your mom is a hoot. If she wasn't called away on a guest emergency, she would have drank me under the table."

Alex grins, knowing I'm being 100% honest. He is the spitting image of his mom, Marilyn, but her personality is on the opposite end of the spectrum. She is cozy and warm, and has a mind as wickedly depraved as mine. I thought her nurturing side derived from raising four children with a somewhat absentee husband, but she guaranteed me that wasn't the case.

"I didn't know evil ran through my veins until I produced mini versions of myself," Marilyn said earlier this evening, her tone half-witty, half-serious. "Alex's dad already had me pulling my hair out, so imagine throwing four babies under the age of five into the mix. I'm shocked they made it to adulthood alive."

"From the way your Ma talked about your Pa, I thought they

were separated." Alex's lips quirk, not stunned by my reply. "It's a pity for her I got my soul-matching skills from my mom. I can't believe it, even thirty-five years later, your Ma is still head over heels in love with your Pa. He must have a magic wand or something." I add a wink to my last sentence, giving it the frisky edge I was aiming for.

When a genuine smile crosses Alex's face, I gesture for him to occupy the seat his mom just vacated. He accepts my offer, just not in the way I was anticipating. Instead of planting his backside in the seat next to mine, he plucks me from my seat, slides into my place, then lowers me to sit in his lap.

My cheeks flare as rampant heat attacks my senses. I could pretend my flaming cheeks are compliments of the numerous pairs of eyes glancing my way, but prolonged gawks are nothing new to me. I get them no matter what I'm doing. Even something as mundane as picking up my dry cleaning in a pair of dirty gray sweatpants and a plain white T gets me eyeballed. The attention used to bother me, but the more regularly it occurred, the more adapted I became.

It is so second nature now, I was genuinely put off when nothing I did secured Alex's attention for more than two seconds when we co-dined at Taste. From his disinterest, it's shocking how far we've traveled in such a short period of time.

Perhaps that's the excuse I can use for not bolting the instant Alex relinquished my hand from his? His unexpected entrance into my life handed me months of sexual frustration, so it's only fair he clears his debt before we move on to greener pastures.

Yeah, right.

As much as I hate to admit it, just the idea of Alex moving

on ensures I won't be seeking my own seat any time soon. Although that doesn't mean I'll go down easily.

"Is there something wrong with the four empty stools beside me?" I glance over his shoulder. As suspected, every eye in the room is on us. "Or the other twenty or so ones scattered around the room?"

My last three words come out in a purr from Alex's beard scraping my nape so he can growl into my ear. "I prefer this seat. Do you have a problem with that?"

He didn't have time to trim his beard, so it's a little more scraggily than it was when we wrestled in the field. I should hate it—*I should hate him*—but his Viking facial hair doesn't just have my insides purring like a kitty; it makes my heart gallop as well. I've always gone for sophisticated, clean-cut men. I had no clue what I was missing out on!

"I *do* have a problem with you stealing my seat. . . *if it improves my chances of getting spanked.*"

When Alex's brow gets lost in his hairline, I lift a recently replenished martini to my mouth to hide my smile. His lips aren't moving, but I don't need him to speak to know what he's thinking. He's shocked by my confession, and, if the thickness in his pants is anything to go by, incredibly turned on. I can understand both his responses. I don't relinquish power—*ever!* But this is different. We're even, which means the occasional switch up is okay.

Furthermore, the horribly depressed state my vagina was in the past two months has all but vanished from his devotion, so shouldn't his dedication be rewarded in the most wickedly spectacular way?

I swallow my glass of martini in one gulp, pop the olive

between my teeth, then slam my glass onto the polished bar so firmly it nearly snaps from my determination. "I'm horny. We should fuck."

Alex coughs, choking on his spit. "What?"

I swivel in my seat, my desire intensifying when I feel him thicken beneath me. "I'm horny. We should fuck," I repeat more slowly and seductively. Well, as seductively as I can since I'm three-quarters drunk. It was delivered a little more slurred than I would have liked, but the alcohol thickening my veins adds a husky edge to my voice I can totally pull off.

Alex's sober eyes bounce between mine. He reads the eagerness, determination. . . and unfortunately, the glassiness in my wide gaze.

"How about we get some nutrients in your belly to absorb the slosh in there—" He presses his finger to my lips when I attempt to interrupt him. "Then. . ." he keeps me hanging long enough I'm on the verge of sobriety before suggesting, ". . . we'll discuss the possibility of fixing your dilemma."

"No deal." I shake my head. "I'm not *discussing* anything." I air quote part of my statement. "What is there to discuss? I'm horny. You have a cock—*a very stupendous one*—and I want it in my mouth. No discussions needed."

"Rae. . ." He sounds as if he is in pain. "Fuck me. You can't say shit like that to me."

"Why not?" My question is so loud, I swear half the continent hears me.

"Because you're drunk."

I furiously shake my head, adding to the giddiness clouding it. "I'm not drunk. I'm tipsy, quite possibly on my way to being drunk, but I'm *not* drunk. Not yet, anyway."

He smirks, more amused by my tirade than angered by it. "You haven't eaten since the plane. Your dad will kill me if you live off olives for another night."

"Don't worry, he'll kill you just for the naughty thoughts streaming through my head."

Alex scoffs. "So I'm to blame for your depraved mind?"

He stands, taking me with him. I wait for him to place me onto my feet before nodding. "As far as my daddy is concerned, I was a good country girl before the city-slickers had their way with me."

I said my comment in jest. Alex didn't hear it that way. "Had their way with you? What's that supposed to mean?"

I shouldn't love the jealous possessiveness in his tone, but I do. "You know what city folks are like when they have a naïve, country girl in their midst." I scrape my fingernails across his chest that is suddenly thrusting hard. "They take advantage."

Grinding teeth sound through my ears before he demands, "Give me names, Rae, and I guarantee the only things they'll take advantage of are the hours their cellmates are sleeping."

Even though the raw aggression in his tone kickstarts my libido, it isn't strong enough for my hazy brain to miss the vital point in his confession. He just admitted he has the ability to detain criminals. If that isn't a critical clue to his real job description, I don't know what is.

"Wanna protect me, big boy?" I giggle, weakening the angry lines staining his gorgeous face.

"More like wanna kill for you."

His comment is missing the playfulness of mine. He's being one hundred percent honest, making me suddenly fretful for the person stalking me. If Alex is right, and Danielle isn't the only one wanting to hack my private parts into pieces, they better hope the authorities find him before Alex does, or he might not get out of this situation alive.

"How about we save the body maiming until after we've eaten?"

Grateful for the invisible white flag I'm waving, Alex stops flexing and unflexing his fists. "Are we eating in or out?"

I shrug. "Depends."

He shadows me out of the bar, slicing the curious glances directed our way from half a dozen to just a few. "On what?"

I stop halfway down an elegant hall. It has all the pretty knickknacks you'd expect at any high-end B&B; there is just one difference: there are dozens upon dozens of personal photos scattered throughout.

"On if you brought a change of clothes. I'm not going anywhere that sells food with you looking like that." I fake a gag as I drag my eyes down his frozen frame.

My pulse thrums when I take in his casual T, faded dark blue jeans and sneaker-covered feet. His laidback look should have my libido crawling back into the hole it only found its way out of days ago, but for some reason unbeknownst to me, Alex rocks the casual look.

His hair is spiked at the front from his fingers constantly running through it, and his beard isn't the only thick thing on his body. His biceps. . . *God.* Men could train for three hours a day for over a year, and they still wouldn't compare to his. They're mouthwateringly scrumptious and barely hidden by the short cuff of his t-shirt.

"You don't like what I'm wearing?" Alex's hand makes the

trek my eyes just traveled. "You didn't mind it when you chose it for me to wear this morning."

"That was different. One, that was this morning. Casual chic is perfectly acceptable for early wear. Two, the concierge didn't have many options at his disposal. When forced to pick between jeans or cargo shorts, only one choice can be made." I gag for real this time. No grown man should wear cargo pants. "And three, one way or another, I'm determined to see you naked. If that can only be achieved by demanding you change your clothes, so be it."

Alex drags his hand across his beard, hiding his shit-eating grin. "For a drunk lady, you certainly have a way with words."

"I'm not drunk. . . " My words trail off when he slings his arm around my waist and guides me toward a hidden stairwell on my right. "Where are we going?"

Please say guest bedrooms. Please say guest bedrooms.

For once, my prayers are answered when Alex answers, "To the guest bedrooms." His eyes lower to mine to take in my gleaming eyes and the sultry curve of my lips. "Supposedly I need to change."

I got Alex naked. It was for barely ten seconds, but his stacked abs, tight V muscle, and mouth-watering guns have kept the furnace in my belly nicely stoked the past three hours. That, and the female members of his family. They tease Alex and his older brother Grayson nearly as relentlessly as me. I've laughed so much tonight, the vigorous activities Alex and I undertook last night aren't the sole cause for my aching stomach. His family is a hoot, as laid back and down to earth as Alex could be if he'd just let go of the reins for a second.

He doesn't need to drink. I haven't touched a drop of alcohol since we joined his family for dinner, and I'm having a blast. I've always assumed family gettogethers would be a snooze fest without a bottle of wine. Alex's family proves that isn't the case. They downed the booze while my veins thrived off their dynamic.

I love how close-knit they are. Watching Alex dote on his mom and sister amplified the crush I've had on him since we bumped heads in the elevator. There is nothing more sexually appealing than seeing a man treat a woman right. Alex can be a little aggressive, and his domineering outside of the bedroom frustrates me, but the respect he shows his mother makes him ridiculously hot.

I've given in to my temptations many times tonight. We've laughed, shared sneaky kisses, and even a handful of feather-like touches have occurred under the table. Usually, I'm against touchy-feely PDA's, but just like the bricks I've attempted to rebuild around my heart, Alex knocks them down. I want him to smother my neck in kisses, feel his hot breath on my skin as he makes me melt underneath him. I want everything he is willing to give me, and then I'll return the favor in a way that will blow his mind.

I squirm in Alex's lap when I fantasize about the hungry, frenzied kisses we've shared so far in our relationship. In the past forty-eight hours, we've experienced them all. The tender ones, the ravenous ones, the ones that make you forget what day of the week it is. I thought our first one was so fire-sparking as it was fueled by pent-up lust. I was wrong. Every one we've had since then strengthens what I've always known: Alex can kiss. His plump lips and the power he has over his tongue is mesmerizing, but his beard... god, it adds an element I've never experienced before.

I hate the wiry hair covering his jaw because it hides an asset he should exploit, not conceal, but the more times he runs his scruffy Viking beard down my neck, the more I fall in love with it. I want to feel it scratching every inch of my skin, to have it coated in both my scent and my arousal. I want it to tickle my neck before he drags it through the wet dampness between my legs. I want it so bad, and I want it now.

I wonder if Alex can hear my private thoughts when his cock throbs in his trousers. He grows against my thigh, teasing me as insistently as I've badgered him tonight. His thick fingers dig into my hip as if he's lassoing a rope around me, tethering us together with invisible bindings I'll never be able to unknot.

Daringly, I press my lips to his ear and murmur, "I want to rip your clothes off and fuck you so bad."

He continues his conversation with his brother without a single hitch in his breathing, but I know he heard me. His fingers flexed against my hip, and don't even get me started on the region my mind can't be deterred from.

"I've been a good girl. I played house. Now give me my reward."

My comment is in jest. We've spent the last several hours surrounded by his family, but not once did I feel uncomfortable. I didn't even balk when his mom slung her arms around my neck to hug me goodnight. I may have even initiated the farewell with his sister. I'm not suddenly overcome with friendliness, I just knew the faster they called it a night, the faster I'd get Alex naked. My plan went off without a hitch until it hit a snag I never saw coming: Grayson and his inability to take a hint.

If I didn't know any better, I'd swear he's purposely foiling my ruse. I've waved a white flag in his eyes many times tonight, but not once has he seen it.

With a grin, I stuff the figurative white flag into my pocket before replacing it with the more risqué, *you'll never be able to miss it* flag. This one is red and fiery, as obvious as the sexual tension teeming between Alex and me.

Alex's eyes stray from Grayson midsentence when I twist in his lap. "Don't mind me; I'm just slipping under the table to help myself to dessert."

My last two words come out in a purr, the sting of Alex's fingers as he struggles not to respond to my tease too pleasurable to ignore.

Staring down at me, his gorgeous face strains as his nostrils flare. He seems conflicted, as if he can't decide whether to spank the sass straight out of me or strangle his brother for not taking a hint.

I'll take either. The friction between us is so great, someone is bound to get massacred no matter what. Although I'd prefer the torture be inflicted on my needy pussy, Alex doesn't just destroy my horniness when he's burrowed inside me, he screws up my heart as well. You'd think that would dampen his appeal. It doesn't. Not in the slightest. If anything, it makes me want him even more.

Besides, didn't he tell me to run to him when I need him? *I need him.*

As if he heard my private thoughts, Alex returns his eyes to Grayson. "Say goodnight."

I assume he is talking to Grayson until he squeezes my hip. My eyes bounce between two pairs of identically devastating blue eyes for several seconds. I've missed something. I have no idea how, but I'm not surprised. Even the most important men in my life flee to the back of my mind when I'm transfixed by my desires.

"Goodnight, Grayson," I murmur like a good, obedient puppy.

With a smirk that reveals he didn't miss the cheek in my tone, Grayson dips his chin. A stab of urgency bolts through my body when Alex plucks me from my chair. He races through the dining room at The Manor, his focus on the hidden servant stairwell we used earlier today.

"Do you know how hard your teases made me? I've been pitching a fucking tent all night long."

The gruffness of his words tugs the coil in my womb, giving it a rough yank.

"I sat across from my mom with a swollen cock. Fuck, Rae!"

I shouldn't smile, but I do.

Seeing my smile, Alex works his jaw side to side. "If I weren't dying to hear you scream my name, I'd tie you to my bed, step back, then wait for you to beg me to touch you."

My steps slow to half their natural stride. *That doesn't sound like fun at all.*

Before I can voice my utter disgust, Alex ducks his head to align our lips. He doesn't kiss me like I'm hoping. He keeps his mouth a half an inch from mine, teasing me as I have done to him all night. The sweet scent of his breath fanning my lips adds to the chaos low in my stomach, but it's only to blame for one-tenth of my turmoil. His eyes, my god. They render me completely and utterly speechless. He stares at me like he'll never take another breath if his air isn't shared with mine. Like he doesn't see the barriers I do. As if he wants me as badly as I want him.

Spurred on by the power his eyes radiate through me, I close the distance between our lips. Our kiss is cruel and vicious, and I love every fucking minute of it. It is one of those kisses that scores your heart, ensuring you'll never forget it for decades to come.

My body tenses as the thrumming sensation strives to break free of its restraints. I groan into Alex's mouth, my throaty moan a warning of how close to detonation I am.

"God, yes," I moan over his lips when he bands my legs around his waist.

My nails dig into the hard slabs on the top of his shoulders when he rocks his hips forward. While grinding his rock hard shaft against my begging clit, he carries me across the room. His steps are as hurried as my fingers are working on unfastening the buttons of his dress shirt.

By the time he breaks through the curtain hiding the servants' stairs from regular guests, I have his shirt off his shoulders. The stairwell is dim, but it doesn't hinder my eyes' ability to absorb his wide shoulders, tattooed pec, and the tiny sliver of leather stopping us from becoming one.

"Not here," Alex groans in pain when my hands shoot down to his belt. "My family uses this stairwell. They like midnight snacks."

His words are telling me no, but his body is saying the

opposite. Every word he speaks coincides with a rock of his hips. He's torn, and for once, it doesn't fill me with worry. I know he wants me so bad, he'll take me any way he can get me. Family hallways included.

"Then hurry. I'm dying."

He moves faster than I expect. He climbs the stairs, throws open his childhood bedroom door, tosses me on the bed, then frees his cock from his pants in a record-setting pace.

I stop smiling at his eagerness when he positions his glistening crown between the seams of my pussy, which is clinging to my damp panties. I wiggle, hating the thin piece of cotton separating us. I was pro-latex before Alex, but now condoms won't be the only thing on my shit list. Panties will be scribbled on the line beneath them.

Who knew a sexy undergarment could be a cockblocker?

Spotting my agitation, a smug grin crosses Alex's lips. I buck my hips upward, trying to seize some of the control he always steals when my smarts are trapped by lust.

"Still," he growls through clenched teeth, his struggle as real as mine.

"I will when you me give me what I want!"

"Not yet."

Pulling my panties to the side, he rubs his cock through the folds of my pussy, coating himself in my juices. Considering we did nothing but kiss, I should be ashamed about how wet I am. Unfortunately for all involved, I've never heard of the word "timid," much less used it to describe myself.

A long, quivering moan simpers through my lips when Alex's engorged knob breezes past my clit. I arch my back, seeking more direct contact. I nearly beg when he pins my hips to the bed by splaying his hand across my stomach, but I stop short—*thank god.* I don't need him to get me off. I have everything I need right here.

My lips part to suck in much-needed air when my hand slithers to my soaked center. After lubing up my fingers, I move them to the little nub seconds away from imploding. My clit is thrumming, dying to crash through the lust cloud surrounding me. A few flicks and I'll be done, my greatest desire taken care of.

I toy with my clit for barely a second before Alex snatches my hand away. The fury roaring through my body triples its heat when he pops my glistening fingers into his mouth. He growls a menacing groan as his tongue laps up evidence of my excitement.

Once my fingers are sparkling clean, he raises my arm above my head to join its lazy counterpart. While one of his hands holds both mine hostage, his other makes quick work of the clothes dividing us. Since I'm only wearing a skirt and a blouse, the process occurs a lot faster than I expect. We're back to his cock teasing my slit within seconds, the clear liquid seeping from his crown revealing he is struggling as immensely as me.

"Please—" I stop myself again. *I will not beg.*

Alex doesn't give in so easy. "Please. . .?"

He dips his cock an inch inside of me before withdrawing it, rubbing it against my clit, then reinserting it again.

He does this another five times before shameful plea after shameful plea spills from my lips. "Please. Please. Please."

Each beg gets me another inch, but it's still inches away from what I need.

"Please, what?" he pushes, his tone as thick as his delicious cock.

I grit my teeth from the mirth in his tone. If I weren't so goddamn horny, I'd knee him in the nuts, throw him off me, and take care of business myself. Regrettably, he isn't the only one aware my self-pleasing mojo disappeared the instant he arrived in the picture.

With that in mind, I growl, "Please fuck me."

"Hmm." Alex twists his lips as if he is contemplating my suggestion. "I might consider it if you use a few more manners."

The gall of him!

I knock his ego down a few pegs by snarling, "Fuck me or bring in someone more capable of doing the job."

That untwists his lips by hardening them into a firm, straight line.

Not so smug now, are you?

The minute I return to Ravenshoe, I'm sending the chatty baker a dozen roses. Jealousy can make men stupid, insolent little boys, but it can also bring out their dominance. Alex won't fuck me into submission, though. He'll utterly destroy me for every man after him.

Goodie.

His destructive path starts at my breasts. He kneads and fondles them until my nipples harden into points. After he's caressed them long enough I'm on the brink of insanity, his attention drops a few inches. My moans urge him toward the area weeping for his attention. Thankfully, he doesn't keep me waiting for long. With one hand needed to pin my arms to the bed, he spreads the lips of my pussy with his index finger and thumb before circling his lips around my clit. He sucks it into his mouth gently, causing my thighs to shake.

My eyes stop rolling to the back of my head halfway when he growls against my slick sex, "Don't come."

Huh? He didn't just say what I thought he did, did he?

He does a long lick to the area mere seconds from shattering before locking his eyes with mine. I don't need him to repeat his demand to know of its existence—his eyes say it all—but just in case they don't, he reiterates, "Don't come. If you do, it will be the only orgasm you'll have tonight."

Before I can announce my utter disgust at his request, he pushes two fingers inside of me. I know what he's doing. He wants me to defy him, to show I have no control over my body when it comes to him.

The only thing I'm going to show him is how stupidly wrong he is.

No one controls me. Not the man finger-fucking me to the point of oblivion, or the one who ensures my tummy never goes hungry. I might work in a male-dominated industry, but I don't work *for* them. *I* make them who they are. *I* make them better people.

The grunt Alex releases matches mine when I use all my strength to curl my legs around his waist and flip him over. He acts surprised by my grapple for control, but the faint grin tugging at his lips gives away his true feelings. He wants me to fight, because he doesn't want a wallflower. He wants an equal, so that's precisely what I'll give him.

With my now free hands spread across his sweaty pecs, I lower myself onto his cock. A pleasurable burn overwhelms me as I take what I need.

129

When my backside hits Alex's chunky thighs, I swivel my hips, taking even more of him inside of me. Even with my spikes hackled, it feels unbelievably good to be filled by him. This is sex. It makes me feel dirty. Wanton. Downright fucking filthy. But it also makes me feel incredibly free.

I feel the latter more than anything when I'm being consumed by Alex. In this moment, as I'm blinded by the raging inferno brewing between us, I could imagine myself falling in love with him. Not just a fleeting fling that burns as fiercely as my lungs do when he enters the room or my pussy aches from taking a man his size. A long commitment. A mutual devotion. *True love.*

After taking an unsteady breath to calm the nerves taking flight in my stomach, I rise to my knees. Alex's fingers flex against my hips. "Not yet." His words are more like groans. "I need a moment. You have no idea how fucking sexy you look right now. Fierce. Strong. You're making me so unhinged I've lost my fucking mind, Rae, but I don't give a shit. They can have it all, everything I have, as long as I never have to give you up."

See? That's what I was talking about when I said he destroys both my pussy and my heart. The look on his face as he relishes being surrounded by my heat is as sexy as fuck, but it does weird things to my insides. Things I've never felt before. Things I'm scared of. It makes my earlier statement not a possibility, more a certainty.

I thought I was incapable of love. Only now do I realize I've always had the ability, I just never had the right man.

That's all set to change now... *maybe?*

12

Alex

"You're braver than me." Ralph, local hooligan/rifle range manager, doubles his grin before handing me a loaded gun. "She's got that killer gleam in her eyes your dad always told me to watch for. As far as she's concerned, the target isn't the only fool standing in this range, waiting to be shot." He nudges his head to the paper silhouette. "Do you want me to draw some coconuts on his crotch? Make sure her aim is real precise?"

Rolling my eyes at the jest in his tone, I ensure the safety on my gun is on before making my way to Regan. She's standing at the entrance of the firing range, looking as out of place as she did last night when I forced her to take the reins in our exchange.

Don't get me wrong, I have no qualms accepting any power Regan is willing to give me, but last night wasn't about that. I can't gripe about us being equal if I don't occasionally hand over the controls. Regan is fierce, stronger than she'll ever know, but her fierceness grows tenfold when she lets herself go. If she needs to reign supreme to achieve that, so be it. I didn't lie when I said she is so far above me, I'm afraid I'll never catch her. I still can't believe she is here now, in my hometown, wearing teeny shorts and one of my shirts twisted into the middle of her stomach.

Besides, she's as sexy as fuck when she's grappling for power. I love that she has a backbone, and she's not afraid to use it. That means she'll forever walk beside me, not behind me.

Hearing my approach, Regan spins around to face me. She's nervously chewing on her lower lip. "Is this really necessary?"

I arch a brow, answering her without words. We've had the same conversation four times already this morning. This is as necessary as my heart's ability to pump blood.

"You are *not* at any time to touch the trigger until you're ready to shoot. Do you understand?"

I wait for her to nod before placing the gun in her hand. Her brows furrow as she stares down at it, but she doesn't dump it and run as I anticipated.

When I told her we were going to a shooting range today, she flatly denied my remark as if it were a suggestion. Pity for her I wasn't joking. There is a deranged man threatening to harm her. Anything I can do to make sure she is prepared for his attack, I'll do. She has a gun. She has the confidence to fire it. Now, with my help, she'll have the skills to protect herself. I'll never let anything happen to her, but I can't be her shadow 24/7. My parents' story is living proof of that.

My dad believed keeping my mother in the dark would

ensure her safety. It nearly cost him everything. I won't let that happen to Regan. Her attacker is smart. He's hidden his tracks so well, even Grayson is having a hard time locating him. But I've studied criminals long enough to know he won't stop until he accomplishes what he set out to achieve. Stalkers don't fail and give up. They keep going until they've either killed their victim or themselves. There is only one result I'm aiming for: the latter.

After curling myself around Regan's back, I show her the stance required to fire a high caliber weapon without injuring herself. "When you're handling a gun, you must maintain gun safety at all times. Don't load a weapon unless you plan to fire it. Keep the safety on at all times, even when the gun isn't in use, and *never* point it at anyone unless you're hoping they'll die."

Her pulse quickens during my last sentence.

"I asked Ralph to put on a suppressor to dampen the noise and smooth out the recoil. It won't be like that when you're firing in haste. Despite what Hollywood tells you, most perps don't use silencers."

Her panicked eyes lift to mine, reminding me she needs more protection than just a few rules. I stop feeling her pulse thrum through my body when I move to the bench at our side to secure a set of earmuffs and protective glasses. Regan reveals she's been paying attention when she lowers the gun so it points just left of her shoes instead of my chest. A ghost of a smile cracks onto my lips when I spot the heels she's wearing. They're the same pair she threatened to gouge my eye out with months ago. I still can't believe that was only a little over two months ago. Feels more like a lifetime.

After putting on Regan's glasses and earmuffs, I don my own set. Her pulse returns to its frantic pace when I curl my body over her back and raise her hand again. "Stop panicking. This can be as much fun as it is a lesson," I shout to ensure she can hear me.

"Shooting a guy in the gonads to stop him from hacking me to pieces is not my idea of a fun time."

My throat works hard to swallow. Just as her tone insinuated, she's aiming extremely low on the paper silhouette. She's not here to take him down. She's aiming to hurt him as badly as he wants to hurt her.

"Aim for his chest." I smile when she huffs. "It is a broader area, meaning you're less likely to miss."

I can't see her, but I can imagine her rolling her eyes. "Watch your thumb. You don't want it anywhere near the slide." She nods, remembering the run down I gave her on gun safety during our travels. "Your fingers also shouldn't be anywhere near the cylinder. That fucker burns."

In the corner of my eye, I spot her lips curving high. She's probably remembering my whine last night when I showed her the burn I got during my first trip to the range. I was six and shit scared of firing a gun for the three years that followed. Thankfully, my father showed me what I'm hoping Regan will soon realize: guns can be as much fun as they are dangerous.

My eyes stray to the target to calculate its distance before returning them to Regan. Ralph brought the target a few feet closer. It's a smart move. If a new shooter has confidence in their precision, they'll be more likely to continue with lessons. If they fail on the first go, or worse, injure themselves, they'll be reluctant to return to the range. Considering I want Regan's marksman skills to be on par with mine, making her comfortable is a step in the right direction.

I switch off the safety, then press my lips to the shell of Regan's muffs. "Alright, when you're ready, fire at your target."

Usually, at this point in a lesson, I'd step away from the recruit. I don't go far. I stay close enough they can sense my presence, but far enough to show my confidence in them. But since Regan isn't a cadet, and I can't be reprimanded for my cock getting cozy with her ass, I'll stay put.

I'll never see marksmanship training in the same light now.

"Come on, Rae. You've got this," I encourage when she stalls firing. She has her arm up and ready, her eye glancing down the sight. She's just frozen. Mute. Shit-fucking scared. "Take charge like you did last night, baby. Show them fuckers how it's done."

She exhales loud enough for me to hear through my earmuffs before firing off a shot. I don't know if the unfavorable nickname is the cause for her sudden burst of determination or because she's noticed the handful of gun-toting men hovering close to watch the spectacle of Barbie unleashing her anger.

They've underestimated the strength of my girl, but it won't be long until they discover what I learned the moment I laid my eyes on her. She's not just strong. She's fucking dynamite.

The vein in Regan's neck flutters when the bullet pierces the left upper quadrant of the paper silhouette.

"Again."

This one shreds the paper silhouette's stomach in half.

"Again."

She continues firing until the magnum is depleted of bullets, and the paper target is hanging by a thread.

135

"Now switch on your safety and lower your weapon."

She does as requested without hesitation.

"Well done," I praise when Ralph drags in the target. Every bullet hit the target, one in a spot I'm certain Regan aimed for.

"If a bullet to the heart doesn't kill him, I'm sure the loss of his cock will make him wish he were dead."

I laugh when her comment forces the men circling us to wither away. I swear some even grab their crotches on their way by.

Regan stops smirking like the cat who swallowed the canary when I say, "Get your finger off the trigger. None of them are your targets." I nudge my head to the handful of men happy to risk their lives to continue enjoying the visual. "Me, on the other hand..."

Regan's smile steals my words... and perhaps my jealousy.

Our time at the range goes better than I could have hoped. Regan's confidence fed off the adrenaline racing through her veins, and the worry her eyes have held since Friday night is almost gone. Although real life scenarios will always be more harrowing than any amount of practice, workable knowledge will lessen the terror. I hope Regan is never in a position in which she's required to protect herself, but if the unfortunate occurs, I'm confident she has the skills to safeguard herself.

Regan's eyes swing from the road to me when I ask, "Wings or cob loaf?"

If I didn't know her as well as I did, I'd be worried by her quietness. Fortunately, I'm pretty clued in when it comes to her emotions. She's not quiet as she is angry. She's absorbing all the information she's been overloaded with the past four days. It's smart for her to do. The more prepared she is, the less carnage there will be.

"Does your ma make the dressing for the wings?"

I shake my head. "Her cooking specialties don't branch into poultry. There's a wings joint a few miles from The Manor. It's not up to my mom's caliber, but they're pretty darn tasty." *Not as tasty as you*, but I'll keep that info to myself.

Seeing Regan like that, a gun holstered dangerously low on her waist, and her hair pulled away from her face to ensure it didn't hinder her long-range sight. . . *fuck!* Every fantasy I've ever had was played out today. I can't wait for Halloween. Regan has mentioned she plans to attend a costume party dressed as Jeannie from *I Dream of Jeannie*, but if I have my way, she'll be a walking wet dream—a blonde Lara Croft.

After quickly adjusting my crotch, I shift my focus back to Regan. She's tapping her index finger on her lips as if she's contemplating. I know she isn't. She's loved the time we've spent with my family as much as I have. So much so, she suggested we return home after our five-mile run this morning to eat breakfast with my family instead of the little café we ran to.

She muses for a few more seconds before saying, "I've never had cob loaf before, so I choose that."

"Alright." I steer my dad's truck to the left, pretending her decision solely resonates around her stomach's cravings instead of her heart's.

We travel two miles before flashing lights cause my foot to

slip off the gas pedal. I pull up next to a state trooper directing us to the opposite side of the road. "What is it?"

There must be something in my tone that displays my authority, or perhaps the fact my family is well known around these parts, because he answers with no hesitation, "Bad traffic accident. Two fatal. One badly injured."

"Are medics on site?"

He nods, his cheeks whitening.

"First to arrive?" Sympathy echoes in my tone. I can still recall the first time I was assigned to a homicide. It was a home invasion gone wrong. Quick, relatively clean death, but still hard to stomach.

"Yeah, it's. . . ah. . . not pretty. That's why we're directing people to go via Trate." He points to a street sign a few spaces up from us. "Travel half a mile before taking a right on Howdy. That will pop you out the other side."

"Alright, thanks."

I jerk up my chin in thanks before pulling my truck onto the opposite side of the road. The fire crew on site have done a good job concealing the wreckage, but nothing can hide the sight of two bodies lying roadside covered by white sheets.

I cut the corner of Trate, praying I'll save Regan from a visual I know will shred her heart into a million pieces. I'm not fast enough, though. If the way her spine snaps straight isn't enough of an indication she spotted it, the harrowing sob rumbling in her throat as she tries to maintain her composure is a surefire indication.

"Rae," I say her name as painfully as my heart is bleeding from the pained expression etched on her beautiful face.

Realizing there isn't a single thing I can say to help her

through this, I unlatch her belt, seize her wrist, then drag her across the leather seat until she's nuzzled under the crook of my arm.

There are a thousand sayings filtering through my mind. Quotes on sympathy, handling grief, and how she's the bravest woman I've ever met, but no matter how hard I try to fire them off my tongue, I can't get them out. She needs comfort, not words. Assurance, not regrets. But more than anything, she needs me. So that's precisely what I'll give her.

I pull her in even closer before flattening my foot on the gas pedal. My dad's truck is an old girl, but she's quick off the mark.

By the time Regan's shaking begins to settle, I'm pulling into the driveway of The Manor. I park near the valet, leave the keys in the ignition, then slide out the driver's side door, taking Regan with me.

"How about we shower before we eat? We smell like lead."

She doesn't, but it's a good excuse to give her a few more minutes to compose herself before my family swarms her for the third time. My silent comfort eased the pain in her eyes, but the fact she didn't jerk out of my clutch the instant we entered The Manor proves she still has a little way to go.

Regan's frantic nod matches the thump of our feet hitting the landing at the top of the stairs. As I chaperone her to my room at the end of a long hallway, she takes in the family portraits dotting the walls. They're similar to the photos my mom shared last night but ten times their size. They were professionally taken the day before my dad started his new placement over a decade ago. They include the same six faces: me, my parents, my two brothers, and my sister, Darcy.

I won't lie; the jealousy that roared through Regan's eyes

when Darcy leaped into my arms yesterday afternoon was one of the best moments I've ever had. She can deny it all she likes, but I know she was seconds from yanking Darcy off me by the strands of her hair. It's lucky I had a vise-like grip on her hand or nothing would have stopped her. Regan doesn't seem like the type to get jealous, but just like her presence affects my mind, she's learning nothing is as it once was.

My arm slips from Regan's shoulders when she freezes halfway down the hall. "Your aftershave is a peppery scent, a spicy palette that elicits thoughts of hard fucks and painstakingly vivid dreams about trekking through the wilderness to find the beastly man hiding behind the smell."

The cocky expression on my face fades when she murmurs, "My anger at being ditched made me mistake his aftershave as yours. I thought the smooth, velvety scent wafting in the air was anger seeping from my pores." She fiercely shakes her head, eradicating the last of the grief in her eyes. "It wasn't. It had a smooth, velvety texture to it, with a pinch of vanilla that had me recalling tranquil gardens and lazy lovemaking on a sandy shore." Tears prick her eyes when she adds on, "It was a smell I've experienced only once before. It was on my darkest day. That's why I was confused. My woozy head had my wires crossed. It wasn't your scent I was smelling Friday night in my apartment. It was Luca's."

I take a step back, shocked. "What are you saying, Rae? That Luca's not dead? That he's the man stalking you?"

She shakes her head once more. "No. That isn't what I'm implying at all. Luca would never do this to me or you." She scans the angry bump on my right temple. "But I think I know who did."

She pushes past me and charges down the hallway. She makes it ten steps before she realizes she has no clue which room is which. All the doors in The Manor are identical.

Hearing her unasked question, I point to a room two doors down on my left. I shadow her into my room, my steps stiffer than hers. I feel sorry for the guests in the room below ours. My angry stomps sound like an elephant sprinting away from the trapeze line.

With a grunt, a tear of a zipper, and a hoist, Regan flops onto the pristinely made bed in the middle of our room to fire up her laptop.

"What are you looking for?" I join her bedside.

Her throat works hard to swallow before she forces out, "Do you remember the confession I let slip after rolling my mom's Jeep?"

She waits for me to nod before murmuring, "Luca and I were fighting that night because I walked in on him in a compromising position... *with a man.*"

Her last three words are barely whispers. She hates that she's sharing stuff she swore she'd never share, but I already have a gist of what happened, and she knows it.

"Luca tried to brush off their exchange. He said what I had saw wasn't real, that they were just fooling around, et cetera, et cetera."

"What most men say when busted having an affair," I interject, my tone snarkier than I anticipated.

Since I'm only working with half-truths, my jab at Luca's integrity isn't surprising, but with neither of us having the time nor the means to discuss the situation, I offer her an apologetic grin before gesturing for her to continue.

141

She does—thankfully. "The *person* Luca was with that night was unappreciative of his recollection of events. At first, he took his frustration out on Luca—"

"Then it switched to you?" I read between the lines.

She nods. "I knew everything he screamed at me was true. I could smell Luca's cologne all over him, not to mention see the honesty in his eyes. He was in love with Luca. . ."

She slows her words to suck in some quick breaths, hoping they'll help ease out her next set of sentences.

Eager to save her from the turmoil, I fill in, "You knew he loved Luca because his eyes reflected your own."

She nods again, but it's not as determined as her earlier ones. Tears gloss her eyes as her hands ball into fists on her keyboard.

The sound of teeth grinding together fades when I curl my hand over hers. "Work with facts, not emotions. Facts are evidential. Emotions are fact-blockers. If you can keep your emotions out of it, you'll find the truth lying beneath them."

Once the groove between her brows soothes, I ask, "You said on the plane that you forced Luca to pick. How did you do that?"

She licks her dry lips before answering, "How any irrationally jealous teenage girl would. I told him it was either his new friend or me. He couldn't have us both."

Her face screws up as if she can't believe how naïve it was for her to do that. I'm not surprised. She was just a girl who believed she was in love. I'm quickly learning that fascination and love are too entirely unique emotions. Don't ask me how I've suddenly gained this knowledge, because there is no way in hell I'll give you an honest answer, but I'm reasonably sure Regan is slowly unearthing the same wisdom.

"Luca picked you?" I ask, questioning the obvious.

"Yes. . . well, after a slight deliberation."

My grip on her hand tightens when reality smacks into me. "Did this deliberation occur in front of the man responsible for the ultimatum?"

Shame floods her face before she nods. "Hence the need for my laptop. It's probably nothing, but the look he gave me that night—*God*. It made me want to hack myself into little pieces."

I stop recalling the pain, disrespect, and humiliation that rained down on me when Regan picked Isaac over me in that field all those years ago. I barely knew her back then, yet I was devastated I was put second, so I can imagine how immense the pain was for the man Luca dissed.

With this in mind, I snag Regan's laptop. She looks like she wants to argue, but my next set of questions stuffs her retaliation back down her throat. "Do you recall if Luca said the man's name? Or was he friends with him on any social media platforms?"

My fingers flying wildly over the keyboard nearly drowns out her faint reply, "No. That's why I was so shocked by what I walked in on. Luca had never mentioned him, much less hung around with him before."

The little vein in her neck works overtime as her eyes flicker. "He had a bomber jacket slung over his bed. It had the same emblem as Luca's football team emblazoned on the back. He was either a part of Luca's team or a member of their cheer squad— you couldn't use the emblem unless you were on their team."

143

I look at her as if she's grown a second head. My nose wasn't buried in a book my entire college career, but that seems a bit excessive.

Regan slaps my arm, her playfulness a welcome addition to our exchange. The tension was getting so muggy, sweat is beading my nape. "Cattle aren't the only ones branded, Alex. If you didn't have teenagers copying your style, you were in the wrong crowd."

I wink, revealing I'm proud of the determination in her eyes before shifting my focus back to the task at hand.

A few keystrokes later, I ask, "This emblem?"

I have a picture of Luca and Regan up on the screen. Luca is wearing a red bomber jacket, and Rae is tucked under his arm, wearing his jersey number on her cheek with paint.

When she nods, barely holding in the tears filling her eyes, I yank her cellphone out of my pocket. She watches me curiously when I snap a photo of the emblem.

Happy I have an unpixellated shot, I hand Regan back her laptop, then run a reverse image search on her phone. Within seconds, numerous matches pop up.

"Who needs facial recognition software when you have Google?" I'm smiling, blind to the fact I'm dropping hints left, right, and center on what I really do for a living.

I'm not looking forward to Regan discovering the truth, but the past four days has made my worry less obvious. She won't be happy when she discovers who my target is, but I've dug my footholds into her deep enough, she'll at least give me a chance to explain myself before she bolts.

"Do any of these men's faces ring a bell?" My low tone indicates I'm more worried about losing her than I'm letting on.

She scans three pages of photos before frustration clutches her throat. "How many groupies did his team have?"

Failing to recognize her question is rhetorical, I scroll to the very bottom of the page. "Only fifty-eight pages to go."

She groans. "Is there a quicker way? We'll be here all night at this rate."

"I can probably refine the search by adding hair and eye coloring."

I do exactly that when she passes on the information I'm seeking. It narrows our list of suspects to thirty-eight pages. It's still a long list, but not as bad as it was.

A few seconds later, Regan freezes as if a lightning bolt sparked through her brain. "Can we narrow the demographics by adding a fraternity? I confronted Luca at the man's frat house."

Hope flares through my eyes as I nod. "I've never been overly good with this techie shit, but I learned a few things at the academy."

There I go again with another little snippet of my real life. If I didn't know any better, I'd swear Regan swapped the water in my bottle for vodka. My lips have only been this loose once before: the night Dane and I got rip-roaring drunk after graduation. Waking up with my head in a bucket of vomit, my feet bare, and my body stripped of clothing ensured it was the last time I used alcohol to enhance my excitement. I doubt it will take more than a glass for me to tiptoe to Drunkville as I haven't touched a drop of alcohol in over six years.

Within seconds, the list of candidates has significantly narrowed. Only twenty-three men remain.

"Stop. There," Regan shouts, halting my scan of the photos mid-scroll.

I zoom in on the picture she is pointing to. She takes her time appraising it, wanting to ensure she has all her t's crossed and i's dotted. I understand her need to be sure. The message scribbled across her vanity was filled with hatred, but this isn't an accusation she wants to throw out without due diligence.

Furthermore, Luca died years ago, so why would her stalker wait so long to seek his revenge? She did go a little off the radar after Luca's death, but she was very much present in all aspects of his life before and after his death.

After tracking her finger down the man's profound nose and extremely sharp jaw, Regan says, "That's him."

"Are you sure? Take another look just in case. We don't want to start an investigation on an innocent man. Just an accusation like this can ruin a man's credibility for years to come. . ."

I stop cautioning her when she points to the unnamed man's dainty, feminine hands. The tick in my jaw ramps up as my nostrils flare. I remain quiet for several moments, sucking in enough oxygen my lungs stop demanding air, but not enough to weaken the red-hot anger heating my cheeks.

Two taps on a phone screen, and one screen shot later, I fire off a message to an unidentified number on Regan's cell.

"Now what?" Regan asks when I toss her phone to her side and flop my back onto the bed we're sitting on.

I rake my fingers through my hair as my eyes stray to the ceiling. "Now we do the one part of my job I hate more than anything." I exhale deeply. "We wait."

"Wait?! We can't wait."

Hearing nothing but utter desperation in her voice, my eyes

lift to Regan's. "As frustrating as it is, this is a part of the process. The information you recalled will be a great help; we've got a lot to work with."

"But?" she asks, hearing it hanging the air.

"But. . . as much as I'd love to pin his nuts to the wall for what he put you through, I can't. Not without ensuring the evidence stacks up. A lot of men wear vanilla-scented colognes. Nearly as many of them have feminine hands. The likelihood of him having both those features *and* a prior run-in with you lowers the possibilities of this being a mix-up, but we still need to assess the probables. I made a mistake once thinking Danielle was the only perp on our radar. I won't risk a second fuck up."

A sudden wish not to be able to read her as well as she can me smacks into me when I see the words she can't express in her eyes. She's not worried I'll fuck up; she's petrified I'll fail her. I'm not talking in the physical sense. It's an emotional upheaval she's worried about the most.

This woman is more detrimental to my sanity than the world's most potent drug. She makes me heedless, which, quite frankly, I'd hate. . . if I didn't love it so much.

"How long of a wait are we talking?"

My brows perk up from the uneasiness in her tone. "An hour, possibly two." I scan her body. "Plenty of time for dinner."

The low growl of my words has her forgetting the seriousness of our exchange faster than I can snap my fingers. Good. She doesn't need to panic. I'll never let anything happen to her.

"And perhaps dessert?"

I return my eyes to hers. They're the most devastatingly

beautiful they've ever been. "*And* dessert. No ifs, baby. I work off facts, not assumptions."

Rolling her eyes at my term of endearment, she tosses her laptop to the side before hooking her leg over my waist. We groan in sync when her quick straddle of my hips has my cock grinding against her rapidly dampening crotch.

"Since you only work off facts, let me give you a few." She waits a beat, needing a minute to control the fire running rampantly through her veins from having intimate parts of our bodies sitting so close together. "First, don't call me 'baby' or any other throw-away name. I'm not your baby. I'm also not your girl." When I attempt to talk, she talks faster. "But I do love it when you call me Rae, so if you need a nickname, stick with that."

My lips furl before my chin meets my chest, soundlessly calling in my defeat.

"Second, I think we've both established that we have some weird, unexplainable connection going on." When I nod in agreement, she adds on, "Then can we stop pussyfooting around? I'm not glass. I won't break if handled roughly. I'm reasonably sure the handprint you left on my ass proves that without a doubt."

My cock rapidly thickening beneath her makes her last fact the hardest of them all to absorb. "And third, but not at all least, if this man is responsible for what happened in my apartment Friday night, we need to tread lightly."

I stiffen. Unfortunately, not all the rigidness is confined to my zipper region.

"I don't want him to get off scot-free; I'd just rather not have another spectacle like the one at Luca's memorial. Danielle's defense has created quite a lot of gossip in my hometown, gossip I'd rather avoid."

I peer up at her, shocked she's aware of the false accusations Danielle is slinging her way. I wasn't aware they were common knowledge.

"I spoke to Ayden after our run this morning. He wasn't impressed he had to go out of his way to track me down. I thought you were going to update him when we landed?"

"I did—just twenty minutes after he would have liked."

From Ayden's reaction, anyone would swear I had shipped Regan to the Bermuda Triangle instead of Washington DC.

"Ah." Regan's brows lower as her lips turn downward. "I take it your conversation didn't go well?"

I twist my lips to hide my smile. Regan acts tough, but she hates the idea of me getting hurt. "My life was only threatened three times in ten minutes, so that's somewhat of an improvement."

Regan laughs. I can tell she feels guilty about her brother's bossy demeanor, but she heard the jest in my tone. She's also grateful I'm taking her family's overbearing personalities in stride. A lesser man may have run for the hills, but I'm not a lesser man. What I said to Regan on the plane is true. I'm not going anywhere.

My eyes slowly drift to Regan's when she says, "Your ma is right. You're a good man, Alex Rogers." Her praise is unnecessary, but fucking great to hear.

"Hmm." She squirms as if my deep, thick voice rumbled through her body. "Let's see if you're still saying that in the morning."

The tension in the room evaporates when I complete the

maneuver she pulled on me last night. In under two seconds, she is beneath me, panting, smiling, and it is all done without a single bit of hesitation crossing her mind. Who in their right mind has time for anxiety when you've got a man as strong and protective as me glancing down at you with lust and admiration in his eyes?

Not anyone sane.

I wake up the following morning to six unread text messages, four unanswered calls, and an exhausted Regan wrapped around my body. Within twenty minutes of sending Brandon an outdated copy of the suspect's photo, we identified her perp, but with his funeral occurring a mere nine months after Luca's, we soon hit a snag.

Jaxson Kittson's life oddly mimicked Luca's. He was the popular jock with a beautiful girlfriend on his arm a majority of his senior year at high school before he scored a highly sought-after scholarship to play football. Unlike Luca, he came out his first month of college.

From what Brandon unearthed in the short window I gave him, Jaxson and Luca met at an LGBT support group at college. Although Jaxson encouraged Luca to reveal his sexual orientation in his own time frame, the exchange between Luca, Regan, and himself saw his stance drastically change. He was the one who leaked the recording of Regan and Luca arguing, hence making him partially responsible for Luca's state of mind the night he died.

I thought this knowledge would ease Regan's grief, but strangely, it had the opposite effect. At first, I thought her devastation came from discussing Luca and the secret she kept on his behalf for years, but as our conversation continued, I realized I had it all wrong. She wasn't upset because I knew Luca's secret; she was devastated she didn't know his.

Luca never told her he was attending an LGBT support group. As far as she was aware, he had no intention of revealing his secret for years, if ever. She didn't care about him wanting to live the life he was born to live. The fact he lost his faith in her broke her heart more than anything. She wanted to support him as I did her last night. Luca never gave her the chance.

After freeing one arm from being entangled around Regan's naked frame, I attempt to snag her cell phone off the bedside table. I stretch with all my might, but it is just out of my reach. I'd have no trouble attaining it if I weren't concerned about waking Regan, but after the night she had, she needs her sleep.

I want to pretend my chivalry stems from aiding Regan through her grief, but my ego isn't willing to take a back seat. Some of her tiredness has nothing to do with Luca and every-thing to do with how we settled her heartache.

Regan is a sexually promiscuous being. She knows what she wants, and she uses all her strong points to get it. I love that about her. When she expresses herself without concern on how I will react, it frees me from worrying that I'm taking advantage of her. . . I won't say vulnerability. Regan may be sleeping, but even a murmur of a word close to "vulnerable" would have me skinned.

I pull Regan in close to my chest before my eyes drift around my childhood bedroom. It's pretty bland compared to the girlish palette of Regan's room. I was one of those adventurous kids, the ones who rarely spend a moment of their time inside, so I guess that could explain its dull appearance. That and the fact this is more a hotel room than my actual bedroom.

With a husband constantly on the road and four children under the age of five, my mom took over The Manor from my great aunt. Everyone said she was crazy—I still think she's a little nuts to this day—but I understand her need to keep her thoughts occupied. Regan was only out of my sight for eighteen hours, and I thought about her the entire time, so I can imagine how often my mom's thoughts stray to my dad.

My parents have an odd relationship. What Regan said two nights ago was right: they're smitten with each other, but it's not in an *all-encompassing, must spend every single waking moment with each other* way. The bouts of separation their relationship constantly face have strengthened them as individuals. They enjoy their alone time before coming together to relish the benefits of having someone at your side, fighting with you instead of against you.

I'm hoping to have a similar relationship with Regan. At times, the Bureau does me wrong. There have been many occasions I've wanted to hand in my badge. But, in reality, the good far outweighs the bad. Furthermore, being a federal agent is a big part of who I am. I trained for my position for years, way before I joined the academy. This life is in my blood as surely as Regan has burrowed herself into my heart. They are both there —permanently—never to be removed.

I'm just praying I can keep them both.

The quickest squeeze of my heart wakes Regan from her restless sleep. Her eyes dart around my room in confusion before she gingerly lifts her head off my chest. The beat of my heart returns to its normal rhythm when the panic on her face relaxes upon spotting me. She was hesitant to come here, but the more time she spends here, the less reluctant she is. I'd say my mom and sister have more to do with that than me, but I don't mind claiming a small slice of the victory pie.

"Good morning." Her usually smooth voice is groggy from just waking up. "Have you been awake long?"

I shake my head. "I just woke." I tuck a wayward strand of hair behind her ear, hoping it will hide my lie.

The lazy smile on my face turns genuine when I spot the cause of her hair being stuck to her face. She has a smidge of icing smeared from her right ear to the little dip in her collarbone. The generous swell of her breasts must have distracted my tongue before I cleared all the evidence of the impromptu buffet I served on Regan's gloriously naked body.

"Well, good morning to you too," Regan purrs in a husky moan when I scoot down low so my tongue can fix the injustice it made last night. "Next time, feel free to help yourself before I wake up. I've always wondered what it would be like to be woken by a man eating me for breakfast."

Her voice jumps a few decibels at the end of her statement, her response a consequence of my teeth sinking into her sugary skin. "Switch that generic statement to one more specific to the individual standing before you, and I may consider testing out the theory tomorrow morning."

As her eyes drop to mine, her legs scissor together. Even with her arousal slowly stirring, she slits her eyes to fake anger.

154

"That means I'd have to wake up in *your* bed tomorrow morning. I don't recall this being a long-term arrangement. I thought we were having a bit of fun?"

"Oh, we'll have fun alright." Her stomach muscles tense when I drag my beard down them, only stopping when the scruff on my chin grazes her milky-white thighs. "We're going to have so much fun, you'll forget what day of the week it is."

Before she can respond, my tongue lashes her glistening slit. I groan, loving the odd combination of sweet and tangy stimulating my taste buds. The frosting I slathered her in last night is invisible, but its super sweet flavor is still detectable.

"You taste like vanilla frosting," I groan before my tongue completes a second long lick of her pussy.

When I suck her clit into my mouth, I expect her thighs to sweep open. Instead, I get them clamped around my head. "About the frosting. . ." Regan waits, huffs, then continues. "Last night was. . ."

"Fan-fucking-tastic. The best sex I've ever had," I fill in when she pauses for the second time.

The honesty in my tone weakens her thighs grip on my head. "Yes, all of that, and. . ."

I peer up at her, catching a glimpse of her lustful eyes over the bountiful swell of her breasts. "And. . .?"

She seems torn. She's clamped my head to ensure I can't budge an inch from her intoxicatingly delicious pussy, but she also appears as if she doesn't want me to touch her with a six-foot pole. How do I know this? She's giving the same look I tried to force on my face the night I took her to my apartment. I can't believe that was only last week. If feels like a lifetime has passed since then.

After a deep inhalation that inflates her chest, Regan pushes out, "Why do you have multiple tubs of frosting at your apartment? For how many tubs you have, you clearly have a purpose for them."

I smile. It is a dick move for me to make, but you can't hear the jealousy in her tone. She's riled up, ready to pounce on any woman who dares get within an inch of me, and I fucking love it.

I use my shoulders to break through the firm hold she has on my head before slipping two fingers inside her. Her pussy rallies against the intrusion, equally torn on whether to accept my advance or reject me. They clamp around my thrusting digits as well as her pussy milked my cock last night. The glistening of her arousal on my fingers increases with every pump they make, undermining her efforts.

When my thumb presses her clit, all protests vanish. Her thighs sweep as her lips part, the moan rumbling in her chest the most seductive of them all. I continue my campaign to remove the groove deep between her eyes for the next several minutes.

Once I'm satisfied it's gone, I say, "The cans in my pantry are empty."

Regan's eyes snap to mine in an instant. As her lips harden into a straight line, the color on her cheeks changes from blooming in ecstasy to fuming with anger. It takes me a few seconds to comprehend her fury, but when I do, it thickens my cock even more than her snug pussy hugging my fingers. Her sights aren't just locked on any future women in my life but my past companions as well.

After a quick shuffle to ensure she can see the effect her

ownership has on me, I advise, "They aren't empty because I used them on anyone. They're good at hiding things. Stuff you don't want anyone to see or have stolen."

"Like?" The huskiness in her voice makes my chest balloon. She's angry, but more than anything, she's trusting. She has no reason to believe me, yet she does.

"Driver's license. Keys. Pretty much anything." The glide of my fingers eases with each syllable I utter. "Thieves aren't known for their smarts. They only look in suspect places. If you want to keep your valuables, hide them in plain sight because safes are the first thing criminals hit."

"Hmm." I feel her hum vibrate the tips of my fingers. "That's smart. My boss has said that before too."

The jealousy on her face earlier morphs onto mine. *What could Isaac have to hide? He's the reason honest men like me need to stay on our toes.*

Not liking how slowly I'm grinding my fingers, Regan lifts her back off the bed. After slinging her arms around my neck, she bridges the small distance between us. My teeth grit when her change in position makes my fingers slip from her snug canal. I'm not mad she's stopped me; it is the warmth of her pussy responsible for my grinding teeth. It's hovering a mere inch from my cock, and her magnificent tits are splayed across my pecs. I'm in pure fucking heaven, which means I'm also fighting with all my might not to come like a fool who can't control himself.

The chances of shaming myself double when Regan slowly lowers herself down my cock. She takes it slow, relishing every inch as she goes. By the time she has my cock swallowed inside of her, the energy bristling between us is rampant, hot and sticky, as damp as her slit.

"I've never had sex before breakfast. Did I die and go to heaven?"

I flex my cock, voicing my appreciation of her praise without words. Her pussy is so snug, she feels every vein pulsating through me. She gasps at my cock's frantic throbs as her head falls forward. Precum squirts from my crest when her tongue glides up my nape to gather a bead of sweat there. Although she was the one lathered with whipped sugar, our entanglement in the hour that followed transferred some of the residue to me.

"Mmm. I'll never eat frosting again without thinking about you."

Her comment annoys me more than it pleases me. She's talking as if last night will soon be a memory. I don't mind that she'll never consume a sugary treat without me entering her thoughts; I just hope she's not seeing us as a temporary thing. I have too much at stake for this to be a few casual weeks twisted between the sheets. And I'm not solely referring to my job.

I tug on her hair, bringing her eyes back to mine. The walls of her pussy clench around me as she cries my name. I jerk my hips up, meeting her pumps grind for grind. She starts chanting "yes" on repeat as her pussy grows slicker, but not once do her eyes leave mine. *This. . .this* is where the magic is. The pull. The connection. The unbelievably crazy sensation that has me wanting to claim the world as surely as I'm claiming her.

I fight her for control, begging to steal the reins from her grasps, but when she hands them to me, I only take half. I want us to be even. One complete unit.

Her head falls forward when I release my firm grip on her hair, giving her back some of the power she awarded me. She rewards my gallantry by adding a squeeze to every descent she makes. Her pussy worships my cock as her eyes reveal she appreciates my ability to share. I'm not talking about other people. She does a good job of pretending she's not as deeply invested in our relationship as me, but I know she's as opposed to sharing as I am when it comes to anyone outside of this room. That's why her hackles were raised over the frosting. She wants our dining experience to be solely ours. No interference. No outsider influence. Just us.

The closer she gets to orgasm, the closer her eyelids become. Just before she rides the wave of euphoria, they fully close. I watch the expression on her face change from possessive to claimed as her lips part and the flush descends from her neck to above her thrusting chest before I succumb to the sensation gripping my sack.

My breathing levels as a tingling sensation races up my shaft. Feeling the heat of my cum shooting inside of her, Regan buries her head between my pecs. Her hot breaths fanning my chest keep spawn pumping out of my cock for the next several long seconds. I give her every drop, loving that my scent isn't just imbedded on her skin. I'm also inside of her.

Usually, the thought of having unprotected sex would give me hives. I've never once forgone protection, but just like every aspect of my life, nothing is as it was before Regan entered the picture. I trust her. But even if I didn't, I'm not scared about being tied to her for life. If anyone should be panicked by that notion, it should be Regan, not me.

I'll do anything to keep her in my life. Nothing is above me.

Not a lifetime commitment. Not the chance of losing my coveted position.

Not even the murmur of three little words way too early to say in our relationship.

"I love you."

I fucked up.

Regan didn't freak at my declaration of love as I had anticipated. She didn't have anything to say. Not a single fucking thing. At first, I wondered if she heard me. I was so close to saying it again when her eyes met mine. One glance, and I knew she heard what I said. She was stunned, a little taken back, and, I think, remorseful.

The last one pissed me off. I didn't expect her to say it back, but remorse? That was the last thing I expected to see when I imagined her response. I've never said those words to another woman before. I've never been in love, so there was no reason for a heartfelt declaration. Still, I anticipated more than I got from Regan.

She wasn't cruel. We've spent the last half hour in the shower removing the icing my tongue failed to lap up last night, but the out-of-control energy that generally bristles between us isn't as palpable. Don't get me wrong, our mutual attraction is as strong as ever, my fuck up just weakened it a little.

You can be assured it won't happen again.

Leaving Regan in the shower to shampoo her hair, I make my way back to the main area of our room. I whip off my towel, dump it halfway across the room before throwing on a pair of jeans and a casual shirt. I don't know why I'm in such a hurry to get dressed. Anyone would swear she hacked up my ego instead of my heart. I guess to some people they are one and the same? Unfortunately, I am not one of those men. I'm confident enough to proclaim that I rock her world between the sheets. Outside of them. . . clearly I need to up the ante.

When I throw open my bedside drawer to gather some socks, my eyes drop to Regan's cell phone sitting on top. It is flashing the same alerts it had earlier this morning. She has six unread messages and four unanswered calls. Although I'm highly suspicious all the messages are from Isaac or someone on his team who can't stay the fuck out of Regan's life, I pretend they're for me. It makes it less guilty this way.

The text messages are as I anticipated. They're all from Isaac. The first three are requesting an update on how she is. The last is approval for Regan to have a support beam installed in her bedroom as per her request earlier this week. Although my inquisitiveness piques from her request for a load-bearing beam, I set it aside for a time when I'm not confused. I'm swimming in so much confusion right now, I feel like I've drunk a gallon of whiskey. Considering I haven't drunk a drop of alcohol in over six years, you can be assured that isn't the case.

After switching Isaac's messages back to being unread, I dial Regan's voicemail. A slight trickle of deceit seeps into my veins when my eyes stray to the bathroom door to ensure Regan is still in the shower. She hasn't done anything to grant my distrust. It's just habit.

The first three voice messages follow a similar path as her text messages. They are Isaac—*again*. Checking in—*again*. I delete his messages, more to cover my ass than the jealousy burning in my veins. I don't know how to make voicemail messages appear unheard, so I'll tell Regan he called before suggesting she call him back.

The tightness in my jaw firms when the final message plays. Although the person isn't speaking, I recognize his heavy wheezing.

"Fuck. . ." A long delay ensues before Brandon adds on, "You need to get a new phone. Preferably one without trackable content installed." His voice is snarky, clearly unimpressed he can still only reach me via Regan's cell.

I hear him take several steps before a door shutting bellows down the line. "Call me on this number as soon as you get my message." He rattles off a New York cellphone number before disconnecting our call.

Although I don't have a piece of paper or pen at my disposal, I don't need one. The panic in Brandon's tone ensures I don't miss a single cryptic clue in his message, much less the number he requested me to use. He was climbing the stairs of our dungeon-like office. How do I know this? The faint chime that squeaked down the line just before he slammed the door. I set up tripwires on the back entrance of our office during the first week of my placement. The bell's chime is extremely faint, but for an officer trained to assess every noise, it doesn't need to be loud.

That's another reason I'm stumped on how someone snuck up on me. The janitor couldn't have entered HQ without me hearing him because I have every entrance wired with barely audible alarms. There is only one way he could have snuck up on me unaware. . . he was already in the building.

Fuck.

Before my notions can run wild, Brandon answers his ringing cell. Just like every time he's taken my calls, his greeting isn't what you'd expect. "Where are you?"

Not a peep escapes my lips before he quickly adds on, "Actually, don't tell me that. I can't guarantee there aren't any ears in this room."

I hear a chair scrape down the line before Brandon starts walking again. This time, he doesn't exit the back entrance of HQ, he escapes via the front door. The humming of heavy traffic and the squawk of hundreds of pedestrians assure I can't be mistaken.

Once the droning noises kick up to an ear-piercing level, Brandon says, "I followed Isaac's head of security through a back entrance last night. He was seeking the same time frame of data I was."

My teeth grit. "Regan mentioned something about him having her followed home. For safety or something. . ." *More like Isaac's inability to cut the cords he strangles all his staff with.* "Did he find anything?"

"Yeah. There's a CTV camera in a building across the street. He found footage of Regan and you exiting the alley."

"Isaac has footage of us. . . *together?*" My eyes stray to the bathroom door as my heart rate picks up speed. My ruse is coming undone more quickly than I'd like.

"Had," Brandon corrects. "It took a bit of work, but I got two steps in front of his hacker. Anything he got is either unreadable or old footage."

"Old footage?" Confusion rings in my tone.

"Yeah. Last night wasn't the first late night walk Regan has taken through Ravenshoe."

I swear I'll have no teeth left by the end of today with how hard they keep clashing together. "So what's with the urgency? Your demand for secrecy made it seem like you had more than a desire to fan your peacock feathers."

Brandon takes my dis in stride. "I do." Another succession of footsteps bellow down the line. "I wasn't the only one piggy-backing off government servers last night. There was another source. I followed the trail they left behind. It took me straight to. . ."

"HQ," we say in harmony.

"Yes. How did you know that?"

I smirk, fond of the shock in his tone. "When listening to your message, I heard the bell above the back door of HQ ding. That didn't happen the night I was jumped."

"You boobytrapped HQ."

Since Brandon isn't asking a question, I don't answer him.

My swollen chest grows when he faintly murmurs, "Fucking brilliant. Why didn't I think of that?"

I could give him a few pointers, but there is no time for that. I just heard the conditioner lid crack open. We've got five, ten minutes tops.

"Did you follow the source back to anyone unusual?"

I can't see Brandon, but I can picture him shaking his head

when a whooshing sound trickles down the line. "That's the issue. There is no source. That station is empty."

"So someone took up residence in a vacant cubicle for the night; that's not a big deal."

Brandon laughs a mocking chuckle. "It is when they don't sign in to the Bureau's mainframe while doing it."

His reply stumps me for all of a second. "What about the surveillance from the alley? Did you conduct searches for anyone exiting or entering in the timeframe I gave you?"

"Yes." His swift reply relays his eagerness. "It hasn't found a match. *Yet.* I uploaded the footage to a shared server in case you want to view it. Might trigger something."

I drag Regan's phone from my ear before the entire sentence leaves his mouth. With my mind hazy from a lack of sleep and perhaps fewer brain cells since I fried many while climaxing the hardest I've ever come—*before fucking things up as I've never done* —it takes attempting to log in four times before I remember the FBI database is still in the stone ages. If you aren't on a PC, you won't be granted access.

"Hold on," I say to Brandon before tossing Regan's cell onto the mattress to fire up her laptop.

My lips twist when it requests a code. Remembering her lack of security, I hit the zero button four times. *Rejected.* I go through the standard password hack every agent uses before calling in a techie for help. Target's birthday. *Fail.* Their mom's birthday. *Fail.* Pet name. *Fail.* I punch the keys a little harder when I input my fifth attempt: Isaac Holt. *Fail.*

Fuck yeah!

Allowing my ego to get the better of me, I type in my name. *Fail.*

Fuck it.

The cusses keep coming when reality smacks into me.

I type my last try slowly, more out of respect than anything: Luca. *Bingo!*

In a few more keystrokes, I'm logged into the Bureau's main network. May as well not be; I have no fucking clue where to go from here. After reattaching Regan's phone to my ear, Brandon directs me on what to do.

Before a minute has passed, the video surveillance from across the street of the alley streams from Regan's laptop.

"How do I rewind it?" I ask Brandon when the footage rolls past Regan and me entering an idling cab.

"I downloaded stills onto your hard drive—"

"That wasn't what I asked," I cut Brandon off. "I asked how do I rewind the footage? I'm not interested in what you've seen. I've got my own set of eyes, which means I have an entirely different perspective."

I run a hand along my scruffy jaw, recognizing that I'm taking my frustration out on the wrong person. "Can you show me how to work this thing? *Please.* There's a reflection in the cab window I want to take a closer look at."

"Alright."

Thirty seconds after agreeing with my request, Brandon somehow takes control of Regan's computer. I don't know how, and in all honesty, I don't fucking care, because within seconds of him taking over the reins, I'm peering at the man I saw in the back quarter panel of the taxi's window.

I stare a long, penetrating glare. I've seen him before; I swear I have. "Can you run his face through facial recognition?"

"Already on it." Brandon's reply is barely heard over the

clicking of a mouse. "I sent duplicate photos to the printer at The Manor's reception desk. They're a little grainy, but not any worse than they are on screen."

"We have a printer at the main desk?"

When Brandon makes an agreeing noise, I balk. One, how does he know where I am? Two, how does he have access to our printers? And three, how the fuck can I get him on my team permanently? Having someone this quick off the mark would be a brilliant move. I've had techies who knew their way around a computer, but none have been this skilled. Brandon must have flown under the radar at the academy, because he would have been nabbed by a more senior supervisor than Theresa if they were aware of his skillset.

After logging me out of the Bureau mainframe and removing any traces of my steps from Regan's computer, Brandon logs out of her device. I need to get the printouts before they disappear into the sinkhole that apparently eats paperwork owned by my family, so I shout to Regan that I'll be back in a minute before hotfooting it into the hallway.

I dip and weave between guests preparing to spend their day viewing the monuments in Washington before taking the servant stairs two at a time. Halfway down, the reasoning behind the perp's familiarity smacks into me. He's the man who flew with us business class to Texas. The smirking fucker who picked a seat across from Regan when there were four better options at his disposal.

My pace slows even more as the knocks keep coming. I thought telling Regan I loved her *way* too early in our relationship was my most worst fuck up this week. Clearly, I overlooked my previous incidents. Theresa had footage of Regan and me on the plane, photos that could have only been taken by someone nearby, i.e. the chairs opposite us. Then the "janitor" who smacked me over the head entered HQ without notice, meaning he was there before everyone left. . . or he never left.

That can only mean one thing.

The man stalking Regan isn't a stalker.

He's one of us.

He's an agent.

15

*A*lex loves me.

He *loves* me.

I thought the shrilling of my pulse in my ears made me mishear what he said, but the instant our eyes connected and held, I knew what I heard was true. His eyes were brimming with vulnerability, and his jaw was in a firm, determined hold.

They weren't the only telltales signs, though. It was the impact his words caused my heart that was the biggest indication. Luca told me he loved me all the time. He expressed it with words, without words, and sometimes even in writing. I thought it was true love, the type that makes it hard for you to breathe, but only after hearing the same words spill from Alex's lips do I realize they weren't the right words for Luca and me to use.

Don't misunderstand me. We loved each other with everything we had; we just weren't *in* love with each other. We had

170

mutual respect, understanding, and the ability to destroy each other—just like Alex and I have.

I tried to say something back to Alex. With my tongue and heart twisted up in knots, it would have never been the words he wanted to hear, but it would have been better than silence. I care for Alex. I have wild, crazy feelings for him I've never felt for anyone, but until I've had the chance to sit and reflect, my emotions will remain unvoiced.

I was hoping to explain to Alex that I needed some time to think before responding, but unfortunately, I lost the opportunity when he stood from the bed and headed for the shower, taking me and my exhaustive post-climaxed body with him.

His playfulness in the shower as he removed traces of our fun night from my body had me believing we successfully dodged the awkwardness of his confession. Regrettably, his quick dart from the shower ten minutes ago dampened my hope.

I take my time shampooing my hair, hoping a little distance will lessen the sparks that forever fire between us. When I step back and evaluate things with a level head, I can understand Alex's blurt of affection. The tension that bristles between us is phenomenal. I've always wondered if instant attraction was a thing or something romance authors made up to sucker readers into believing their characters fell in love on the very first page.

Now. . . now I need my head examined.

This kills me to admit, but I want to say it back. *Like, what? Who the fuck am I?* The only time I've fallen in love the past five years was when they redesigned the butterfly clip. Now instead of just giving you a little buzz, it sends you rocketing toward orgasm within seconds of switching it on. I don't fall for people, much less a man I know is lying to me.

Ugh! I can't even blame my stupidity on tequila. I had a few scrumptious cocktails last night, but I steered clear of any that bring out my stupid. It was probably a combination of sugar, heartache and a hot, virile man.

Learning that Luca had a second life that excluded me stung like a thousand bee stings. Instead of giving me solitude to deal with my hurt, Alex kissed every welt, patched up every scar, then made me forget I was hurt to begin with by cherishing me as I've never been cherished.

Now his dropping of the "L" bomb makes sense. Our exchange last night was filled with so many emotions, they were bound to spill over to this morning. I'm shocked it didn't occur earlier. That's how perfect last night was.

Not feeling as deflated as earlier, I rinse out the last of the conditioner from my hair before switching off the faucet. Just as I grab the towel Alex left for me, I hear him shout that he'll be back in a minute. The urgency in his tone returns my heart to the frantic rhythm it thumped when he said those three little words, except it isn't leaping with worry. It's bounding with hope.

It spikes even more astronomically when I enter the main area of his room. My laptop is sitting on the edge of the bed, open and switched on. My steps slice to half their natural stride when the cursor suddenly bolts to the top right-hand corner.

What the fuck?

I sit next to my laptop before dragging it onto my lap. The dampness of my finger makes the touch pad a little unresponsive, but even after drying it, the curser doesn't move as randomly as it did earlier.

After a quick glance at the door separating Alex's room from the hallway, I fire up my internet browser and log into the search history. It shows no new results for today.

My lungs saw in and out when I drag my cursor to the locked file hidden between folders of useless photos and documents. I don't know why I'm being so pedantic. I doubt anything on my laptop would be of interest to Alex, but I have a moral obligation to uphold. Nothing in this file could hurt me, but the man I'm paid to protect. . . in the wrong hands, this file could spell disaster.

I suck in a relieved breath when it shows my last login to this secure file was four months ago. That sounds about right. Four months ago was when a woman with half a brain decided to submit her third request for child support. Hell will freeze over before Isaac pays a dime for a child that isn't his. This isn't a standard case of a naughty weekend gone wrong. Despite Theresa Veneto's claims, the paternity of her child is not in question—*not with my client, anyway.*

Her underhanded tactics to deplete Isaac's fortune of millions of dollars have already caused her to lose her position at Ravenshoe PD, so she'd do best to tread carefully. Isaac let her off easy the first time. She won't be so lucky the second time around. After the stunts she pulled, he should have had her prosecuted. Instead, all he got was a forced resignation. There were no charges filed, no record of conversation, or steps put in place to stop her from pulling the same tricks on another unsuspecting fool. She just packed up and left town, taking her illegitimate child with her.

Excluding Isaac, Jeremiah is the only one I feel sorry for in this situation. He doesn't deserve to be thrust into the middle of an ugly custody battle when the woman who has his blood knows who his real father is, but Theresa doesn't care. She uses Jeremiah against Isaac every chance she gets. He couldn't even walk down the street without her harassing him. I'm so glad he finally accepted my advice early last year, or he'd still be dealing with her harassment to this day. When you have a leech like Theresa Veneto trying to drain your blood, you must remain cautious. Those little suckers attach to you in places you'd never suspect, weakening you with every suck until you no longer have the will to live.

I shut my laptop screen a little hard. I blame Theresa. Anytime she enters my mind, my thoughts turn sullied. I never knew it was possible to hate someone you've never met. Theresa proves that is a lie. Hate is too nice a word to describe what I feel for that lady. She's scum—and a million other derogative words.

Pushing aside my dislike of Theresa and a niggling doubt in my stomach that just won't quit, I don a semi-casual dress and cute jacket. While dragging a brush through my freshly washed hair, I check my phone to see if I've missed any calls from Isaac. His contact the past two days has been very sporadic. Usually, he's on the ball when it comes to communication.

I'm surprised there are no voicemails, but there are four unopened text messages. The first few are the standard check in ones Isaac conducts three to four times a day. The last one. . . I fan my suddenly heated cheeks.

I'm the first to admit, I'm a sexual explorer. If there's experimentation to be done, and it has an adrenaline-laced orgasm attached to it, you can be assured I'll be the first person to sign up. That's where Isaac's final message comes in, the one giving me permission to have a load-bearing beam installed in my bedroom.

For years, I've toyed with the idea of having a sex swing installed in my apartment. For just as many years, I realized there wasn't much use. I don't—*didn't*—date, and for the rare occasions my battery-operated boyfriends weren't cutting the mustard and I branched out to oxygen-fueled ones, our hookups never occurred anywhere near my home turf.

Up until recently, I held a permanent reservation at a generic hotel, similar to the one I tried to check into after the incident at my house Friday night. But with every new adventure comes a need for new equipment. Although my rules on dating haven't altered, I'm not against bending the rules to cross a few items off my wish list. Inviting Alex for a sleepover doesn't mean anything. We're two consenting adults who occasionally drop immature words like "love," "boyfriend," and "forever" into our exchanges. It's perfectly normal.

My finger freezes halfway across the screen of my phone. *Did you hear the deceit in my tone like I did?*

Yeah, figured as much.

I don't want to date. I just don't want Alex to either. That doesn't mean we're exclusive. It just means we're. . .

I've got nothing. Not a single fucking thing.

Just the thought of Alex with anyone but me annoys the shit out of me. That's the reason I got all alpha-possessive earlier. His love of frosting was displayed in the most brilliant manner last night, but even if he ate it by the tub-full as if it is ice cream, he'd never amass as many containers as I saw in his pantry last week. Thank god the reason behind his obsession was legitimate. I love frosting, even more so now, but I would have hated it if I discovered I wasn't the first woman he's lathered it in.

My wicked thoughts stop as I dial Isaac's number. He might be too busy to talk to me, but I've missed hearing his voice. Excluding family, Isaac has been the one constant in my life the past five years. No matter what happens with Alex, no matter how far we do or do not travel, Isaac's position in my life will never alter.

To an outsider, plucking me from the pool with demands of exclusivity before I had attended law school may seem excessive. To me, it's Isaac. He saw what he wanted and ran for it. I wouldn't necessarily say he molded me into an ideal candidate for his empire, but others may. Do I care about their opinion? Not at all. Isaac has made it very clear I am free to pursue other opportunities at any time I see fit. All he requests is a month's notice.

With how well he pays, you can be guaranteed I'm not going anywhere anytime soon. But even if he paid me in peanuts, I still don't see the facts altering. I love my fancy apartment, designer clothes, and heels like every other red-blooded American woman, but those are materialistic things. They'll never make me happy. Alex's abrupt entrance into my life proves that more than anything.

I'm drawn from my naughty thoughts when Isaac's deep timbre sounds down the line. "It's about time you called me back. I nearly sent out a search party."

I roll my eyes. "By search party, do you mean Hunter?"

Hunter Kane is Isaac's head of security. He's also a brilliant hacker. If you want to know anything about anyone, Hunter is your man—although he came up empty-handed when I requested surveillance from outside of the warehouse Isaac and I are hoping to turn into a bustling nightclub.

Isaac's laughter joins mine. "He's already been called in. Did you want me to call him off?"

"Yes!" My girly screech bounces around Alex's bedroom. "You're such a worrywart. I told you I was heading out of town."

"At the same time you asked if you could have a sex swing installed." He's more shocked at my admission that I want him to yank Hunter off my tail than my request.

"I didn't ask to have a sex swing installed. I requested a load-bearing beam—"

"Which every man with half a cock knows is code word for a sex swing."

It is lucky I can hear the mirth in his tone or I'd be suspicious he was jealous. Even though I know he isn't, I can't help but ask, "Jealous much?"

That cuts his laughter in half. "I wouldn't say jealous, more concerned. You've been a little off the past few months. At first, I thought it might have been family issues." The way his tone dips at his last two words reveals whom he was referencing: Luca. "But your uneasiness didn't weaken as usual, not even after a visit home." He pauses, exhales deeply, then asks, "Are you homesick?"

I shrug. "A little." Not how he's thinking, but with me having no better explanation for the crazy emotions bombarding me, I don't have any other words to offer him. Except perhaps, "I've met someone."

Isaac inhales a sharp breath. "The same someone you mentioned earlier?"

An agreeing murmur drones through my lips. "We're. . . uh. . . kind of seeing each other?" That came out as immature as it sounds.

"Wow."

Isaac only says one word, but it's the words he didn't express I hear the clearest. He knows I'm a *one date then dump them* girl, so hearing me admit I'm possibly *dating* was as shocking for his ears to hear as it was for my mouth to say.

"It's nothing serious; it's just. . ."

Once again, I've got nothing.

After a prolonged awkward silence, I mumble, "I like him."

A puff of air expels from Isaac's lips. "I'm glad. That's good. As long as he's treating you right, I'm fine with this." His words grow more convincing with each one he speaks. I laugh when he adds on, "I think it might take me a little to adjust."

"You're not the only one."

Another stretch of silence passes between us. Thankfully, this one is more endearing than the first. Isaac rules his business with the rueful reputation he amassed during his college years, but the one sitting in silence on the other end of the line, the one whose breathing is as labored as mine, he's the sole reason I'll never leave his empire. He's more my friend than my employer.

An office chair squeaking into position sounds down the line. "I've got to go. Morgan ordered lime yellow booths instead of the standard black." I giggle like a school girl when he gags. "They remind me of the hideous floral print on my grandmother's couch."

"Aww, don't be too hard on her. She could have ended up with the original flamingo print she ordered."

Isaac growls. "We barely survived that disaster."

Nodding, I laugh. "We still had a lot of fun that weekend, though. Your grandmother kept us on our toes."

"She did. We'll have to go back. . . when you're not gallivanting around the country with random homeless guys." He grumbles his last statement.

"Isaac."

I could say more, but I don't need to. The way his name exited my mouth with a sharp and precise breath exposed everything I needed to express.

But in case it didn't, I add on, "Back off. He's a genuinely nice person—"

"Who's never heard of a razor."

"Thank god for that!" My voice has the country twang I try to hide. "You have no idea how good it feels when he—"

"Regan." Isaac growls my name as seductively as Alex does, except his is laced with disgust instead of unbridled lust.

"Hey, this is what happens when you stick your nose in places it isn't wanted. If you want details, I'll give you details. Big. *Juicy.* Details!"

I feel like I've hit the jackpot when Isaac snaps, "Fine. I'll stay out of your private life if you promise never to put that image in my head again."

"Deal."

I grin like the cat who swallowed the canary. Isaac must be off his game. He's usually as stubborn as me. I've never seen him succumb so quickly before—if ever.

After requesting that I return his calls more diligently than I have been, Isaac disconnects our call. It is only after dumping my phone next to an empty canister of frosting do I recall exactly what he said. He requested I return his calls, as if he called me.

That can't be right. There were no voicemails or missed calls on my phone, just text messages. If it were anyone but Isaac, I would assume he was mistaken, but Isaac is as pedantic about accuracy as he is about protection. This isn't something he'd get wrong.

The desire to shower for the second time this morning rains down on me when I spin on my feet to face the bed. First, my laptop was open and unlocked, now my voicemail messages have been deleted. This can't be a coincidence. It can only mean one thing.

Alex isn't a spy; he's just spying on me.

16

Alex

"**C**alm down and stop talking in fuckin' riddles. How do you know he's one of us?" Grayson's eyes glance down at the photo Brandon printed all the way from Raven-shoe. "Where was this image obtained?"

"The back quarter panel of the taxi that picked us up from the alley. The cab driver must have recently washed his car as the paint was so gleaming, we caught his reflection."

His nose screws up as he takes in the grainy image. "I thought you said there were two perps?"

"I thought there were, but maybe I was mistaken? I wasn't exactly thinking straight since my brain was leaking out of my ears."

Grayson's angry snarl matches mine. "Yet, you still recognize him?"

"Yes! The vision is shit, but you know how on point I am with photographic recognition. He's the same man who flew with Regan and me to Texas last week."

The distrust in Grayson's eyes fades for belief. He's aware I have the most photographic memory in our family because he fought me for the title last year.

"So this photo is evidence—*if you can call it that*—that he may be the man who attacked you, but I'm not connecting my dots the same way you are. How is this proof he's with the Bureau?"

I fill the seat next to him, causing the old wicker chair to squeak from having two grown-ass men sitting on it. "Theresa had photos of Regan and me. . . *together*." He nods, recalling me telling him the same thing two nights ago with the exact same dip in my tone. "When she presented the evidence, I didn't pay as much attention to the non-focal points as I usually do."

"You were distracted by your girl. I get it."

The humor in his tone pisses me off, but I nod all the same. Regan forever distracts me, to the point it is becoming frustrating.

"I assumed the photos were taken by a member of the flight crew via some type of surveillance device as they had a black tinge on the edges. It was only after talking to Brandon did I assess the photos more diligently. The black edging appears to be high caliber stitched cotton, meaning the photos were taken over someone's shoulder—most likely a man's suit-covered one. Add that to the angle of the photos, and you can only reach one conclusion: they were taken by someone sitting across from us. The fucker used my neurosis against me to gather intel on both Regan and me."

Although I can see Grayson is dying to grill me, unlike me, he has no troubles keeping his focus on the task at hand. "Accusing a supervisor of tailing an agent is a risky move, but saying an agent assaulted you. . ." His words trail off as he scrubs his hand over his tired eyes. "That feels wrong just admitting."

Before I can inform him that Theresa gives wrong a whole new meaning, he adds on, "I get where you're coming from, though, and you haven't viewed the info my guys have unearthed the past twenty-four hours. Dodgy has a new meaning now that I've run stats on the head of your unit."

I stare at him quietly. He said he'd look into my case. I didn't realize that meant he'd have his crew working on it as well. Grayson's guys are the cream of the crop, the very essence of what every agent strives to become a part of. They don't work on stalker cases that involve rogue supervisors more interested in netting their targets than maintaining the integrity of their unit. They take down entire criminal associations, terrorists, and serial killers.

Missing my shocked expression, Grayson slouches into his chair. "This guy you're targeting, do you have much on him?"

Shaking my head, I drop my eyes to the photo Brandon printed for me, assuming that is whom Grayson is referencing.

"Not him," Grayson responds, returning my focus to him. "The guy you're at Ravenshoe for. The one who got your panties in a knot whenever your girl mentioned him in a roundabout way during dinner."

A *pfft* noise sounds from my mouth, denying his assumption without words. Regan rarely mentions Isaac or his association when she's with me. Her thoughts are too occupied for *him* to enter the equation.

Grayson nips my attitude in the bud by saying, "I saw the

elevator footage, Alex. She doesn't just have your panties twisted up; she's got your balls in her purse as well."

Although I'd rather knock the smug grin off his face with my fists, I have more important points to work through. I've pussy-footed around for nearly a week now. It's time I start thinking with the head on my shoulders instead of the one between my legs. Regan deserves a man who can both satisfy her and keep her safe. I'm only exceeding in one field at the moment.

"How did you see the elevator footage? I wiped it from the servers?"

Grayson's lips tug high, exposing several pegs of white teeth. "Is anything ever truly wiped?"

I'm tempted to tell him to save his excuses for when I upload the sex tape he made in college, but the squeak of a screen door stops me. Regan storms onto the back porch we're hiding out on. The high slit in her mid-thigh dress steals my devotion for a couple of seconds, but her sassy diva-like attitude utterly consumes it.

I assume her fiery attitude is because she's finally deciphered what I mumbled earlier, but she proves me wrong when she says, "You wiped *my* messages from *my* phone." Her tone leaves no chance in hell I can mistake it as a question. "Why would you do that?"

I nudge my head to the door she just stormed through, requesting for Grayson to give us some privacy. With a shake of his head and a determined stance, he ignores my suggestion. After glaring at him in warning that he'll pay for his stupidity later, I stand from my chair and motion for Regan to join me at the side of the patio. She is as stubborn as Grayson.

With a cocked hip, she spreads her hands across her waist then arches her brow high. Most men would take the shit-eating grin stretching across Grayson's face as appreciation for the spectacular vision standing before him, but Grayson is anything but ordinary. He's not taking in Regan's seductive curves, ample breasts, and drop-dead gorgeous face. He's attracted to her fiery attitude.

Our father might be set in his ways like his father, grandfather, and great-grandfather, but the new generation of Rogers are a cut above the rest. With our father rarely home, our mother raised us, which means we have no qualms respecting fierce, determined women. *And I have no issues subduing them either.*

I step closer to Regan, my chest swelling when the vein in her neck pulsates with every movement I make. "I didn't mean to delete your messages—"

"So you admit you used my phone?" she interrupts, her voice as ice cold as the glare she's giving me.

I nod. "Just like I have since the night in the alley."

That stumps her for all of two seconds. "Allowing someone to use your phone doesn't give them the right to do whatever the fuck they want with it. Those were *my* messages—for *me.*"

"I had every intention to tell you about Isaac's calls, but between being attacked, your discovery last night, and other *matters* this morning, I haven't had a chance."

Regan looks two seconds from ripping me a new asshole, but I'm saved from being maimed when Grayson interrupts, "Isaac?" He scoots forward on his chair, acting as if it's the first time he's heard the name. "You said you're from Ravenshoe, right?" His question is directed at Regan, not me.

185

A sudden wish for privacy crosses Regan's face before she nods once at Grayson's question.

"Is this Isaac also from Ravenshoe?"

Grayson is good. If I hadn't discussed Isaac with him earlier, I'd truly believe he has no clue who he is.

When Regan nods again, Grayson murmurs, "No shit! I had a college friend who moved to Ravenshoe a few years ago. His name was Isaac." He scrubs his hand along his jaw as if he is digging through his memory for clues. "What was his last name again?"

If he's hoping Regan will jump in and save him, he's shit out of luck. She keeps her lips more tightly sealed than mine.

Realizing Regan will never give him the out he seeking, Grayson reveals, "Holt. That's it. Isaac Holt." He gifts Regan the smirk he generally uses when he wants the ladies on his side. "Is my Isaac your Isaac?"

"No," Regan answers without pause, not the slightest bit fazed she has two sets of very dominant, interrogative eyes staring at her. "But I have heard of Isaac Holt. What lady in Ravenshoe hasn't?" My cheeks inflame with anger when she fans her face as if she's suddenly hot. "He has *quite* the reputation." The way her tone dips ensures we can't mistake what reputation she is referring to.

Grayson laughs, shifting my eyes from glaring at Regan to him. "Sounds like the Isaac I used to know. If you ever see him, be sure to tell him I said hello."

"Sure," Regan replies, her tone friendlier than her snarled lips are implying. "Should I refer to you as Grayson, or do you have another alias you'd prefer I use?"

Grayson snaps his eyes to mine, his fury uncontained.

Before half the unasked questions streaming from his eyes can reach my ears, Regan tosses a dozen fake IDs onto the coffee table wedged between us. Half belong to Grayson; the rest are mine.

Grayson launches to his feet. "You told her about the frosting canisters? What the fuck, Alex?!"

Ignoring his angry sneer, I step closer to Regan. I've got more concerns than his private stash being raided. Regan is looking at me in a way I've never wanted. Anger. Betrayal. Disgust. They all filter from her beautifully pained green irises. That far outweighs his need to find a new hidey hole.

Before I can get within touching distance of her, Regan crosses her arms in front of her chest, then locks her eyes with mine. They're brimming with unbridled fury and a shit ton of hurt. "Is Alex even your real name?"

I nod my head. "Nothing I've told you is a lie. My name is Alex Rogers. I was born December 31st. Grayson is my brother. This is the house I grew up in as a child. I've never lied to you, Rae. Not in the way you're thinking."

Relief washes over Regan's face when she hears the honesty in my tone. It doesn't last long. Not even for a second. Her guards are up; her trust is down, and I fucking hate it. "Not in the way I'm thinking? So what *other* ways have you lied to me?"

"We've discussed this. You know I can't. . ."

My words trail off when she squeals in frustration, spins on her heels, then reenters The Manor. I take off after her in under a second, only stopping when Grayson fists my shirt. I can see the worry in his eyes, his panic that I've let Regan crawl so profoundly under my skin I'm not seeing the entire picture, but I can also see he understands my dilemma.

"You need to tread carefully," Grayson warns, his tone unlike anything I've ever heard. "If your findings are true, you could lose her forever."

His words sucker-punch me harder than his fists ever could. That's the last thing I want.

"If the man stalking her is one of us, she'll think everything was staged. The feelings, the trust, it will all vanish." He sounds as if he is talking more from experience than conjecture. "When the time is right, you can come clean, but now is *not* the time."

"She already knows."

Grayson shakes his head. "No, she doesn't. She's running on half-truths—just as you are. Be inventive, Alex, while also doing the job you're paid to do."

His riddled reply piques my curiosity—even more so when he releases me from his hold, snags the printout from the coffee table, then enters The Manor without speaking another word.

I stay on the patio for the next several minutes, running my fingers through my hair and pacing back and forth. I want to tell Regan everything, but Grayson's warning holds some credit. Regan just protected Isaac's identity, which proves she's extremely loyal to him.

Although I can't guarantee that would have been the case if she hadn't caught me in a lie, I must remain cautious. I know firsthand how hard people fight when they feel as if their backs are against the wall. They fight with everything they have, often forgetting who they are fighting for.

I won't let that happen to Regan and me. I'll fight for her with everything I have because I'm used to fighting. Nothing in life ever comes easy for me, so why would I expect love to be any different?

17

J stop shoving clothes into my bag like a madwoman when the creak of a door sounds through my ears. I don't know why I'm being so dramatic. It's hard being angry about having your privacy invaded when you did the exact same thing only minutes ago.

I didn't enter The Manor's large industrial kitchen with the purpose of tracking down information on Alex, but when I spotted the dozen or so canisters of frosting at the very back of a middle shelf, my inquisitiveness got the better of me.

Mostly.

Somewhat

Not even.

I was spying.

The more annoyed I become about Alex deleting my messages, the more logical my quest for revenge sounded. Two wrongs don't make a right, but when you're working off minimal sleep and a brain firing off only two cylinders, even the stupidest ideas seem brilliant.

To be honest, I wasn't surprised when I found the driver's licenses with Alex's photo but alternate names in replace of his. In a world where everyone knows everything, even regular joes seek ways to keep their private information precisely that: private. I'm more angry that they didn't give me anything concrete to explain the stupid feelings I've been bombarded with the past forty-eight hours. I must be in a time warp, as nothing happening can be true. My protectiveness of Isaac is as intense as it's always been, my libido just as strong, but there is something very wrong with this picture.

I don't excuse snooping as if it is a normal thing to do; I don't choose sex over morals, and I sure as hell don't let men weasel their way into my heart with cute words and mind-blowing orgasms.

More determined than ever, I spin around to face Alex. He better be packing heat, as several grenades are heading his way.

My willpower withers when the person entering my room isn't whom I'm expecting. The already elevated beat of my heart doubles when the man's face identifies as familiar.

"You're the gentleman from the plane? The one who sat two seats across from me?"

I don't know why my comments sound like questions. I'm not seeking confirmation. I know what I saw, just as well as I know it's extremely unlikely he was on the same flight as me and is now a guest at the same B&B.

The man stiffens, stunned I've remembered him, but his mouth remains tightlipped. His surprise is warranted. I'm not recalling him because he has a gorgeous face and fit body any red-blooded woman would have a hard time forgetting. On the contrary, being saved from his scrutiny by the handsome man filling the vacant seat next to him is the reason his face is stored in my memory bank. He's not creepy-looking, but the vibes he gives off are.

"What are you doing here?" I feel the rod in my back straightening, taking on the steel strength in my voice.

When he steps closer to me, as if the six paces between us are too great, I hold my hand out in front of my body.

He copies my gesture, but more to say he means me no harm than to keep me at arm's length. "I'm not here to hurt you, Rae. I'm here to help you."

If his use of my nickname doesn't send sirens alarming in my head, the similar size of our hands skyrockets my panic to an all-time high. His hands don't match his round face and deep timbre. They are dainty and small, quite feminine.

"Help me with what?" I impress myself with how calm my voice is. Probably helps that my suitcase hides the stiletto I'm clutching for dear life.

A condescending smirk etches onto my face when he replies, "Your life is in danger."

No shit, Sherlock.

I force tears to my eyes. "How do you know this. . . unless you're the man behind the threat?"

His balk ripples the air. I've got him stumped, but not enough to restrain his curiosity. "What gave me away?"

I lick my dry lips before answering, "You called me Rae."

He clears the confusion from his face with a quick scrub of his shadowed jaw. It gives away his ruse even more. He's married. He may have removed his ring, but the white band circling his ring finger will take months to clear.

After dropping his hand from his face, he says, "That's your name, isn't it?" His tone is more panicked than threatening.

I shake my head. "No one calls me Rae."

"Anymore," he corrects, proving he knows me more than a random stranger would.

When he steps closer to me, I raise my stiletto into the air. Spotting my weapon of choice, he has the audacity to smile. It's a stupid thing for him to do. Discovering Alex is spying on me already has my mood teetering dangerously on edge; now his arrival has pushed me over the brink. I'm the most unhinged I've ever been.

With a grunt, I push off my feet. I charge for the door he's blocking with his waif-like frame, hoping if I pierce his arm with my stiletto, it will give me enough leverage to escape without harm.

My plan has the effect I am aiming for. He howls like a wolf staring at a moon when my heel breaks through both his suit-covered sleeve and his skin, but he's not down long enough for me to fully flee.

"Let me go!" I scream when he bands his arm around my waist to yank me away from the locked door.

My scream is drowned out by Alex calling my name. He either heard my battle cry or sensed I am in danger. "Rae!"

As the sound of feet stomping up a set of stairs booms into my ears, I throw my head back. Stars dance in front of my eyes when my skull cracks the stranger's nose, making another painful moan ripple from his lips.

"I'll break your nose with my next hit," I warn, my voice strong.

When he fails to adhere to my threat, I throw my head back for the second time. It hurts him more than it does me.

As his hands dart up to catch the blood gushing from his nose, I break away from his side. The tremor of my body rattles all the way down my arm when I twist the old-fashioned handle on my bedroom door. I turn and turn and turn, but it fails to open, and there's no key in sight.

A lack of key won't be an issue soon from how hard Alex is ramming into it. I can hear his grunts through the thick wood paneling, smell his determination. It is only a matter of seconds before he saves me—*again*.

When I advise my attacker that, a loud ricochet zooms around the room. I startle to within an inch of my life when a bullet flies past my ear, rustling my shoulder-length hair on the way by. I want to say the shot was fired from outside of the room, but unfortunately, that isn't the case. It came from my attacker's direction.

"Rae!"

Alex's scream breaks my heart more than the thought of dying. He sounds truly wounded, as if the bullet shredded through my stomach instead of the door jamb a few inches right of my head.

Bile scorches my throat when a deep voice behind me warns, "If you enter, my next shot won't miss."

The bangs on the door stop, but I know Alex hasn't left. I can hear his deep breaths, smell the sweat slicking on his skin. His scent is so profound, the fine hairs on my nape prickle.

"Turn around to face me."

With my arms held out in front of my body and my heart in my throat, I spin as the unnamed man demanded. As suspected, he has a gun, and it's pointed my way.

"Don't make me do this," he pleads when he spots the tears in my eyes dying to stream down my face. "This isn't what I want. I came here to help you." His words are as shaky as his hands. They fill me with panic, even more so when I notice his finger is curled around the trigger.

"Okay." I lower my tone before suggesting, "But we can't achieve that with violence."

I smile, hoping it is as effective on madmen as it is on admirers. It works—somewhat. It has him directing his pistol to just left of my chest instead of directly at it.

I suck in three long breaths before asking, "What do you want to help me with?"

His eyes bounce between mine to check the sincerity of my question. Happy with what he sees, he replies, "They're taking it too far." His voice is weaker than mine, more timid.

"Who?" I have a million more questions to ask, but with my mouth failing to cooperate with the prompts of my brain, I have to settle on any they're willing to express.

The man's eyes drift to the door Alex was in the process of breaking down before he fired a warning shot.

"Alex?" I ask through the lump in my throat.

"Yes." He stops, swallows, then says, "Well, not entirely. . ."

He stares at me as if he's seeking assistance. I don't know why in the world he thinks I can help him. I'm as lost as he is.

"Tell me more!" I choke out in a scream two seconds later when a commotion at his side gains his attention.

I could be wrong, but I'm reasonably sure the noise came

from the bathroom attached to my room—a bathroom with a window large enough for a grown man to climb through.

"Did someone send you here? To help me?"

He shakes his head, its quiver as violent as his chin is shaking.

I hear my heart in my ears when I ask, "Did someone send you here to hurt me?"

He continues shaking his head. "Not this time."

"There was a before. . .?"

Chaos ensues before the entire sentence leaves my mouth. A flurry of blond charges through one door as the wood from another splinters at my feet. The air leaves my lungs in a grunt when a thick arm bands around my waist two seconds later to drag me to the ground. I hit the wooden floorboards with the same loud thud as the unnamed man, but it isn't my body slamming into the ground without concern of injury. It's Alex's.

After gathering me into his chest, he rolls over, sheltering my body with his. I feel his blood surging through his body, smell the testosterone on his skin. It is a virile, manly scent, one I'm certain I've smelled before. His smell makes me woozy; I'm just unsure in my spooked state if it is a good thing or not.

Sometimes, just catching the slightest whiff of a familiar smell causes me more lightheadedness than the strongest alcoholic concoction. Other times, like yesterday afternoon, it bombards me with disturbing memories. Before I can decipher which one this is, Alex pulls away from me, taking the memory with him.

I settle my skyrocketing heart rate before peering in the direction the man once stood. He is hogtied to the ground, his face as red as mine as he strains to breathe through the heavy weight of Grayson kneeling on his back.

"Is she alright?" Grayson asks Alex, who has plucked me from the floor so he can frantically search me for a bullet wound. His quest is so thorough, it's as if he incorrectly counted the number of shots fired in his room.

I cup his jaw to wordlessly coerce his eyes to mine. When I get them, I say, "I'm fine." *I'm confused as fuck, but fine nonetheless.*

The devastation in his eyes cuts through me like a knife. They have the same horrifying look my eyes held when I cleaned away blood and mud from my hands the night of Luca's accident.

I run my fingers through his beard, loving how its thickness can conceal my fingers. After tracing his plump, downturned lips, they continue their trek, only coming to a stop at his ear so I can tug his earlobe.

Alex smiles at my playfulness, the tension in his shoulders relaxing. The wide span of his lips lifts his cheeks, exposing a scar I hadn't noticed before. It is hidden by his wiry beard and blond wisps of hair curling around his face. It is so well-concealed, I wouldn't have noticed it if I hadn't explored his face.

Before I can ask him about the scar, my attacker murmurs, "This is what she wants. Her goal was to force you together."

I expect Alex's face to cloud with the same confusion as mine. Regrettably, that reaction lies solely on my shoulders. He's not confused. He's more annoyed than anything.

Catching Alex's rueful glare, the stranger mumbles, "You're lucky she picked me. I've got a conscience—a wife the same age as Rae. You might not be so lucky next time."

"Lucky? I got lucky! You fired your gun at her!" Alex's violent roar picks up right alongside his anger. "How is that lucky?! You could have killed her!"

When the stranger shakes his head, soundlessly denying his accusation, Alex storms for him. Grayson falls from his back when Alex fists his shirt so he can drag him to within an inch of his face.

"You *never* point your weapon unless you're willing to kill the person you're aiming it at." His hot words sizzle on the man's flaming red cheeks. "That's the first thing they teach you in the academy!"

My eyes rocket to Alex's as quickly as Grayson's. *Is he saying what I think he is? Is he one of them?*

Spotting my inquisitive glare Grayson yells, "Enough!" He nudges his head to me. "Take her downstairs while I sort this mess out."

I glare at him. *I'm not a baby, so he sure as hell can't command his brother to treat me as one.*

"Who wants us to be together?" My question isn't for Alex or Grayson. It's for the man staring at me, pleading for me to listen to him.

When his panicked eyes drift between Alex and Grayson, I plead, "You said you wanted to help me, so help me. Who made you do this?"

He only gets out a "T" sound before Grayson's knuckles steal his words. He's out cold in an instant, the low hang of his head giving me my third bad memory of the day.

18

"He's not even a rookie agent?"

I throw down the file Grayson's men put together after hauling Jay Foster's ass to the local PD office before I plop my backside into the chair next to Grayson. Adrenaline-thickened blood is still roaring through my body, and my panic is still at an all-time high. Three inches—three motherfucking inches to the right and I would have lost Regan forever.

You have no idea how much the thought is tearing me up. Jay is lucky Grayson knocked him out before I did one of the many things running through my head. He wouldn't be facing charges of reckless endangerment with a weapon, conspiracy to commit a crime, and attempted murder charges. His family would be organizing his funeral.

Argh! I should have accepted Grayson's offer to interrogate him in the basement at The Manor. I would have if Regan's welfare wasn't at the forefront of my mind. She's been withdrawn since the attack. That's not unusual. . . for a normal person.

Rae isn't normal. She's so fucking strong, she consoled me when I should have been comforting her. Her silence must center around something else, something she doesn't want to share with me. It's the reason she's sat quietly in the corner of the guest living room the last three hours, as she knows there's less chance of me breaking down her guard in public.

Call me cocky, but behind closed doors, I know she doesn't stand a chance. Out here, being eyeballed by everyone as stunned by the turn of events as me, I take two steps back for each one I take forward.

I wait for Regan to accept the tub of frozen frosting my mom's holding out for her before my eyes return to Grayson. He has an odd grin on his face, like he too is being bombarded with wicked memories from the vanilla scent lingering in the air.

The females in our house see frosting a little differently than us. They use it like ice-cream to combat their emotions. The more they consume when swarmed by worry, the less flighty their brains become.

We don't consume it. We rule it. We govern with it. We use it against them as if they're so stupid they believe an overload of sugar is the answer to everything.

It's a pity everyone in this household underestimated Regan. It is nearly as shameful as her life being placed at risk for the good of the Bureau.

"Did Jay mention a second perp?"

Grayson shakes his head. "He's admitted guilt to your assault and the message left in Regan's apartment, but other than that, he's been fairly quiet. He's scared of the repercussions."

"It's her, isn't it? Theresa put him up to this?" I ask, hearing the words he isn't saying.

Grayson leans back in his chair before resting his left ankle on his knee. "From what my men have gathered, yes. It appears as if she requested for Jay to wear the same cologne as Regan's deceased boyfriend to make it more authentic."

Anger blackens my veins. "Then arrest her."

"For what?" Grayson's deep timbre reveals he's seeking a lifeline rather than dispersing agitation. "Although she stepped *way* outside her box, anything Jay confesses to is hearsay if it isn't backed up with evidence. Furthermore, you know the length some crews go to snag their man. This was just another tactic to bring down a criminal."

"By placing Regan's life at risk?" I lower my voice when Regan's head pops up. "He endangered her life."

Grayson shakes his head. "He threatened her life, but as far as Jay is concerned, she was never in any real danger." He leans forward, recognizing I'm five seconds from blowing my top. "You cited in reports time and time again that those around Isaac were the way into his empire. Theresa accepted your advice. It may not be in the manner you were hoping, but she followed solid intel from a dedicated and well-respected member of her department."

"You follow a lead; you don't force a soon-to-be-agent to harass someone in such a way that they live in fear of their life." I hear my anger roar twice when it ricochets off the living room walls.

Grayson locks his murky blue eyes with mine. "You do if it gives you a way in."

I glare at him, knowing he isn't telling me everything, but also aware he won't hold my hand as I dig through the facts. Just peering into his familiar eyes brings to mind quotes our dad always says, "You don't get anywhere by accepting hand-outs. You have to work for everything you have."

My back molars grind together when the truth smacks into me two seconds later. "She used me to get to her."

Air whizzes from my nostrils, shocked Theresa is this smart. I didn't think she had it in her.

"That's how Josie knew who Regan was. She wasn't on a case the night we went out for dinner; she was leading me to Regan."

"You're a passive, stone-faced agent who could fool a pastor into believing he's a saint... until you're with her." Grayson nudges his head to Regan. "You wear your heart on your sleeve when it comes to your girl. Theresa used that knowledge to her advantage."

"Well she's shit out of luck if she thinks my relationship with Regan will snag her Isaac. Regan doesn't know anything."

My reply doesn't come out as strong as I'm hoping. Regan is innocent, but I'm confident she has Isaac's trust, so that means she's the key we need to unlock Isaac's case. I just refuse to treat her as a commodity.

"What are you going to do?" Grayson asks when I stand from my chair.

I run my hand down the front of my pants, hoping it will calm my anger. It's a woeful waste of time. "I'm going to wring Theresa's neck."

"Then?" Grayson asks, confident there's more.

He's right. "Then I'll tell Regan the truth." When Grayson attempts to talk, no doubt to tell me he thinks it's a stupid move, I continue speaking, "It's the right thing to do, Grayson. If Regan thinks I was only with her to take down Isaac, I'll lose her." The clench of my jaw says the words I can't express: *I'd rather die than live without her.*

Those sixty-five seconds between Jay firing his gun and Grayson taking him down were the lowest sixty-five seconds of my life. In an instant, I understood Regan's grief and why it's taken her so long to overcome it. The pain was intense, worse than anything I've ever experienced.

This is selfish of me to say after all the hurt Regan has dealt with the past eight years, but she survived Luca's wreckage because she's meant to be with me. That was the universe's fucked up way of bringing us together. If Luca hadn't died, Regan would have never worked at Substanz. I would have never seen her dance on stage, and she would have never stolen my heart with a can-can kick and a bright smile.

Theresa thinks she forced Regan and me together, but I know that isn't the case. The crazy, unexplainable thing between us started years before Theresa arrived at the Bureau —way before even Regan realizes.

Once the dust settles, and the world rights itself again, I'm sure Regan will see sense through the madness. I don't believe in psychics and all that flowery shit some women try to pin you with, but I'm so confident Regan belongs with me, we'll work through this *together.*

"Can you watch her for me?" I don't need to nudge my head

to Regan for Grayson to know whom my question refers to. "I need to make a call." *A really fucking important one.*

I grow worried I said my last statement out loud when Grayson's brows pull together. Although I can tell he is dying to grill me, he dips his chin, granting my request.

Regan's eyes track me as I cross the room, but she maintains her quiet front. Not wanting anyone to overhear my call, I use the manager's office at the back of The Manor to make it.

With our last conversation ending on a sour note, it takes Dane a little longer to answer my call than usual. He's delaying on purpose. How do I know this? Where else does he have to go?

"You alright?" I ask, hating the grogginess of his voice when he greets me. Dane's an early riser, and it's late morning. He should have awoken hours ago.

"Yeah, it's just . . .ah. Shit."

I wait, hoping he'll give me more to work with.

It's a long-ass two minutes.

"Listen, I need to talk to you—"

"If it's about our conversation the other day, just stop. I was talking shit, trying to ease your guilt. I'd never fool around on Kristin. You know I think the world shines out of her ass."

There is an edge of honesty in his tone, but not enough for me to fully believe him. He's keeping something from me; I'm just unsure if it's an old affair or new matters he doesn't want to share.

"I wasn't calling about that. I've got some stuff going on that affects us both, so I figured I should give you an update."

Dane breathes noisily down the line, but not a peep escapes his lips.

I use his silence to my advantage. I tell him everything: Regan's threat, my attack on the way out of HQ, and Jay firing at Regan. Then once it is all said and done, I tell him the real reason I called.

"So it isn't just my head on the chopping block if I go after Theresa. Your position is at stake as well. I know how much your family relies on that money, Dane."

My hand stops scrubbing my scruffy beard when Dane growls, "Can you stop playing the fucking sympathy card?" He coughs to clear a croak in his throat. "How many times have I told you? You're not responsible for what happened that night in the field. I got shot, but you didn't pull the fucking trigger."

He has said the same thing numerous times the past five years, but I still take blame. He followed me to back me up. That's how he got shot. If I had acted as an agent that day instead of a man, he wouldn't be paralyzed from the waist down. It doesn't get any simpler than that.

"You don't know this woman, Dane. Theresa is—"

"The spawn of Satan. Yeah, I get it. My brain still works, you know. It is only my legs that are fucked up." He laughs. I don't see the humor in his reply. "After our last conversation, I dug a little deeper into the information you sent me. Danielle didn't seek revenge years later for no reason. She was convinced the time was right. Wasn't hard considering she is mentally unstable. Out of the past five years, she spent three of them volunteering at a local Christian parish."

He doesn't need to spell it out for me. His tone says everything. During our years at the Bureau, we've both seen a lot of the "Lord's good people" who don't understand that no amount of Bible study will cure a sickness inside someone's head.

"Regan mentioned something about speaking with Danielle's pastor in their teen years," I disclose.

An agreeing murmur vibrates from Dane's lips. "Yeah, it helped for a while, but the instant she turned eighteen, she went off the radar, and her files were sealed shut."

My brows stitch. "So how are you aware of them?"

"Let's just say, the less you know, the less likely you'll be indicted."

Dane chuckles. This time, I join him.

"Fair enough."

Usually, I'd give him a lecture on how we are lawmen before we are anything, but since this concerns Regan, the woman I'd rather die for than live without, I'll lay down my moral sword for a real weapon.

A few minutes of silence pass between us. I'd like to say it isn't awkward, but I've never been fond of lying.

"Are you sure you're alright with this?" I ask when the tension becomes too great.

Dane takes a moment to deliberate. I don't blame him. He has a lot to consider. Agents aren't paid well in general, but the pittance they pay first-year recruits is woeful.

My heart starts beating again when he murmurs, "Yeah, I'm good. I've got some tricks up my sleeve."

I wait, knowing there is more.

He proves me right by saying, "But I need you to keep that promise you made to me that night in the field."

"I didn't promise shit."

My voice comes out sterner than I intend. I'm not angry at Dane; I just hate being reminded how close he was to losing his life. When we were hunkered down, waiting for the helicopters that never came, he made me swear that no matter what happened, I'd always take care of his girls. I stalled for as long as I could, but the weaker Dane's pulse became, the weaker my resolve became.

Within a minute, I caved.

A minute after that, the bullets raining down the meadow halted, and we escaped the valley of death we were hiding in. I thought it was a sign that my promise was what saved Dane's life. I was a fool. His life was spared, but my soul is still hunkered down in that field, striving to find its way back to me.

"I'll still get him, Dane. I'll never forget what he did to you." I grit my teeth hard, loathing the grogginess of my words.

Dane's deep exhalation reveals he heard the sentiment in my tone. "That's not the promise I'm talking about."

"I know." My knee bobs up and down as I struggle to leash my anger. "But I'll still keep it."

Dane exhales again, this time more in annoyance than trouble. "You've got to let this go, Alex. It's eating you alive."

I shake my head, expressing my lie without words. It kills me seeing him in his wheelchair, his legs withered, his once six-foot-two frame half its size. That's why I rarely visit him. I can't see him like that and not feel responsible for what happened. Dane was in the prime of his life, and in an instant, it was pulled from beneath him. Neither of us have been the same since.

Regrettably, Dane doesn't need words to catch me in a lie. "You don't even know if it was him. You're working off half-truths."

I laugh. It isn't a pleasant, happy-filled chuckle. "He might not have pulled the trigger, but I guarantee you, he knows who did. That makes him just as responsible."

"There are two sides to every story—"

"Yeah, there is," I interrupt, nodding. "But you only get to pick one side. The right side of the law. He didn't. . ."

My words trail off when the creak of a door steals my attention. My mom's dynamic has flipped The Manor from a cold, rarely booked establishment to one that goes months with the no vacancy sign lit, but it's unusual for anyone to come back here. It's why I chose this area to take my call. I wanted privacy.

"Can I call you back?"

Although I'm asking Dane a question, I don't give him a chance to respond. The click of the ancient phone onto the receiver almost drowns out the scurrying of feet. It's for the best, then the person sneaking up on me unaware won't hear the unclicking of my holster as I remove my gun from my hip.

With my pistol held high and my heart rate out of control, I exit the office at the speed of a rocket. I only make it three steps before a horrifying image blitzes me with guilt.

A gun is pointed at Regan's head.

It's mine.

19

"Jesus Christ, Regan. I could have shot you." Alex holsters his gun before stepping closer to me. "What are you doing back here?"

"I was. . . uh. . ." *Come on, Regan. You don't have air for brains!* "Looking for you."

The anger reddening Alex's cheeks whitens from my reply. He seems genuinely happy about my response, like he isn't associating with me solely to crack a half-decade-old case.

He's a damn good actor.

I don't know how I didn't put the pieces of the puzzle together earlier. The large scar on his knee should have been my first clue, but I brushed it off, conscious men as physically fit as him have many issues with their knees. Then I spotted the faint scar running from his right temple to his left ear. If I hadn't spotted it within seconds of absorbing his familiar scent, I probably wouldn't have paid it much attention. But when you add those three facts with the warning Jay gave before Grayson knocked him out, the evidence seems damning.

I wanted to give Alex the benefit of the doubt, to believe the absolute horror in his eyes when he searched my body for a bullet wound was genuine, but I've learned many hard lessons in my short life. The most imperative is to always trust my gut.

That's why I slipped away from Grayson's watch to follow Alex down here. I had planned to confront him, to call him out as a liar and a fraud, but the remorse in his words when he took his call stopped me. His pain was genuine, and although I'm feeling like a right royal fucking idiot, I didn't want to add to his pain.

It was for the best. If I hadn't held back my desire to gut him as badly as he is gutting me, I would have missed the final piece of the puzzle. Those last words Alex spoke, the ones about choosing the right side of the law, I've heard them before. It was the night I fled Substanz with Isaac. It was one of the very first things the agent who let me flee without shooting me said.

I step closer to Alex so I can run my fingers through his beard as I did earlier. My heart breaks a little when he leans into my embrace, as if he can't breathe without my touch. I wouldn't be touching him if I wasn't seeking a way to stop me from feeling like such an idiot. I missed all the signs—every single one of them!

It's quite pathetic when you think about it. A bit of facial hair and a few inches of growth, and poof, you've got me fooled. God—I thought I was smart. This proves that book smarts have nothing on common sense.

I guess that's why I'm so confused as to why Alex is doing this? Is bringing someone to justice for evading a crime really worth all this effort? I know undercover agents don't follow the norm, but this is taking it too far. I introduced him to my family. I slept with him. I nearly even said three little words I swore I'd never say again, and for what? For it all to be doctored in a case file that will never reach the courts?

The statute of limitation ensures criminal charges can no longer be filed for an offense once five years has passed. That means even if I confess to my sins right now, I'm in the clear. Neither Isaac nor I will face a single second in jail, so there has to be something I'm missing. Even the world's most heartless man wouldn't do this for nothing.

I take a step back when a horrifying thought enters my mind. *What if he isn't after me? What if he wants someone closer to me, someone more powerful and harder to take down?*

The room spins around me as the dots keep connecting. This isn't about me at all. I'm just the pawn he used to reach the king.

Oh god, I'm going to be sick.

"Deep breaths, Rae. Take in some big deep breaths for me," Alex coaches when a panic attack blindsides me out of nowhere. I haven't had one in years, but I'm not surprised I've finally succumbed. This hurts—a lot!

The concern in Alex's tone as he attempts to calm me down steals the air from my lungs more than the reality of our situation did. He used me. He took my heartache, my belief that not everyone is out to hurt me, then tossed it back in my face.

How could I have been so stupid?

How could I let him play me like an idiot?!

My lungs wheeze through the pain shredding them in two when Alex guides me to a chair halfway down the corridor. He dashes away from me, only to return thirty seconds later with a bottle of water and a box of tissues. I don't know who the tissues are for. I'm not crying.

Another wave of stupidity crashes into me when I raise my hand to my cheeks. They're flooded with moisture.

"It's okay," Alex assures when I stop his attempts to soak up the mess. "Shock can take hours to arrive. It's perfectly normal to feel this way after what you went through this morning."

A thousand curse words scream through my head as I stare at him, but not one fires off my tongue. It isn't Jay's attack rendering me a blubbering idiot. It is him, a man I trusted, a man I thought I could love.

"Keep breathing for me, Rae. You've got this. You're so fucking strong, baby, so very strong."

I want to pull away from him. I want to yank his gun from his holster and use the skills he taught me yesterday against him, but instead, I act as the coward I was the night Luca died. I shimmy my shoulders; I put on a brave face, and I act like the world hasn't crumbled beneath my feet.

This is real life. People like me don't get happily-ever-afters and forevers. Ms. Collard warned me what would happen if I "rang the devil's doorbell" too many times. I thought she was an old coot who needed to switch up her reading palette to something more risqué than the Christian romances she devoured four times a week. This kills me to admit, but I should have listened to her.

Luca loved me so I would hide his secret.

Alex pretended to love me to unearth secrets.

Shame me once, fool on you. Shame me twice, fool on me. There sure as hell won't be a third time.

I feel the rod in my back hardening as anger overtakes my devastation. My lungs feel lighter as the sensation that I'm drowning fades. I do have this. I had it before Alex arrived in the picture, and I'll have it years after he leaves.

No, correct that. *After I kick him out.*

He might have chosen me because he thought I was easy prey. He's about to find out the hard way how badly he underestimated me. Luca's death broke me, but it also showed me that I am stronger than I ever gave myself credit for. One person may not be able to take down an army, but she can sure as hell dent their defense.

"That's it, baby. Look at you. I'm so fucking proud of you, Rae; so damn proud."

I continue bombarding Regan with praise, confident every word I speak brings back the woman I'm in love with. I'm not worried that she's finally cracked. I knew this would eventually happen. Regan is strong, but she's been dragged through the wringer the past week. If she didn't eventually crack under the pressure, I would have grown worried she wasn't human.

You can be the toughest and most bravest person on the planet and still be struck down by a panic attack. Some struggle to breathe. Others cry. Then there are men like me who throw hospital equipment around their room like a maniac forgetting their shattered knee can't take the weight of his body. There is no shame giving in to the emotions holding you hostage. Whether it is grief, remorse or fear, you'll never truly be free unless you let go of what's holding you back.

"Do you want some water?" I unscrew the bottle and hand it to Regan before she can answer me. She accepts it, albeit hesitantly.

I stop peering into her eyes over the bottle of water trembling against her lips when someone calls my name. Although I don't need to see the person to know who's demanding my attention, I shift my eyes to them. I'm glad Regan's finally freeing herself from her torment, but I doubt she wants anyone seeing her like this.

Grayson stops stomping down the dimly lit hallway when I shake my head. My movement is meek, but strong enough for both Grayson and Regan to see. At the same time Grayson's throat works hard to swallow, Regan ducks her chin into her chest to hide her tear-stained face.

"*Give me a few,*" I mouth to Grayson, annoyed at his frozen frame. Even a man without a heart would recognize now is not the time for an interruption.

I'm two seconds from throwing Grayson out of the hall by the scruff of his collar when he says, "It's important."

I give him a look as if to say *and this isn't?* My girl is crying directly in front of me, and she's not in my arms. You can't get any more imperative than this.

My jaw clenches when Grayson murmurs, "It's *really* important."

My retaliation snags halfway up my throat when Regan says, "It's fine, Alex. Go."

I shake my head. "No. It's *not* fine. He can wait."

Regan balks as if shocked she comes before anyone. I add to her surprise when I tell her precisely that. "You'll always be first, Rae. *Always.*"

It is a struggle for her to keep her tears at bay, but she does, somewhat. They just pool in the corners of her eyes instead of gushing down her face.

"I've got to pack anyway. Our plane leaves in a little under three hours." She gestures her hand to Grayson. "Go see what your brother needs. I'm sure he wouldn't have interrupted us unless it was important."

Although Grayson hears the slight sneer in her words the same as I do, he dips his head, agreeing with her. "If I don't show you this now, it may not be helpful by the time you get a chance to use it."

I return my eyes to Regan. "Are you sure you're okay?"

"Yes." She breathes heavily, relieved I'm giving in. "I'm perfectly fine."

Her fake grin dampens the confidence in her tone, but I pretend I haven't noticed it. I'm juggling so many balls at the moment, I'm close to dropping them all. If that happens, things could end disastrously.

"Do you know your way back to our room?"

Regan smiles, then nods. Thankfully, this one is more authentic.

"Alright. I'll meet you back there soon, okay?"

When she nods again, I lean in to press a kiss on her mouth. Just before my lips touch hers, she jerks her chin to the right, forcing my lips to land on her cheek. I tell myself it's because she doesn't want me to taste the salt of her tears, but there is a niggle in my gut that makes it hard to walk away from her. But she disappears before I'm even halfway to Grayson, her wish to flee darkening his eyes with as much suspicion as mine.

"Whatever you're about to show me better be fucking good,"

I growl at Grayson, taking my anger out on him instead of myself. I shouldn't be doing this. Regan should always be my utmost priority.

"Have I ever let you down, Alex?"

He sounds annoyed. Rightfully so. He broke two bones in his hand knocking Jay out before he could reveal my secret to Regan, and how do I thank him? I get pissed for him having my back more than I have his.

Remaining quiet, he guides me into a room I didn't know existed. Well, I did, but not like this. The number of men, computer equipment, and state of the art surveillance devices in this old boiler room rivals Theresa's operation. There is just one difference: they have notably more intel on the man we're tracking.

"You're after Isaac Holt?" Surprise echoes in my tone.

Grayson shakes his head. "No. He's small fry compared to whom we're chasing." He taps two fingers on a center photo in a board of many. "Henry—"

"Gottle Senior," I fill in. "*Fuck.*"

My last word is highly appropriate to describe Henry. He is the mob boss of New York City, the cream of the crop on the FBI hit list. He's the motherlode. Crack him, crack several crime syndicates beneath him. We call him the golden hen because every egg he hatches is made out of pure moneymaking gold.

"Is Isaac a member of his crew?" I try to keep hope out of my tone. I miserably fail.

Lucky, because it's bitch-slapped when Grayson shakes his head. "No. They know of each other, but we've yet to link them from a business standpoint."

"How can that be? You know as well as I do that Henry doesn't associate with anyone outside of his *association*." I air quote my last word like an A-grade soft cock. Clearly, Regan isn't the only one still struggling to understand the emotions racing through her veins.

Grayson does a weird shrugging thing. "True, but things are different between them."

"Different how?"

Grayson points to three photos. Vladimir Popov, crime lord of Vegas. Col Petretti, slowly recouping mob boss of the Florida/Hopeton region, and Mario Taleo, suspected leader of a lower Mexican run circuit. "All of these men owe Henry in some way."

My "duh" eyeroll stops halfway when Grayson quickly adds on, "Isaac doesn't. Henry owes him."

He hands me a photo of a man I'd guess to be late twenties, early thirties. He has dark hair, a well-built frame and the same sneer as every man in this room. "That is Henry Gottle Junior."

My lips quirk. *I was unaware Henry had a son.*

"Details are sketchy, but from what we've unearthed, Henry Jr. and Isaac attended the same university. Some shit went down, and Isaac stepped in, gifting him a handful of favors from Henry Senior."

Grayson's intel annoys me more than it pleases me. I don't want to hear that Isaac's connections in his industry started nobly. I also don't know why Grayson is wasting my time with this shit now. He's got nothing useful for me, certainly nothing worth stealing me away from Regan for.

When I tell him that, he smiles. "You asked a question; I answered it." He slaps his hand on my shoulder to stop me from fleeing before saying, "My investigation into Henry isn't why I brought you here. He is." He nudges his head to a photo of Isaac.

"Your cross examination found something I can take him down with?"

Hope flies out the window when Grayson shakes his head. "But I have something just as good. I found a way you can get your man without compromising your relationship with your girl."

Huh? Is he talking in riddles? I've searched high and low the past four months to find a way of taking Isaac down without the ripple effect being passed on to Regan. I've yet to discover a viable path.

"More times than not, it isn't the evidence you find that unlocks a case..."

"It's the person at the helm responsible for the crew's success," I fill in, remembering a quote our dad has often said.

"That's right." Grayson moves to a bulky computer in the middle of the room. "You've said since day one that Theresa wasn't right for this case, that she hinders it more than she helps it."

I halfheartedly shrug. Sometimes my gripes were more out of frustration than Theresa's lack of skills, but I've always believed people are more honest when they're placed in a hostile situation, so perhaps my accusations were honest.

"Theresa isn't the right woman for this case because she can't be objective."

I want to cut in, but my interest in the documents Grayson is bringing up on the monitor is too high to force an interruption. There are court transcripts, requests for paternity tests, and affidavits marked as private. I scan these types of documents day in and day out, but the names across these capture my imagination. They all contain the same two names: Isaac Holt and Theresa Veneto.

"They have a child together?"

Grayson shakes his head before he nods then shakes it again. "No one knows. Isaac refuses to take a paternity test."

His reply doesn't shock me. Isaac would never give DNA willingly.

"Is this him?" I ask, holding up a photo of a boy I'd guess to be approximately three years old. "He has the same cleft chin as Isaac."

"Yeah, he does. Back in the day, that would have been all the proof needed."

I'd laugh if he wasn't being honest.

I lay the photo of the little boy down before shifting on my feet to face Grayson. "How could the Bureau put Theresa in charge of this case knowing the circumstances? This is a clear case of conflict of interest. If Theresa wants to pin Isaac by the nuts for a personal matter, she can't be objective."

Grayson gives me a look. Thankfully he saves his lecture on double standards for another day. I want to pin Isaac's nuts to the wall for a personal reason as well, but my desires are different than Theresa's. Isaac committed a crime, so I'm simply holding him responsible for his actions. Theresa slept with him; now she has to pick off each flea he infested her with. That makes them utterly incomparable.

I stop seeking other reasons my goals are different from Theresa's when Grayson discloses, "The Bureau let her work

219

his case because they're unaware of their connection. These files were so deeply buried, they only surfaced today."

I'd call him out as a liar if I couldn't hear the honesty in his tone.

"This morning?" When he nods, I add on, "Who found them?"

Grayson laughs. It isn't his standard chuckle. "That's the stupid thing. They weren't really found; they kinda popped up."

"Out of nowhere?"

A *pfft* noise escapes my lips when he nods. "No fucking way. Why would they just suddenly appear?"

Grayson pops his hip onto the desk. "Maybe someone has your back?"

"Maybe someone's trying to stab a knife into my back." I scrub my hand across my hairy chin. "Something isn't sitting right with this, Grayson. Info like this doesn't just magically appear. If it was buried as deep as you say it was, someone had to go digging for it."

He glares at me like I'm a fucking idiot. "So you're not going to use it to get Theresa pulled off the case?"

"I didn't say that. I'm not a dumbass. With the right leader steering the helm, this case could be closed by the end of the month."

Grayson's *you're a fucking idiot* glare ramps up.

"But that doesn't mean I'm suddenly a believer in magic lamps with wish-granting genies inside."

"Don't look a gift horse in the mouth, Alex. Sometimes shit is just on your side."

I want to believe him, but things never work out like that for me. If I want something, I have to work for it. It's never handed to me.

"Third phone I've owned in under a week, can you believe it?"

Regan stops peering out the window to shift her eyes my way. She drops them to the new cell in my hand before raising them to my face. Just as she was the hours prior to our take off, she's extremely quiet. She didn't even bat an eye when I paid for us to fly home first class. I don't care about the unlimited drinks and fancy meal the airline clerk tried to sell us with. I just wanted Regan to be comfortable.

The dam sitting in her eyes the last two hours nearly breaks when I ask, "Are you okay?"

I know it's corny, but those three little words seem more important to Regan than the ones I blurted out this morning. It's our thing, our way of checking that the other is okay without overloading them with a trillion questions.

"Yeah, I'm fine. I think I'm coming down with something. I'm not feeling real good." She unlatches her belt before scooting past me. "I might go splash some water on my face to see if it helps."

"Okay. . ." I stop talking when she darts down the aisle like her ass is on fire.

Needing to squelch my instinct to take off after her, I use the plane's Wi-Fi to log into my emails. As promised, Grayson printed, photographed, then emailed me the information he discovered this morning. I smile, confident Theresa won't know what hit her when I arrive back on deck this afternoon.

After a grilling by the top man in Grayson's team, Jay came clean that Theresa was the facilitator of his campaign. She had intel on him, stuff he never wanted his brand new wife to find out about.

Although pissed he didn't man up sooner, I am grateful it eventually happened. Without him and his confession, I'd still be worried about Regan's safety. I'm still cautious; it's just not as dire as it has been. I have eyes on Theresa, many of them, so she won't make a single move without me knowing. Even though I'd like to see her face prosecution for what she did to Regan immediately, I know there is a long, drawn-out process that must occur before that can happen. If I can get her to step away from her position first, then the rest will come —eventually.

Not trusting my internet provider not to screw me over, I screenshot each document and save them to the photo album in my phone. Because Theresa has taken Isaac to court many times, it is a tediously long task—although not as long as Regan is taking in the bathroom.

Suddenly conscious I may have misread Regan's bathroom trip as inspired by anguish rather than lust, I check the location of the first class stewardess. Upon spotting her station empty, my heart rate quickens. Between Grayson's discovery, packing, then traveling to the airport in rush hour traffic, I've barely had a moment to put my hands on Regan. I should be ashamed to admit it's killing me, even more so after what she went through this morning, but I'm not.

Furthermore, if I've learned anything the past week, it's that Regan has no qualms telling me what she needs and how she needs it. Clearly, she needs me as much as I need her.

After unlatching my belt, I track the steps Regan took twenty minutes ago. I'm about to rack my knuckles on the gray door when it suddenly pops open. Spotting the stewardess making her way back down the aisle, I dash inside the tiny cubicle, locking the door behind me.

"That was close," I growl under my breath, pretending I'm afraid of getting busted. It adds extra heat to the energy that forever bristles between us, taking it from a simmer to a full boil.

The little vein in Regan's neck works overtime when I cup her jaw and lower my lips to hers. I've barely gotten in half a lick of her succulent mouth when she mutters, "I'm on my period."

"Oh."

My fingers fall from her hair when I take a step back. It's an asshole move on my behalf, but understandable since I've never handled stuff like this before.

Regan screws up her face in apology. "Yeah, it's why I'm a little off. The joys of womanhood." She shrugs before adding on. "Sorry."

"What have you got to be sorry about?" I prep my stomach when I take a step closer to her, fairly certain of how she'll react to my next comment. "Our time doesn't need to be wasted, though. Your mouth is still in working order, isn't it?"

She socks me in the stomach as I anticipated before skirting past me and dashing out of the washroom. I wait a few seconds before taking off after her, more to hide my smile than my worry about being busted following her out.

I fucking love Regan's feistiness, but since I'm treading in foreign waters, and she's combatting a shit load of hormones, it will be best for me to downplay my happiness at the return of her sass.

The last half of our trip isn't silent like the first half. Regan talks —a lot. I feel like I'm under the lights, being drilled left, right and center about my life before her. If I didn't know any better, I'd swear she is interrogating me. She wants to know where Maxx, my cat, was and why I didn't introduce him to her when we were at The Manor, if The Manor is owned by my parents or do they rent it, and the birthdate of each member of my family.

She made an excuse that her last question was because she wants to add them to her planner to ensure she doesn't miss their special day.

Our exchange is odd—a little sweet—but mainly odd.

"Are you sure you don't want to come up?"

The purr of Regan's words shock me. They are as deep as a pussy cat cuddling up to her owner and as sexual as a tigress in heat.

"I've got wine, tins of frosting, and a few other edible *items* we can test out." She loosens the top button of her blouse to ensure I can't miss what the "other" items on her list pertain to.

I swivel my tongue around my mouth to loosen the dryness there before asking, "I thought you're. . . ah. . . *indisposed?*"

Regan's brows furl for the quickest second before they

smooth back to their original position. "Yeah, so? That just means we have to be more inventive."

I smile, grateful the frisky, fun-loving Regan is back. Although, I will admit, I like seeing her timid side as well. It gave me a chance to show her I can take care of her when needed. She doesn't need to hold the reins all the time.

"I'd love to come up, baby, but I've got a really important meeting I have to attend."

The smell of burning skin lingers in my nose when she glares at me. My ego absorbs her anger as disappointment, but my brain shouts at me to stop being such an idiot.

"I'll drop by tonight, hopefully with some good news."

Regan's slit eyes return to their normal width. "Good news?"

I nod. "Hopefully."

I'm confident I've got enough to take Theresa down, but I'm just as confident she won't go down without a fight. Theresa didn't get to her position by playing nice. She is more ruthless than any male supervisor I've worked under. I used to respect that about her. Now . . . I wouldn't piss on her if she was on fire.

"What type of news?" Nothing but inquisitiveness rings in Regan's tone.

"It won't be a surprise if you spoil it for yourself," I jest, running my finger down the crinkle in her nose.

She folds her arms in front of her chest before drawing away from me with a huff. "I don't like surprises."

"I don't like that you don't like surprises." *Or the way you're looking at me.*

I see Regan's anger work up from her stomach to her throat before she squeals, throws open the cab door we're sitting in, then hightails it to her apartment building. When she enters the idling elevator without a backward glance in my direction, I make a mental note to return with ice cream or chocolate. Perhaps even both.

I want to stay with her, but I need to slay one dragon before returning to soothe another.

Regan

*U*gh! The gall of that man.

I practically throw myself at him, and he rejects me! *ME!* I had no intention of getting him naked—*again;* I just wanted to keep him talking like I did in the plane. It took me a little longer than I care to admit to get over my shock after discovering what secret Alex was hiding, but once the fog cleared, brilliant idea after brilliant idea steamrolled into me.

The one I had in the bathroom in the seconds leading to Alex accosting me there was my most brilliant one yet. Alex can't take me or Isaac down if he's buried beneath a pile of dirt. I don't mean death. Although I'm mad as hell at the way he deceived me, I don't wish him ill harm—unfortunately.

Hard time behind bars, on the other hand, I have no qualms with that.

There is no way what he did to me is legal, so I'm confident this isn't the first time he's done it. I've never had an interest in prosecution, but I did study it in law school in case things with Isaac didn't pan out. All I need to do is unearth Alex's inner-most secrets, then I'll expose them for the world to see. He'll be stripped from his position, dragged through the mud, and then he can become extremely friendly with some of the men he's placed behind bars... and I won't feel an ounce of guilt.

Maybe.

Somewhat.

Not even.

Argh!

I wish I were a vindictive person. It would be a shit ton easier if Alex didn't look at me the way he did. I'm aware people are trained for this; they're taught how to walk, speak, and act to ensure their cover isn't blown, but nothing he did seemed like a ruse. I truly believed he cared about me.

I growl when I catch sight of the hopeful woman in the mirror hanging in the entranceway of my apartment. What a pathetic loser she is. *He lied to you, repeatedly, yet you're still seeking a way to excuse him. You're better than this.*

With sheer determination fueling my steps, I dump my overnight bag, charge into the office Isaac had fitted for me when I agreed to relocate to Ravenshoe, then I fire up the soft-ware program I had Hunter install while I flew home. I have a lot of evidence to process. Names, dates of birth, and the numerous pictures of Alex's family I snapped on my way from the dungeon-like room he was hiding out in when he discovered me spying on him to his bedroom.

In a moment of anger, I tried to convince myself that Alex's family members were agents brought in to fool me. But the longer I stared at his family portraits, the more I realized I was wrong. They don't just have similarities; they have a connection that can't be forced. Their dynamic matches the one I have with my family, so I'm confident they're the one lie Alex didn't attempt to pull over my eyes.

The rest, I'm set to uncover now.

atching Theresa walk out of our office for the final time doesn't feel as relieving as it should. She took my demand for her resignation like a real champ, like it wasn't the first time she's been forced to resign due to a conflict of interest. I thought she'd put up a protest and accuse me of falsifying documents to step over her on the invisible ladder every agent in the Bureau strives to climb. It wouldn't be the first time she's accused a member of her team of doing this, but she didn't sling a single accusation my way. Not one.

I'm fucking shocked.

Perhaps she figures going willingly will lessen the severity of her punishment? In a way, she's not far off the mark. She didn't lose her position at the Bureau today; she is simply not the supervisor of this team anymore. From what I overheard when the head of our region arrived a little over an hour ago, a new interim leader will be decided by tomorrow morning. I really fucking hope she or he has their head more in the game than Theresa ever did, because if they even so much as attempt to pull a stunt like she did with Regan and me, I won't just have them fired, I'll have them arrested and charged.

I don't care what Grayson says, what Theresa did wasn't just wrong, it was illegal. When I have a little more time, I'll look into her scheming, meddling ways with more diligence. But for now, my focus must remain on safeguarding Regan from the backlash of both Isaac and Theresa's injustices. Theresa knows I'm watching, so she won't so much as blink an eye in Regan's direction. Jay is assisting authorities with their enquiries, and Brandon is seeking a more solid match between Isaac and Theresa. It will be only a matter of time before all the pieces slot together. Once we get a full view of the entire picture, then our focus can return to where it should have been all along: on Isaac.

Seeing it is a little after 10 PM, I stand from my chair to gather my coat. It's not cold outside, but I'm a little chilly since it's been over six hours since I've felt Regan's skin under mine.

I dip my chin in farewell to my fellow agents still confused about what occurred this afternoon before heading for the door. I'm not a tattler. I handled Theresa's stupidity; now the Bureau will manage the legal side of her error. As far as I am concerned, my lips will remain shut on this case until it goes to court. If my colleagues want to be updated on what happened, they can read the report once the Bureau uploads it. If that never happens, it's not my problem. I've got enough shit to sort through without adding more.

I make it halfway across the stark, bland office I call HQ before a pair of steel blue eyes stops my steps midstride. I do a double take, certain I'm mistaken. As far as I was aware, he was on the other side of the country. He should not be walking into this office, much less when I'm here.

"Dad?"

He stops talking to a bunch of bureaucrats at his side still seeking a way to excuse their mishap to crank his neck my way. His lips curl up, revealing his wonky smile when he spots me frozen halfway across the room. Although he is hitting close to sixty, I don't miss the numerous female agents eyeballing him when he spans the distance between us.

"What the hell are you doing here?"

The last half of my question is muffled from me wrapping him up in a firm, manly hug. I love my dad, and I'm man enough to admit it. It's been far too long since I've seen him— far *far* too long.

"I was talking to your mother; she gave me an update." His voice is as thick as I remember. Just as stern as well. "Came down to see if I could be of assistance. This mess runs deep. We don't like the Bureau being smeared with dirt like this."

My first thoughts go to Josie. Although she's adamant she didn't know Theresa's game plan, she's taken responsibility for her part in the kerfuffle. It will serve her well. Integrity is a big part of this agency.

I drop back two paces so I can lock my eyes with a pair as equally blue as mine when my dad slaps a black leather wallet into my chest. Although I don't need to see what is inside to know who owns it, I flick it open all the same.

My heart hammers my ribs when I spot my badge and agent ID peering back at me. "Where did you get this?"

"Same place we got this." He hands me my government-issued gun. "She wiped the servers of any evidence of her involvement, but we've got several agents seeking alternative proof."

"She? Theresa attacked me?" I sound shocked. I don't know why. I've always said she has balls of steel.

My dad nods. "Jay was training to join technical support. He'll never have the muscles to lift a man of your size without help."

I halfheartedly nod in agreement, but still, Theresa. . .fuck. My hearing is still ringing from how badly she clocked me. Clearly, she wants more from Isaac than just child support.

My dad's eyes scan the room. Although he'd never say anything, I can tell he is shocked by the conditions we are working in.

"We're waiting on an update on who'll take Theresa's place. Once they're appointed, they can add their own flair to the place." I laugh. It's more a tired laugh than playful. "I'm just hoping they're not stalling because they're planning to shut our unit down. We're here for a reason, Dad. I don't want Theresa's fuck up ruining that."

"It won't," he assures, his tone confident. "The higher ups know who raised you. They trust your instincts. It's why I'm here."

I stare at him, unmoving and unspeaking. *What the hell is he talking about?*

Thankfully, he is accustomed to my rare stumped states.

With a laugh, he says, "They want you to lead this team. Bring this case to fruition."

"I can't—"

The arch of his brow cuts me off, then his stare tells me everything else I need to know. This is why he came here; he

233

knew I'd turn down the promotion the instant they suggested me as Theresa's replacement.

"If mom updated you, you know why I can't accept."

He steps closer to me, ensuring his words are only for my ears. "Is she innocent?"

My spikes hackle just from him asking. "Of course she is. I wouldn't be with her if she wasn't."

"Then I don't see the problem."

My heart rate kicks into gear as fast as my fists clench. "The problem is, you haven't met Regan. She's stubborn, fierce." *The fucking love of my life.*

My dad's smile reveals he heard the words I didn't express. "She sounds just like your mother."

"Precisely. That's why I can't do this. You saw what it did to Mom. You nearly lost her. Don't make me suffer the same fate."

"Your mother and I have been together for over thirty years."

"After she nearly died—*twice!*" I lower my voice, which lowers the number of inquisitive eyes glancing our way. "I'm not you, Dad. I wouldn't survive seeing Rae go through that."

He does a good job hiding it, but I see the pain in his eyes when he says, "You think it was easy for me? Those where the hardest years of my life, but lessons were learned, sacrifices were made. We'll never make the same mistakes again."

"No, we won't. Because I won't let them happen." My eyes dance between his, which are now wetter than they were when he arrived. "Tell your colleagues I said thank you and that I appreciate the opportunity, but I'm not accepting the position. I'm doing what you should have done for Mom. I'm putting Regan first."

He's stiffer when I hug him this time around, but I don't hold back. Men in our industry lose their lives every day, so I'll never say goodbye without ensuring he knows what he means to me.

Just before I pull away, he yanks me back. "I'm proud of you, Son." The crack of his words nearly have me coming undone.

"Right back at ya." I squeeze him extra tight before pushing off my feet and charging for the door.

The instant I step onto the cracked concrete outside of my office building, the weight I expected to lift from my chest when Theresa was removed from her position finally shifts. My exchange with my dad felt wrong but right at the same time. Wrong because I feel the promise I made to Dane slipping from my grasp. Right because everything I said to my dad was straight-up honest. Regan needs to come first. She comes before anything and anyone.

Even me.

23

Regan

Six hours and not a single shred of evidence. I've used every resource at my disposal, and I've yet to find a single fucking piece of intel on Alex. I'm not talking evidence to convict him for life; I'm talking anything. There are no driver's licenses, no electric bills. Not a single thing. His apartment isn't even registered in his name. It is as if he doesn't exist.

How can I catch a ghost in the act if he's invisible? It's impossible!

I slump into my office chair with a groan. I'm exhausted, both physically and mentally. I'm also slightly hormonal. Most of my lie in the washroom earlier today centered around fleeing Alex's touch before my stupid ass libido could overrule my astute head, but a very small portion of it was true. I'm not PMSing, though. I'm ovulating. I'm one of those weirdo creeps who can tell when her egg is about to shoot out of her ovary because I get a little cranky, a whole lot horny, and a bit more slimy downstairs.

Sorry, I know, too much information. It was just another example of how stupid I've been the past week. Even with having the Depo shot, if I notice even one of the three signs I announced earlier, I don't let a man within two feet of me. 99.9999% is not 100% accuracy, so you can be damn sure I'll never risk being in the 00.0001% category of women who get pregnant on contraception.

Did that thought enter my mind this morning when Alex and I smeared the sheets with more than just frosting? Yes, it did. Did I listen to the warning alarm sounding in my head? No, I didn't.

See? What more proof do you need about how stupid I've been?

I stop reprimanding myself when the buzz of a doorbell ricochets through my apartment. It could be anyone, but considering it is nearly 11 PM, and I failed to update Isaac on my return to Ravenshoe today, I'm reasonably sure it is the one man I never want to see again. The one I want to hurt as much as he's hurting me. *The one I'd give anything to wake up tomorrow morning and find out this is all a lie.*

I hate what this is doing to me. I'm a confident, fierce woman who is letting a man crumble me into half the woman I am. I'm stronger than this, and I will survive this.

With sheer determination guiding my steps, I exit my office, dash down the hall, then climb the three stairs of my foyer. I don't look in the mirror like I usually do before greeting guests. I know what will reflect back at me, and I'm not willing to let that woeful wallflower waste another minute of my time wallowing in self-pity.

A manly scent smacks into me when I swing open my apartment door. The virile scent scarcely registers on my libido's radar. It's struggling to ignore something much more tempting than the scent of an alpha male on the hunt. It's fighting to contain the lips wrangling her into a submissive, no backbone loser.

Alex is kissing me. Not a little kiss. Not one I'll forget within the next week or the next year. He's *kissing* kissing me. A kiss that makes me forget all kisses before it. A kiss that ensures I'll never forget him and the impact he's had on my life. *A kiss that breaks my heart even more.*

He nips, and he bites, and he holds me captive without a single part of his body touching mine other than his mouth. It is awe-inspiring and devastating at the same time. Is it possible to love and hate somebody at once? If you had asked me last week, I would have laughed and said you're questioning the wrong person. I'm incapable of love. Now I wish Alex had never re-found my heart. I wish he had left it buried deep in the hole I shoved it in eight years ago—because living without a heart was better than living with a broken one.

"Fuck, I've missed you," Alex murmurs over my lips. "Is that corny for me to admit? Does it make me a soft cock to say I've been dreaming about your lips, taste, and smell the past seven hours?"

When he steps back, I drop my eyes to his chest. I'm strong, but I'll never be strong enough to look him in the eyes without feeling like an idiot. The drop in my gaze reveals more travesty. He's come bearing gifts. He has ice cream, two tubs of Chinese, and a giant slab of milk chocolate.

"I wasn't sure if you had already eaten, so I grabbed enough for us both." He enters my apartment like he owns the joint, his steps confident. "We should probably get the ice cream into the freezer before it melts." His thick beard doesn't impede his cheeky grin when he mumbles, "It's probably nothing but slop after that kiss."

When he hovers closer to me as if he is planning to kiss me again, I point to the kitchen. "Freezer is that way."

While he unpacks the Chinese, I head to the freezer to place the ice cream inside. It's weird how well we play house. I guess it shouldn't be. I did just say "play."

A suggestion Alex's mom made to me in jest yesterday smacks into me when I open the freezer to discover a half-empty bottle of vodka inside. "Slip some vodka into his drink. He'd never know. Might loosen him up a little."

Loose lips do sink ships.

"Are we celebrating anything in particular? Or do you always go all out on Thursday nights?"

Alex stops spooning fried rice onto a plate to lift his eyes to mine. It hurts, but I maintain his eye contact. "There was a development at my work today. The odds swung in my favor."

I shouldn't trust the honesty in his eyes, but I do.

"So you're happy about the outcome?"

He nods. "It's best for all involved."

I stupidly move close enough to him, he can band his arm around my waist and tug me into his chest. My heart twists in despair when he presses his lips to my temple.

"Do you remember that whiny two-faced bitch you mentioned earlier?"

"The one from three whole days ago?" The sarcasm in my voice conceals my anger. He really does think I'm a naïve idiot.

Alex laughs, then nods. "Yeah, her. She was transferred to another department today."

"Oh." My heart rages out of control. *Boom-boom. Boom-boom.* It chops up my words when I ask, "Who's taking her place?"

His balk reveals more than his words. "Ah... we don't know yet. Hopefully someone good."

He presses his lips to my temple for the second time before he relinquishes me from his grasp so he can return to serving our dinner. The low hang of his head ensures I'm aware I'm not the only one now having a hard time maintaining eye contact.

Two tubs of Chinese, half a container of ice cream, and five spiked drinks later, Alex is looking a little tired. His tipsy state reveals he'll be more of a touchy-feely drunk than a talkative one. Although I've unearthed more about him the past two hours than I did the prior week, I still need more. More alcohol and more talking will equal more time in anger management for me, but it will be worth it. I fucked up, so it's my job to fix my mistakes, *isn't it?*

"We should go out and celebrate your victory. It's Thursday night. That's practically the weekend." I drag him to a standing position. It takes a mammoth effort. *My god, I forgot how much muscle weighs.* "Let's go dancing."

He gags. "Dancing. No. I'm tired. It's been a long-ass week."

His slurred words encourage my pursuit. "And I'm full of beans, so we're going dancing."

I lug him to the door, barely missing his whine about there being much better ways to burn off energy than dancing. It's closely followed by a grumble about stupid womanhood ruining his fun.

"Be a good boy by following my lead, and I'll show you how a period doesn't necessarily mean no sexy time."

My waggling brows freeze halfway. For just a nanosecond, I forgot this is a ruse. We're not going out because I'm buzzing on excited adrenaline. I'm pissed off, annoyed as fuck. I am *not* looking for excuses to justify his betrayal. I'm seeking a way to destroy him. . . and hopefully find a magic cure to soothe the nicks my heart incurred during the process.

"Careful." I lean Alex on the back quarter panel of a taxi before handing the driver some bills from my purse.

His eyes flare from my generous tip before they lift to mine. "Are you sure you're okay getting him inside? These old relics don't have elevators."

I groan. It matches the one Alex makes when his stomach threatens to spill for the third time the past ten minutes. In desperation, I took him from feeling the pleasant buzz of alcohol to being rip-roaring drunk in under two hours.

Guzzling vodka as if it is water will do that to anyone, much less a man who hasn't touched a drop of alcohol in years.

I should have handed him a real bottle of water the instant his words started slurring beyond recognition, but when my vindictive bitch claws are out, I have a hard time reeling them back in.

I shift my eyes back to the driver. "Three flights of stairs, what's it gonna cost me?"

"Rae. . ." I stop tiptoeing out of Alex's room when he murmurs, "Stay with me."

I shake my head. "I can't."

I'm not being mean; I truly can't. The guilt on my chest feels like an elephant is sitting on me, trapping me as desperately as Alex's deceit blindsided me. This is the reason revenge never works, because neither party feels good once all is said and done. Luca's death should have taught me that, not the pained groans of a man I hardly know.

"I've got stuff to take care of. I'll see you in the morning. Okay?"

I don't know why I lie. Perhaps I hope it will ease my guilt enough I won't smell the alcohol leeching from his pores. It's suffocating his manly smell as effectively as the vodka drained the color from his cheeks. He looks truly unwell.

"Please, Rae. I don't feel good."

No, I guess you wouldn't since you drank a fifth of vodka in under an hour.

"I can't—"

"Please, baby."

His throwaway nickname should annoy me more than it pleases me. Unfortunately, it doesn't. It reminds me of good times more than bad, and how for a whole week, I thought I was more than just a pretty face.

My lips shake when I begin to speak. "I can only stay a little while. I do have important things I need to take care of."

Hearing the uneasiness in my voice, Alex lifts his head from the pillow to glance my way. I'm shocked he has the strength to do that. "I understand. Thank you."

I smile to hide the wobble of my top lip. "You're welcome. Now scoot over."

After a deep breath to expel my nerves, I kick off my heels, then slip between the sheets. Bad move. Everything I am losing is now displayed directly in front of me. It hurts. It hurts so fucking bad.

Alex inhales a sharp breath. "Rae, baby, are you crying?"

I shake my head, sending tears flinging off my cheeks. "I'm not crying. You're just drunk, that's all." My quivering voice ruins my campaign.

Vodka fans my lips when Alex laughs. . . or is he groaning? I can't tell. "I'm not drunk. I don't drink. I'm just a little unwell." His glassy eyes bounce between mine for several seconds before he murmurs, "Perhaps I'm love drunk?"

"Please don't," I beg through clenched teeth, consumed by an equal amount of anger and resentment.

I may not know this man, but I've studied him enough the past week to know some of his telltale signs. His eyes are blazing with the same ownership they held in the wee hours of this morning when he told me he loved me, and the thickness bracing against my thigh hasn't been hindered in the slightest by his intoxicated state. He wants to ravish me—both my pussy and my heart.

"We are *not* going there again."

Alex scoots down the bed so we come eye to eye. He takes his time assessing my wide eyes, tear-stained cheeks, and downturned lips as if he's not viewing them through a kaleidoscope.

"That's it, isn't it?" he asks a short time later. "What I said to you this morning scared you? That's why you've been distant?"

The pain in his words cuts through me like a knife, but I do a good job of pretending my heart isn't being torn in two. "No. Don't be ridiculous. I get it was a heat of the moment thing." *That you were playing the part.*

"Playing the part?" Alex asks, clearly confused.

Oh shit, I said that out loud?

I roll my eyes like it's no big deal. "You know? The act guys play when they want to get in your panties. They'll say anything if it gets them laid."

Some of the haze in Alex's squinted gaze shifts toward anger. "I was already in your panties, so why would I say it if I didn't mean it?"

I want to say, *because you're playing me for a fool.* Instead, I settle on, "You were caught up in a moment. It's fine. I know you didn't mean it."

His fingers flex on my hip, notifying my body of his touch even more readily than the hardness it's struggling to ignore. It's now acting as traitorous as my heart.

"I *did* mean it."

I shake my head violently. *Now I feel as drunk as Alex is.*

"I did, Rae. I meant every fucking word. How can you not believe me? I've been acting like a lovesick idiot all week." The slur of his words doesn't lessen the impact of them. "I get it's early. I understand it's scary. But that doesn't make it any less real." Tears burn my eyes when he locks his with mine to declare, "I'll give up everything I have before I give you up. Okay?" He wipes away my tears with the back of his hand before repeating, "Okay?"

I shouldn't nod, but I do. You can't see what I'm seeing. Even through the haze, his massively dilated pupils, and the low hang of his lids, his eyes aren't the ones of a liar. He's either telling the truth, or I'm a complete fucking idiot. I really hope it isn't the latter.

"Okay. Go to sleep. We'll talk more in the morning."

I tickle his beard in a soothing manner, hoping the gentleness of my touch will lull him to sleep. This isn't a conversation I want to have in general, much less with a drunk man.

"Promise me you'll be here in the morning, Rae." His words are slower, more relaxed. "I want to wake with your hair fanned across my chest like I have the last four days."

I run my thumb along his little scar hidden from view before nodding. "I'll be here."

"Promise me."

My chest rises and falls three times before I stammer out, "I promise."

My pledge gives him the comfort he needs to fall asleep. It also eases my heartache a little. He let me leave without injury that night at Substanz. He didn't have to. He didn't know me, so he had no reason to believe me when I said I wasn't a prostitute, yet he still did. He gave me his faith even though I didn't deserve it, so shouldn't I do the same for him?

Perhaps he doesn't know I'm Rae from Substanz?

Maybe he'll be as blindsided by our bizarre connection as me when I expose it to him?

I don't believe in miracles, but I never thought I would be capable of falling in love either.

I wake up a little after 5 AM. That's not unusual. Before Alex, I pounded the pavement for two hours before the sun even rose. I feel like running now; I'm just not sure if it is to burn off excess energy or confusion. It's probably a bit of both.

Alex groans when I roll him over so he is lying on his back. He barely budged an inch all night. I guess when you consider the alternative, I was extremely lucky. Last night could have ended a whole lot worse than it did.

While rubbing a kink in my neck, I head into Alex's tiny kitchen to hunt down some pain medication. Two tablets for me to ease my aching head, and three for Alex's thumping head he's yet to become aware of.

I find a bottle of pain medication rather quickly sitting on the top of his fridge. Now all I need is a glass to fill with water. Since Alex's kitchen is one tenth the size of mine, that doesn't take long to discover either. It is in the bottom cupboard on my left, just to the right of a stack of open shelves. He has the usual items: old bills, dated magazines, and two frosting canisters.

I shouldn't pry, but as they say, curiosity killed the cat.

The first tin of frosting has the same fake IDs I found in the pantry at The Manor.

I wish the second was just as innocent.

I've never paid much attention to how large frosting cans are. You wouldn't think by looking at them that they're capable of hiding a cell phone. Not just any cell phone either, a highly recognizable one, one I last saw when it slipped from my grasp and fell down a grate an hour before I bumped heads with a stranger in an elevator.

Here it comes again. The steamroll of idiocy is smacking into me once more.

While leaning my back on the kitchen counter to take in some deep breaths, my eyes float around Alex's kitchen. They don't travel far, only to a sleek-looking laptop hiding beneath a stack of papers.

My heart rate that hasn't settled since yesterday morning bangs out a new tune when I recall Alex telling me his laptop was at the shop. Although he could have had it returned by now, I don't know when. Excluding today, he's rarely left my side. I'm not overly friendly with computers, but Bosco, the only IT shop owner in town, is a sleaze I'll never forget. Even though I agreed to be his fake date at the annual cook off his family holds in Miami each year, it still meant my laptop was returned a week later. Alex doesn't have boobs and ass on his side, so he will be required to wait the general six to eight weeks every male resident of Ravenshoe waits.

After a quick glance over my shoulder to ensure I'm still

alone, I pull Alex's laptop out of its hidey hole. No passcode, no lock code, and no fucking chance in hell Alex can pretend he didn't know me before he knocked me out. There are photos—dozens of them. Most are of me running, but there are the occasional ones of me out of my active gear. I'm either staring into space or wiping away the tears I pretend don't fall at the same time every night.

My hand rattles when I run my finger over the touch pad to open up his emails. He's smarter than me. He doesn't leave an obvious paper trail. Other than a few emails about Danielle, his inbox is empty.

I curse into the brisk morning air when an email lands in his inbox out of nowhere. Its loud whoosh sounds like a siren roaring through Alex's apartment since not a single noise can be heard—not even Alex's faint snores from earlier.

Clutching at my chest to ensure my heart remains in place, I return my eyes to the screen of the laptop. The cause of my near heart failure is an email from someone named BJ. The subject requests for them to have an urgent meeting, and it was sent only thirty seconds ago.

Confident I can make the email look unread with one quick click of a mouse button, I open it.

Alex,

We need to meet. Preferably outside of the office. It's in regards to the information we obtained about Theresa this morning. Please delete this message once you've read it. I also sent additional details to your phone.

BJ

After reminding myself time and time again that there are plenty of women in the world named Theresa, I assess BJ's email more diligently. What information is BJ referring to? Alex couldn't have helped him this morning, as he was with me all morning. He never left my side. . . except when he consigned me all the hot water so I could wash my hair. I found my open laptop on the bed following this.

You son of a bitch!

After tossing his laptop back in its rightful spot, I charge into Alex's room. I'm not planning to wake the ass-peddling, lying son of a bitch. I want proof.

Proof he's a liar.

Proof he's a user.

Proof I'm the biggest fucking idiot in the world for ever believing a single word he said.

I find what I'm hunting for a few seconds later. His brand new cell has only been in his possession a few hours, but since I overheard the customer service representative showing him how to activate his phone using iCloud connectivity, I'm hoping it will hold the clues I'm seeking.

I hit a snag when my swipe of the screen requests a lock code. I try every combination I can think of before the iPhone locks me out of his device for five minutes. Five minutes might not seem like a long time in a standard, everyday life, but when you're seeking answers while only two seconds from losing your shit, it feels more like a death sentence.

"He broke your trust first," I assure myself as I call a frequently dialed number on my cell.

Even with the early hour, Hunter answers in a timely manner.

"I need your help," I demand, rudely not offering a greeting.

I hear Hunter scrub the thick beard on his jaw before he replies, "Anything."

He knows he owes me, so this will make us even.

Over the next ten minutes, Hunter walks me through the process of hacking into Alex's phone. At the start, he was hesitant as to why I couldn't ask Alex his details, but a quick mumble about Alex being an adulterer changed Hunter's prospective.

Hunter hates cheaters, so much so, he offered to drain Alex's bank account of the scarce funds he has before guaranteeing to fleece any family money he has coming his way in the distant future.

I thanked him for the offer but said it was unnecessary. I wish I wasn't so quick to refuse when the evidence in Alex's phone turns damning.

Although his iCloud account has yet to sync with his photos, the handful in his album take care of the last thread binding my heart together. Add them to the messages BJ sent every hour on the hour the past eight hours, and I can only reach one conclusion: he used me. Not to get to Isaac. Not to have me face charges over half a decade old. He used me to advance in his position at the Federal Bureau of Investigation.

That *boss* he spoke of, the one he appears to hate, she's the same woman my boss loathes. Their reasons for dislike are vastly contradicting though. Isaac can't stand Theresa Veneto because she's dragged him through three years of legal battles in an attempt to pin an illegitimate child on him. Alex hates her because she's higher-ranked than him.

Well, was.

From BJ's messages, it's obvious she was removed from her position last night. Either Alex didn't get BJ's messages strongly urging him against using the information he discovered this morning, or he didn't care about his advice because each message received reveals BJ's growing agitation.

3:45 PM – We need to talk. It's urgent.

3:55 PM – Is this the right number? Why aren't you replying?

4:10 PM – I know you think you've struck gold, but don't use the information you unearthed about Theresa.

I didn't think you could feel someone's frustration via a text, but BJ's next one proves me wrong.

4:15 PM – Alex, fuck! Call me before you do something you'll regret.

That's around the time Alex dropped me off at my apartment.

4:35 PM – You did it, didn't you? You used the information. What the fuck were you thinking? Having her removed from her position won't help.

5:35 PM – This won't end well. No matter how well you spin it, this won't end well.

6:35 PM – I thought you were about the department, not the glory?

7:35 PM – I tried, man. I really tried.

Clearly, Alex isn't the only one who hit the bottle tonight. BJ's next message is riddled with spelling errors.

8:35 PM – I should hadn in my badge now, save htem coming to serach for it. You should tell her, Alxe. She deserves to know.

Even heavily intoxicated, Brandon can tell right from wrong.

It's a pity Alex can't.

25

"*R*ae?"

You have no idea how hard that was to say. The burn in my throat is so horrific, even a three letter name is too much for me to handle. What the fuck is wrong with my throat? Did I swallow razor blades last night? And my head, it's thumping even more now than it did when I was knocked unconscious.

My legs feel like dead weights when I swing them over the bed. I scan my bedroom, aware of where I am, but having no recollection of how I got here. The last I remember is entering Regan's apartment. My god, our kiss. It was the best we've ever had. It tied me to my woman even more, ensuring the decision I made last night was a step in the right direction.

I shuffle across the wooden floorboards of my apartment like an old man who can't bend his knees. I don't know why I'm searching for Regan. A woman with an aura as strong as hers can't hide in a crowd, much less a dingy, cramped apartment. I can still smell her scent lingering in the air, though, so she must have left some time in the last hour.

A groan rolls up my chest when I spot my phone sitting on the dining nook in my kitchen. It's barely 6 AM.

Upon spotting no unread messages or emails, I log into my contacts and fire off a message to Regan.

Me: *I'm sorry about last night. Must have eaten something bad. I'm going to go die in bed for a few more hours. If you don't hear from me by lunch, call in the coroner.*

I laugh before hitting send. It is an apologetic but fun message, kind of similar to how I'm feeling.

Although I won't fully rest until Jay is behind bars, and Theresa is as far from Ravenshoe as possible, my eyelids aren't giving me any other options. The instant my head hits my pillow, I crash for a solid ten hours.

My head is still thumping when I return to the land of the living, but it has nothing on the mad beat of my heart. Regan still hasn't made contact. I have no missed calls or text messages. We generally communicate in person, so I could excuse poor technology skills as her lack of contact, but I know how fanatical she is about returning Isaac's messages. If she's not messing up the sheets with me, she's rarely seen without her cell phone in her hand.

I scrub the sleep from my eyes as I dial Regan's number for the fourth time today. It rings and rings and rings, but she fails to pick up. I leave a message before sending her another text. They're similar to ones I've already sent.

Me: *Call me as soon as you get this. I don't think you should be alone right now.*

My girl is strong, but she's been through so much the past twenty-four hours, I'm sure she's struggling to recognize herself.

I shower, dump my sweat-riddled clothes into the washing machine, then head to the kitchen for a strong, dark brew. Another thirty minutes have passed, and there are still no calls or messages from Regan, so I do what all desperate men do. I call in back up.

Brandon's contact is as stifling as Regan's. My calls go straight through to his voicemail, meaning he is either on another call or his phone is dead. I leave him a voicemail like I did on Regan's phone, but my tone is more anxious now and slightly more panicked.

When another thirty minutes pass with no contact, my heart thuds into my ribcage as my feet pound the concrete stairwell of my apartment building. I charge down them, my steps so frantic, I misdial a frequently called number several times during my short trip.

I stop hailing a cab like a madman when the FBI switchboard operator answers my call two seconds later. She dispatches me through to the Ravenshoe division even faster than that.

"I'm Alex Rogers, requesting an update on a target." I rattle off Regan's details to the agent who accepted my call.

My graceful slide into the back of the cab turns into a thud when he updates me on Regan's location.

"Are you sure?" I double-check while pressing my phone closer to my ear, certain I heard him wrong.

"Positive," he replies, his tone relaying his confidence. "She hasn't left her apartment since she entered it early this morning."

"Okay. Thank you."

I throw bills at the cab driver, encouraging him to floor the gas.

We arrive at Regan's apartment with a record-setting pace under our belts. After awarding the cabby's tenacity to wrangle the populated streets of Ravenshoe into being his bitch with a few more bills, I enter Regan's apartment building. I take a quick detour through the service room hidden at the back of the foyer to ensure the security wires I cut last night are still tethered.

I'm not surprised when I notice they've been repaired. Isaac is as pedantic about personal safety—*or should I say staff scrutiny?*—as he is about concealing his criminal activities from the eyes of the law.

After my pocket knife makes quick work of the freshly installed wires, I take the emergency stairs two at a time. I could ride the elevator, but a conversation I had with the security personnel of Regan's building last night changed my mind.

He said they were in the process of having additional security measures implemented in Hector. That usually means CTV cameras in layman's terms.

The situation in my stomach worsens with every stair I climb. I'm not worried Regan is injured. My girl is fierce, and I'm confident she can protect herself. It is the niggle in my gut warning me that my world is about to be upended causing my weighted steps.

By the time I reach Regan's floor, I'm sweating profusely and wheezing like Brandon did when he busted into the hallway to say he spotted Regan's stalker reentering her apartment. The memory reminds me that I should give Brandon an update on Regan's case. He probably has no clue her stalker wasn't really a stalker, and that Jay was merely one of the many suckers Theresa snagged in her web of deception the past year.

My bangs on Regan's door match the mad thump of my head. I don't know exactly what I ate to make me feel like this, but I'm never eating Chinese food again. I've never been so unwell.

"Rae?" I bang again.

This time I only get two thumps in before the door swings open. Instantly, my woes are a thing of the past. Regan's hair is wet and swept to the side, exposing inches of her ravishing neck. Her smell is fresh as if she's recently showered, and her face is. . . vibrant and red.

Hmm, that's odd.

"Are you okay? I've been calling you all day."

She steps away from me when I attempt to cup her jaw to kiss her hello.

"What's going on?" I lift my hand to my mouth and breathe

out to make sure the acid scorching my chest isn't affecting my breath. My teeth still smell minty fresh from their recent brushing.

I drop my hand from my face. "Did I do or say something wrong last night? I'm having a hard time remembering anything." I chuckle, hoping it will lighten the mood. It seems to have the opposite effect.

"You need to leave." Regan's pitch is as sharp as her lips are furled.

"Okay," I reply, stunned by the severity of her tone. "I'll leave. . . once you tell me what's going on."

Her already narrowed eyes slit even more. "I don't need to give you an explanation. I just need you to leave."

I shove my foot in the way when she attempts to slam her door in my face. The width of my boot means I can only see half of her, but it is open wide enough I can't miss the agitation crossing her face.

"What the hell is going on, Rae? We were fine last night, so what happened between now and then that's gotten you all worked up?"

Her pupils dilate as she fights hard to ignore the moisture teeming in them. "Nothing happened. I'm just done."

The sneer of her words shock me, but not as much as what she has to say next, "I told you at the very beginning, if I want you, you'll know. If I don't, you'll know that just as quickly. I don't want you anymore." Her tone dips during her last sentence.

"That's not true," I deny, shaking my head. "You wouldn't be standing here on the verge of tears if you didn't want me. You want me; you're just scared. It's okay, baby. We can work through your confusion together—"

Her hot breaths fan my lips when she throws open the door and screams, "I'm not confused! I'm also not an idiot!"

One tear and my entire fucking world implodes. "Baby, please don't cry. I never said you were an idiot. I'd never think that about you. . ."

My words trail off when I spot the quickest flurry of black in the far corner of her living room. It wasn't a small shadow dancing in the late-hanging afternoon sun. It was the size of an adult. A male adult.

When I lean to the side to investigate the situation more thoroughly, Regan follows my lead, blocking my view.

This bombards me with anger. . . and perhaps a shit ton of jealousy.

"Do you have someone in there with you? Someone who's welcome to stay while you shower and parade around in that?" I gesture my hand to the satin slip she's wearing that shows off more of her skin than it conceals. "Is that what this is all about?"

Regan straightens her spine as if she's going to deny the accusation in my tone, but something changes her mind. It could be the plea in my eyes or the fact she failed to locate the outline of my gun on my hip. If she thinks me being unarmed will stop me from retaliating if *any* of the horrid notions running through my head are true, she's poorly mistaken. I don't need a gun to disperse my anger. I only need my fists.

After a quick swallow to eradicate the fury in my tone, I ask, "Who's in your apartment, Rae?"

An expensive men's cologne darkens my cheeks when Regan steps closer to me. She is determined, unstoppable, and on a mission to tear my fucking heart in two. "I know who you are. I know what you did." Her voice is barely a whisper, but I hear every word she speaks. "You lied to me." Her voice rises as she fights to hold back her tears. "You deceived me."

I shake my head, my panic at an all-time high. She looks truly broken, but even more concerning than that, she believes I broke her.

"I've never lied to you. Not once."

She grabs something off a drawer on her right before thrusting it into my chest. A few loose papers haphazardly fall to the ground when I twist the manila folder around to face me.

Oh fuck, I'm fucking dead.

The folder is filled with numerous printouts of the surveillance images I have of Regan on my laptop. They show the timeline of when my obsession started—right back to her Substanz days.

I feel the train jump off the tracks when Regan sneers, "You're a liar, a user, and a cheat." She pauses as if it is a struggle for her to deliver her next set of words. "So I returned the favor."

I'm blinded by tunnel vision, swarmed by rage. "You returned the favor? What the fuck do you mean, you returned the favor?" Nothing but absolute agony echoes in my tone.

Regan smiles. It's not one that makes me feel warm and fuzzy. It tarnishes her beautiful face with hatred and makes my heart feel like it's swimming through tar.

She steps closer to me, bringing her eyes in line with mine. "It doesn't feel good, does it? Do you feel stupid? Like you should have been smart enough to see the signs? I understand. I felt the same way." She glares at me in disgust. "I'm seeing things more clearly now, though. It was fun while it lasted, but it's time for me to stop fooling around with the minor leaguers and step back into the game with the big hitters where I belong."

She uses my utter bewilderment—*and perhaps blinded-by-fury rage*—to her advantage by slamming her door in my face.

26

I stop staring at the ceiling of my entrance way when a deep voice rumbles through my shattered core. "Everything okay?"

Isaac sets down a glass of whiskey before crossing the room, his hands delving into his trouser pockets on the way. He's been as quiet as me today. If I didn't know him as well as I do, I'd assume discovering me with tears flooding my eyes was the cause for his discontent.

It's a pity I know him better than that.

It's also a pity I threw him into the deep end with me.

Nothing I said to Alex was true. There has never been anything between Isaac and me. There will *never* be anything between Isaac and me. That's why I can prance around in front of him in a satin slip as Alex so angrily pointed out. We don't have that type of relationship. Isaac sees me as his friend, not a plaything for him to dominate or control. *Or ruin.*

I only said what I did because I wanted to hurt Alex in the

most painful way. I've only known him a short period, but I'm well versed on his jealousy issues. I wouldn't have been so game if he were carrying his gun, but with the playing field even, I unleashed a side of me I haven't seen in years. It wasn't pretty, and in all honesty, I'm a little ashamed of how I acted, but after all the evidence I unearthed the past six hours, it won't take much to have my stupidity excused.

"Regan?" Isaac queries, making me realize I didn't answer his first question.

"Yeah, everything is fine."

I've said the same thing to myself numerous times the past twelve hours.

I'm fine.

Isaac's fine.

Everything is fucking fine.

Except my heart. It's stuffed. Broken. Shattered into a million pieces.

"Then why are you upset? I haven't seen you like this since. . ." His words trail off like they always do when he mentions Luca.

I didn't know it when we met, but I wasn't the only one who had suffered the loss of a loved one. Isaac's grief was even fresher than mine when he blindsided me with a proposal to join his empire. I think his girlfriend's death was one of the reasons he chose me. I was nothing like Ophelia, yet everything like him. We both suffered heartache at a young age before fighting through our grief to achieve everything we have.

You'd think once Isaac reached the pinnacle of success, the struggle would stop. It hasn't. It's grown worse. Envy is a horrible thing. It makes decent men crooks and already bad men even more unhinged. The instant you hit success, prepare yourself for the onslaught. Resentment, greed, bitterness, you'll face it all. It won't matter how you achieved your triumph, you'll never be seen as anything more than a fraud. Someone must have helped you. Someone must have paid your dues on your behalf. They look for any excuse they can find as to why their life doesn't emulate yours instead of striving for their own greatness.

I thought Alex was above that. He doesn't have any money—I don't know a single non-corrupt member of law enforcement who does—but he didn't seem to care. He has the confidence and charisma that makes people look past the low digits in his bank account, and for what that lacks, his ability to lie without a single bit of hesitation firing in his eyes will take care of the rest.

"I. . . uh. . . discovered something a little concerning when I was away." I grit my teeth, loathing how weak my voice is. I sound like a whiny baby overdue for a bottle.

Isaac nods but remains quiet, encouraging me to continue. I would like to say it helps, but with my mind as twisted as my gut, I can't fire any words off my tongue. I feel like an idiot, but instead of being able to hide my shameful face until the storm rolls over, I have to confess my sins to a man who has only ever looked at me with pride in his eyes. This sucks. It's worse than when I had to explain my final paycheck from Substanz to my father.

I fobbed it off as a weekend gig at a local burger and fries joint, but my father is way too perceptive for that. I swear he nearly had a coronary. His face was as red as mine when it dawned on me that years of hiding never really hid me. Jayce knew where I was. Dwain knew where I was. It was just a rookie FBI agent left in the dark.

"Do you remember that FBI Agent from Substanz?"

"The one who got shot?" Isaac correctly guesses.

I nod. If I hadn't read the reports on Alex's injuries in his recently uploaded iCloud file, I would have never believed his kneecap was shattered by a bullet. Only two days ago, he carried me up a flight of stairs before tossing me on a bed without a remote hint of strain crossing his face. At the time, I was so impressed by his stamina, my ego fed off the testosterone pumping out of him. Now, just the thought of what we did that morning makes me sick. I've witnessed firsthand the tactics people use to get what they want, but Alex's ploys were excessive.

My eyes float up from the floor when Isaac cups my cheeks as he did earlier today. None of my tears had fallen, but he had his thumbs at the ready, prepared to catch them if they did. Isaac hates tears, so much so, I faked having a lash in my eye as the reason for the moisture brimming in them. He never found the felonious lash, but his hunt gave me a few seconds to gather my composure.

I begin to prepare my defense when Isaac says, "You discovered what happened to him." He's not asking a question, he's stating a fact. His tone assures I can't mistake this.

I nod again, causing Isaac to cuss. That's more surprising than my stupidity the past week. He's known to drop the occasional F bomb when things don't go his way, but in his day to day life, he rarely swears. I think it is out of respect for his grandma. . . or perhaps fear? She smacks him up the head if he so much as says "damn."

A gold cufflink on Isaac's sleeve blind me when he scrubs his jaw. "I was hoping you wouldn't find out. It's not something I want you to take blame for."

"How can I not accept the blame? I brought him into our lives."

Isaac vehemently shakes his head. "We've discussed this many times the past five years, Regan. Nothing that occurred that night was your fault."

I endeavor to correct him that I'm no longer referring to the incidence at Substanz, that I mean Alex's reappearance in our lives, but Isaac's next set of words steal mine. "I've been sending money to his family for years. I know it won't change anything, but it lessens my guilt—somewhat."

I take a step back, perplexed. "What family are you talking about?" My voice is the strongest it's been today. "He doesn't have a family that needs looking after."

Isaac's brows furrow, stunned by the demand in my tone. It isn't a bad shock. He's glad I'm emerging from the dark cloud that's been hovering above my head since I invited him into my apartment over an hour ago.

Air vacates my lungs in a rush when Isaac discloses, "His wife is a strong and proud woman, but their daughters were in the forefront of her mind when she accepted my offer of assistance."

Have you ever submerged yourself so deeply in your own body, you feel like you're looking at yourself from the outside in? That's what I'm feeling right now. I'm here, but I'm not. I can't breathe. I can't speak. All I can do is sit back and watch the hurt fester in my stomach until it eventually boils over.

Alex didn't just deceive me. He lied to his wife—the mother

of his children—and at the same time, he forced me to become someone I never wanted to be. He made me the other woman.

"I need to go home."

"Okay," Isaac says slowly, surprised by the rapid change in our conversation.

He shadows me into my bedroom, only chuckling with half the energy he used earlier when he took in the sex swing he had installed this afternoon. I roll my eyes before snagging a suitcase out of my walk-in closet and tossing it onto my bed. I can't believe I finally built up the courage to express my desires without shame, only to have them thrown in my face. I've learned my lesson. I won't let it happen again.

The smug grin on Isaac's face clears when he stops taking in the woven seat on the sex swing to pivot around to face me. "You're leaving now?"

Feigning ignorance of the panic in his tone, I nod.

The worry clouded in his steel gray eyes intensifies. "If this is about the agent—"

"It has nothing to do with him," I lie. "There's just stuff I have to take care of. My sister. . . and brother. You know, *stuff*." I'm two seconds from punching myself in the throat for how stupid I sound. "Do you think you can hold down the fort until I get back? I'm sure it will only be a few days."

I'm not running away like a coward. I want to fix the mistakes I made. But I can't do that here. Just seeing Alex for those two short minutes upended the courage I built this morning to tell Isaac about the FBI's unfair investigation into his empire.

Although I'm still planning to update him on everything I know, I refuse to let Alex make me look like an idiot for the third time in under twenty-four hours. I need to ensure all my t's are crossed and i's are dotted before I come clean to Isaac.

I doubt he has anything to be worried about, though. I scoured the evidence Alex had in his phone for hours this morning. He has nothing on Isaac—not a single fucking thing. And he'll never get anything—because I'm going to make sure he doesn't.

I didn't study to the point of exhaustion for seven years to let a man with no morals judge Isaac's integrity. I did it to stop precisely this: the corrupt, unworthy men and women who don't care whom they have to trample to get what they want.

Isaac pays me extremely well, and he's about to get all his money's worth in one sitting.

a technician I've never met before jumps out of his skin when I throw open the surveillance van door half a block down from Regan's apartment. I'm not here to spy on her or soothe the sting my ego just sustained. I'm here to amass evidence, to prove I know my girl better than anyone.

She's angry. Rightfully so. She caught me in a lie. But she's not an adulteress. She doesn't believe in tit for tat or seeking revenge because she knows it causes more harm than it does good, so I'm confident she'd never stoop to those levels.

She's mad, that's all.

I remind myself of that time and time again as I flash my ID at the stunned agent before taking his spot in front of a bank of monitors. I remember the lazy smiles she gives me when she wakes, how she smells like flowers while her skin tastes like honey, and although shock was the first expression that crossed her face when I told her I loved her, it wasn't her only response. She was pleased—somewhat angry—but mostly pleased.

The confidence hardening my spine bristles when I rewind the surveillance footage back far enough to discover the identity of the man in her apartment. Isaac greets Regan in his usual way, with a kiss on the cheek and a brief hug, but his caress this time around goes a little longer than I feel comfortable with.

"They're just colleagues," I remind myself. "She has no interest in him whatsoever. . ."

I stop talking out loud when Isaac cups Regan's jaw. Because the security dome is directly above them, and Regan's head is hanging low, I can't see what his thumbs are caressing. I assume it is her cheeks, but I can never be called rational when jealousy is sluicing my veins.

"What's he doing?" I ask the techie, my tone blunt.

He stops quivering in his boots to assess the surveillance footage. "Rubbing her lips?" he suggests a short time later.

My furious roar bellows through the van. "Why would he do that?"

The techie shrugs. "I saw him do it last night before he said goodbye to his date."

His Adam's apple bobs up and down when my growl ripples through the air.

"Or he could be wiping her cheeks? I can't tell from this angle. He's probably caressing her cheeks." He sounds as if he is striving to convince himself as much as he is me. "Yeah definitely a cheek rub. He would have kissed her by now if he was going to. . . "

Silence overtakes his words when Regan shifts her head upwards for the quickest second before she drags Isaac into her apartment by the lapels of his suit jacket. Although pain was the first thing I registered in her eyes, there was also a snippet of deceit in them.

While working my jaw side to side, I take a mental note of the time in the far right corner of the monitor. That scene was recorded over an hour ago.

It doesn't mean anything. I trust her. She wouldn't hurt me like this. Rae is many things, but she could never be accused of having a cold heart. She'd let her heart stop beating before she'd use it against anyone.

"What other activities have been recorded today?"

The technician's eyes drop to the movement register we log into evidence every day. "Not much. I just reestablished our connection after a glitch, and before that, Isaac was recovering from a late night." The waggle of his brows expresses the words he didn't say.

"What was this delivery?" I point to a note he jotted down on a separate piece of paper. Since the delivery wasn't for Isaac's apartment, it isn't documented the same way.

"It wasn't really a delivery, more an installation." The quiver of his lips mince up his words. "Here's a copy of the invoice."

He is gripping the paper so hard, I nearly rip the one page document while accepting it. His panic is respected when I scan the business name at the top of the invoice: *Naughty Boys and Girls.*

The reflux I've been struggling to ignore the past hour triples its burn when I discover the product Regan ordered to have installed. There are no fancy codes to decipher or cryptic names. It is as obvious as the sun hanging in the sky: *one premium leather interwoven sex swing.*

I throw the invoice onto the keyboard as if it scorched my hand before slumping low in my chair. It still doesn't mean anything. Not a single fucking thing. Regan is an adventurous woman. She could have arranged for this to be installed weeks ago.

Argh! That tightens my jaw even more. Just the thought of her with anyone but me has me craving a rampage.

Hoping to weaken my anger, I run my eyes over the invoice once more. I take it in with the diligent eyes of an agent instead of a jealous, scorned man. The invoice is dated with yesterday's date. An additional fee of five hundred and fifty dollars was negotiated for an urgent installation. That price would jump to a thousand dollars if it was done in under twenty-four hours.

I'm not surprised. Isaac is infamous for his impatience.

I freeze as sick fear makes itself known with my gut. She wouldn't. She couldn't. The invoice was paid with the same company credit card we have in Isaac's file, but Regan doesn't see Isaac like that. I'm tired and a little under the weather. I'm not seeing things clearly. Right?

Right. Then why are my legs stomping the pavement as I race back toward Regan's apartment?

The pain ripping through my chest is intense, worse than anything I've ever experienced. It's so bad, I'll happily blow my cover to more people than just Regan if it stops the feeling of a grizzly bear shredding me to pieces.

I know Rae. I know this is not her. But him. . . I don't trust him. He gives orders without any concern for the families left behind when he issues the sentence of death. He mocks and ridicules those he believes are beneath him to make himself feel better. He'd even go as far as stealing another man's woman just for the hell of it.

He's not doing that to me.

He stole my soul years ago.

He cannot have my heart as well.

Just before I enter the revolving door of Regan's apartment building, I'm grabbed from the side. My anger reaches fever pitch when I'm thrown against a brick wall before my chest is pinned by a forearm. Shock, anger, and downright fucking fury pumps into me when I discover who is stopping me from righting the wrong done five years ago.

"Let me go, Brandon."

I don't give him a chance to respond before I switch our exchange from a verbal confrontation to a physical one. I fling him off me as if he is weightless, the pain burning me alive from the inside out swallowing my morals.

Brandon is stronger than his meek demeanor gives him credit for. After picking himself off the floor, he curls his arms around my torso and holds on to me tightly. His strength impresses me, filling me with just as much determination to destroy him as badly as I am planning to destroy Isaac.

"You have two seconds to get your fucking hands off me before I. . ."

Years of training nearly go down the drain when my fist almost finalizes my sentence. The only reason it doesn't is because of what Brandon murmurs next: "I know you're angry. I know you're mad about what did or did not happen between them, but there are more important things at stake right now than your ego."

Shocked by the absolute agony lacing his words, I stop struggling against him. Realizing I am no longer fighting him, he drops his arms and takes a step back. My lungs saw in and out when I pivot around to face him. I'm not tired. Before Regan entered my life, I trained a minimum of two to three hours a day to maintain adequate fitness for my role. It's the expression on Brandon's face causing my windless response.

His expression mimics mine to a T: the hurt, the pain, the gut-wrenching sorrow. If I didn't know any better, I'd swear he was the one who forced Regan and Isaac together.

The reason for his pain is answered in the most horrific way when he murmurs, "Dane is dead."

To be continued in Couple on Hold!
Available now.

If you want to hear updates on the next books in the Infinite Time Trilogy, be sure to join my **readers group**: Shandi's Book Babes

Or my **Facebook Page**: www.facebook.com/authorshandi

Isaac, Hugo, Hawke, Ryan, Cormack, Enrique & Brax stories have already been released, but Brandon, Grayson and all the other great characters of Ravenshoe will be getting their own stories at some point during 2019/2020.

Join my READER's group:
https://www.facebook.com/groups/1740600836169853/

Subscribe to my newsletter to remain informed:
http://eepurl.com/cyEzNv

If you enjoyed this book please leave a review.

ALSO BY SHANDI BOYES

Perception Series:

Saving Noah

Fighting Jacob

Taming Nick

Redeeming Slater

Saving Emily *(Novella)*

Wrapped up with Rise Up *(Novella - should be read after Bound)*

Enigma:

Enigma of Life

Unraveling an Enigma

Enigma: The Mystery Unmasked

Enigma: The Final Chapter

Beneath the Secrets

Beneath the Sheets

Spy Thy Neighbor

The Opposite Effect

I Married a Mob Boss

Second Shot

The Way We Are

The Way We Were

Sugar and Spice

Lady in Waiting

Man in Queue

Couple on Hold

Enigma: The Wedding

Silent Vigilante

Bound Series:

Chains

Links

Bound

Restrained

Psycho

Russian Mob Chronicles:

Nikolai: A Mafia Prince Romance

Nikolai: Taking Back What's Mine

Nikolai: What's Left of Me

Nikolai: Mine to Protect

Asher: My Russian Revenge

Nikolai: Through the Devil's Eyes

RomCom Standalones:

Just Playin'

The Drop Zone

Ain't Happenin'

Christmas Trio

Falling for a Stranger

<u>Coming Soon:</u>

Skitzo

Trey

Made in United States
Orlando, FL
27 January 2023

29111823R00157